UNDER
NORTHERN STARS

Also by William MacLeod Raine
in Thorndike Large Print

GLORY HOLE

UNDER
NORTHERN STARS

WILLIAM MacLEOD RAINE

Thorndike Press • Thorndike, Maine

Library of Congress Cataloging in Publication Data:

Raine, William MacLeod, 1871-1954.
  Under Northern stars / William MacLeod Raine.
  p. cm.
  ISBN 0-89621-918-6 (alk. paper : lg. print)
  1. Large type books. I. Title.
[PS3535.A385U5   1989]   89-33947
813'.52--dc20   CIP

Thorndike Press Large Print edition published in 1989 by arrangement with Houghton Mifflin Company.

Large Print edition available in the British Commonwealth by arrangement with Patricia Raine Barker.

Cover art by James B. Murray.

UNDER
NORTHERN STARS

CHAPTER 1

A Traveler Hears a Bullet Whine

The first hours of swift, desperate racing to escape had lengthened into dragging days, the days into racking weeks. Hard and tough though he was, inured to the saddle from childhood, he felt wearily that he had been traveling half a lifetime. Only his iron will had kept him going.

From the moment when he had plunged into the desert with the man-hunters behind him, the flight had been a nightmare. Fever had burned him up, and chills had sapped the strength from his supple body. Worn and sick, he had clung to the horn because of the indomitable doggedness in him that made quitting impossible. Delirium and pain and exhaustion, and, after the wound began to heal, hunger . . . Silent eons of loneliness . . . The spur of fear pricking him . . . And, in this Northland, vast white stretches desolate and bleak . . . Snow blanketing the hills to the end of the world.

At least he had reached a far country where

he ought to be safe — if that was a word to use in connection with one who had a reward on his head, dead or alive. By dodging towns and circling ranch districts, he had avoided capture. He believed his pursuers had lost track of him.

The thought gave him a grim smile. He did not know himself where he was. For many hours he had been enmeshed in hills, had wound up draws, climbed prongs, reached summits from which he could look on white land waves rolling away like the waters of an interminable sea.

A chill wind was blowing down from the Arctic. The day was cold, and would be colder, he guessed. There was a taste of more snow in the air. Already a flake or two had melted on his cheek. He yearned for a roaring fire under a roof, for warm blankets, for the savor of hot coffee and bacon in the frypan. Instead he would have to put up with a windy camp in a draw and rabbit stew cooked in a skillet while the storm swirled about him.

He was an outdoor man, used to his own company, but there had been times during the journey when he would have mortgaged his future for the sight of a kindly human face, for the sound of a friendly voice. It was so now. The solitude was oppressive. It carried a threat with it. In such a waste of bleak space a lone man was a helpless atom.

The sounds that notified him of the presence of another were sinister — the whining of a bullet, the crack of a rifle. Instantly he slid from the saddle and dived through a tangle of plum trees to the bed of a creek He listened. The slap of running feet came to him. Someone was flying along the ridge back of him, intent on swift escape.

The traveler changed his rôle from hunted to hunter. He plunged into the thicket of wild plums, burst into the open, and ran obliquely up the slope toward the ridge. If possible, he intended to find out who had shot at him and why.

Dusk had fallen, but he made out a figure scudding along the rockrim. Fifty yards in front of it was a horse. As the pursuer cut across to head off the fugitive, he saw with surprise that the other convergent runner was not a man, but a boy.

The lad caught his foot in running cedar, stumbled, and went down. He was up again in an instant, but that lost second decided the race against him. Unable to reach the horse, he turned to defend himself.

Too late to check his rush, the traveler caught the gleam of a knife. The blade ripped into his shoulder and sent a flame of fire scorching through him.

The fingers of his left hand closed on a small

forearm, those of his right on the handle of a quirt suspended from his wrist. Savagely he swung the lash. Like a furious snake it wound around the slender limbs clad in blue Levis. The victim fought to break away, and in retaliation kicked at the other's shins. The torturing quirt fell with implacable rhythmic regularity and half-circled the writhing legs. There was not strength enough in the struggling figure to free itself from the grip of steel binding the arm.

The man with the whip heard with no pity the gasp of the tortured youth and was not moved by the agony of shivering flesh. But the wailing cry which broke from the lips when pride and courage collapsed stayed his hand.

Startled at it, he loosened his hold and stepped back. For that scream of pain had come from a girl. He stared at her, astounded. Her breath came in ragged sobs. But she was still a young Amazon. In spite of the physical torment it mirrored, her look flamed hatred and defiance. The eyes in the small contorted face were like live coals.

"Hell's bells!" the man exclaimed.

She took advantage of his amazement to turn and bolt for the horse. But he was too quick for her. As she was pulling herself into the saddle, he dragged her down. She flung her slim body against his and tried to trip him. They struggled, knee to knee and thigh to thigh. Her leg locked under his, but she had not power enough to make him lose balance.

His spur became entangled in running cedar. Fast in each other's arms, they plunged to the ground. He was underneath, but he easily turned her over. Before he pinioned it, her hard little fist beat again and again in wild fury against his twice wounded shoulder.

"You damn li'l' wildcat!" he cried angrily.

He clamped thighs and knees to the slim strong body that tossed to and fro trying to dislodge him. It was as though he were taming a bucking bronco.

Suddenly she gave up struggling. "Let me go!" she demanded urgently.

"Not till I know why you shot at me and knifed me," he told her harshly.

"Let me go!" she repeated, and though it was still an imperative he sensed terror riding in her voice. "You'd better let me go, or . . ."

The threat died away unspoken. He wondered what she would have said. Perhaps in the words she had not uttered there might be an explanation of her attempt to kill him.

"Go on," he jeered "If I don't turn you loose — what then?"

Her body twisted beneath him and her white teeth snapped at his hand.

"Better stop that," he said grimly, "unless you

want me to wear you out with my quirt."

"Let me up, you coward!" she cried desperately.

"We'll see about that."

Already he had been swept by a wave that seemed to lift all the weight from his body. He had set his teeth and fought it back. Now it poured over him again, took him from his feet, and seemed to toss him high above a tiptilted world. His head sagged, and he slid down into the brush cedar.

She pushed him aside, rose, and ran to the horse. What had occurred to save her she did not quite know. It did not matter. She was free. Not until she had swung to the saddle did she look back at him Then it was to make sure that he had not followed.

He still lay where he had fallen, face down, his head in the brush. Was he dead? Had that bullet fired from ambush reached a fatal spot? Or the knife-blade which she had thrust in terror? So much the better. Other men could live in peace if Clem Oakland had been blotted out. They need not walk in danger of their lives.

But even as she dug her heels into Gypsy's ribs and put the pony to a lope, fear knocked at her heart. She had never before seen a man pass from violent, lusty life to utter stillness. Even in the few minutes since the shot had been fired the storm had increased to screaming fury. The snow was coming in gusty swirls. The bite of the air was bitter, and the shrill whistle of the wind held an ominous threat. Clearly a blizzard had brewed in the mountains and was sweeping the hills. It was going to be a wild night. One caught without shelter . . .

If there was still life in that prone figure, the searching cold would obliterate it. Well, was she to blame because at last he had met the fate long due? His record of persistent outrage against those she loved condemned him. Why think of him now? Judged by what men said of him, he had never known pity for others.

But to ride away and leave him there wounded, too broken to crawl to shelter: she could not do that. One would not treat a dog so on a night like this. Evil though he was, the man was a human being.

She turned Gypsy and rode back, all her judgment in hot rebellion against the weakness of such a return.

CHAPTER 2
Molly Gives First Aid

After she had swung from the saddle, the girl moved forward warily. Through the snow pall it was impossible to see for any distance, and she did not want to fall into a trap.

The man was still there — and alive. For his drawling voice flung a jeer at her.

"So you came back, to make sure you'd killed me."

"Can you travel?" she asked.

"It's the one thing I do."

He was sitting up, his right hand resting on the hip close to the butt of a Colt's thirty-eight. Even then, with diverse currents dragging at her mind, she had an impression that his sunken eyes mocked her.

"I'll get your horse," she said.

"You're full of Christian kindness."

She remounted and vanished into the whirling white of the storm. It was a long time before she returned leading his sorrel. Even in those minutes the temperature had fallen noticeably.

14

"I thought I'd never find your horse," she explained, bringing it close for him to mount.

He pulled himself to the saddle, his body and limbs dragging as though they were weighted.

"Sure you can ride?" the girl flung at him, curtly.

"Yes, ma'am. I learned when I was a li'l boy."

Abruptly she turned away. He caught at the bridle-rein of her pony.

"You wouldn't leave, would you, without giving me a chance to thank you for all your friendliness? First, the pill you sent to me. Then the nice playful jab with the knife and the caresses with your fist. Don't you reckon you ought to tell me the name of my good Samaritan so I can remember it in my prayers?"

"Let my rein go," she ordered.

"Better not go without your rifle and your knife. You might want 'em again."

The girl jerked at the rein to free herself and Gypsy went into the air. The unexpected movement broke the grip of the man.

Into the white desert the girl vanished. She was presently aware that the other horse was following. Its nose pushed past her until the rider was knee to knee with her.

Even the sound of the wind had deadened in the blinding snow. The world was narrowed to a space the boundaries of which could be touched with the outstretched hand.

"Getting its back up for a ripsnorting night," he shouted.

She thought she knew a way to get rid of him. "I'm Molly Prescott," she said, flinging the information at him against the storm.

"Pleased to meet you," he said derisively. "After a fellow has been shot at and gouged by a young lady and after he has skinned her with a quirt, they're well enough acquainted to swap names. Mine is Jeb Taylor."

"That's a lie," she called to him scornfully. "I'm headed for home. Unless you want to meet my people, you'd better light out."

He laughed hardily. "That's right. It is a lie, though I don't know how you knew it. As for meeting your folks, I'm real anxious to see them so I can congratulate them on having such a nice gentle young lady in the family."

She said no more. Her mind became preoccupied with another problem. They were lost. All sense of direction had been wiped out by the dense stinging walls of white which pressed upon them.

"I don't know the way," she said at last, screaming the words.

"I've been guessing that for quite some time," he cried back. "How far is it to your place?"

"Four or five miles."

"Could your bronc find it if you gave him his head?"

"Don't think so. He never had any sense."

"How about the creek? If we worked back to it, would we run into any ranches along it?"

"There's a deserted cabin about half a mile from where we were."

"We'd better try for it."

"Can we find the creek?" she asked.

"By following the dip of the ground. I'll lead. Stick close to me."

The intense cold of the air, thick with gray sifted ice particles, searched the warmth of their bodies and sapped vitality from them. They came to a little draw, went down it to the creek, and turned to the left.

He waited for the girl to draw alongside of him.

"Is the cabin right on the creek? And on which side?" he asked.

"Close to the creek. On the left. Just the other side of a barbed-wire fence," she told him, cupping her mouth with a hand to help the words carry.

The horses plowed through the drifts along the creek bottom until barbed wire stopped them.

"There's a gate," Molly said. "I'd better lead now. I know where the cabin is."

A moment later she stopped and slid from the pony. "Here it is. We'll have to unsaddle and turn the horses loose. No stable here."

It was a log cabin with a dirt floor. The latest occupant had left a rough homemade table, two stools, and a wooden bedstead mortised into the wall.

"We won't freeze for a while, anyhow," the man said.

He rubbed together his numbed hands until he could use the fingers, then built a fire with the slats of the bed as fuel. As the leaping flames in the open fireplace lit his face when he leaned forward to arrange the wood, Molly watched him curiously, not untouched by surprise.

The gaunt bearded face gave her an impression of a harried man, one driven by desperate circumstance. He seemed haggard and worn. The sunken eyes were savage but not feral. She had not expected Clem Oakland to look like this. He had been described as vainglorious and smug in his effrontery. The insolence of the man who had called himself Jeb Taylor was sardonic rather than arrogant.

"I'll look after the fire. You'd better 'tend to your hurts," she told him.

"So I had," he agreed, and added a rider impudently. "But ladies first. You have a few wheals as souvenirs to remember our happy meeting."

Angrily, she flushed. Pains from the stinging quirt still ran across her thighs. "I suppose you're awf'ly proud of having whipped a girl," she said scathingly.

He had untied a frying-pan from his saddle and was rummaging in a gunny-sack, but he turned round to meet without apology the blaze in her eyes.

"I'm pleased I didn't know she was a girl till she'd eaten quirt a while," he said coolly.

"Probably that's the way they treat women where you come from."

"When they forget they're women," he amended.

He stepped to the door and scooped up a panful of snow. This he held over the fire until it melted. Slicker, coat, and vest he discarded, after which he opened the shirt and very carefully began to work it free from his shoulder.

"Hope you'll excuse me for turning our happy little home in the hills into a hospital," he said with a sarcastic grin, "but since you've furnished the patient, I reckon you won't complain."

She did not answer. Her fascinated eyes were fixed on the red stain that had spread over the shirt, a stain still wet and soggy. Chill dismay pressed upon her heart. Had the thrust of her knife been responsible for this? She had only flung out her hand in self-defense. She had not meant to do more than keep him away. Yet perhaps he might die here, in this cabin, while

19

they were shut in by the blizzard far from medical aid. It was a dreadful thought. If he did, she would be a . . . No, not that. She pushed the word away from her.

"Won't you let me help you, please?" she begged.

His hard gaze swept over her. "If you'll promise not to be – impulsive," he mocked. "I don't like to interfere with a lady's pleasure, but I have to draw the line at letting you beat on my shoulder with your fist."

Molly disregarded the gibe. "Hadn't I better cut away the shirt?" she asked.

"No. It's the only shirt I have. Soak it loose."

He had drawn a piece of clean linen from the gunny-sack. This she used as a sponge. The muscles of his lean jaw stood out like ropes, but he did not once wince while her fingers were very gently peeling the shirt from the shoulder.

"Wash it," he ordered curtly after she had done this.

In washing the wound, Molly made a discovery. The slash of her knife-blade had been imposed upon a half-healed scar.

"There's an old wound here," she cried "I don't mean old, but one not made to-day."

"Correct," he admitted grimly. That was all. He offered no explanation of how he had received it.

"Just a minute," she said, and turned her back on him.

The girl was fumbling with her attire. He heard the rip of tearing linen. When she turned to him, her face was flaming. In her hand was a long strip of cloth. She used it to tie up his shoulder. His immobile face registered no sign that he was not used to having young women supply bandages to him from their underwear.

Impassively his gaze took her in while she worked. She was young and vivid. Her movements had the swift grace of one whose muscles cöordinate perfectly with a quick mind. He guessed in her the buoyancy of health. Her hair, abundant and wavy, was a shade deeper than coppery gold. The eyes, set not too close, were blue as a mountain lake. Tiny freckles were sprinkled lightly across the bridge of a piquant nose. In spite of her Levis, her high-heeled boots, her boyish shirt and Mackinaw, she bloomed eternally feminine in the shadowy half-lights of the grimy cabin.

"That will have to do," she said at last, frowning at the makeshift job she had made of the bandage.

Carefully she slipped the shirt over the wound and buttoned it, then held vest and coat while he put them on.

"First time I ever had a valet," he said, with a grin. "If I was Jay Gould I'd take you on permanent."

She froze up, swiftly. He need not think he could get familiar with her because she had helped him in his need. Now she could afford to snub him. Since the discovery of that earlier wound, her conscience no longer stabbed. The responsibility for his plight was not hers.

His words had been casual, by way of thanks, with no ulterior meaning, but he did not take the trouble to explain. She could think what she pleased. He was not interested in placating a girl who could fire from cover at a man to kill. The thing was hard to believe. If he had not caught her in the act, he would not have thought it possible. She had not even taken the trouble to deny it, probably because she had known it would be of no use.

He broke the rest of the bed slats and renewed the fire. The wind tore furiously at the cabin and howled down the chimney. From the two-pane window he looked out on the swirling wilderness.

"I wouldn't wish this blizzard on my worst enemy," he said evenly. "Kicking up its heels for a stemwinder, looks like."

"Wouldn't you wish it even on a Prescott?" she asked, with a flash of bitterness.

He turned to look at the girl. It was dark in the hut except where the fire flung shafts of fantastic light-leaps. He could not see the ex-

22

pression of her shadowed face. What did she mean by that?

There were some things he meant to know. On what provocation had such a girl fired from ambush to kill another human being? Had she mistaken him for someone else? Or had she been urged by the desire of collecting the reward? Three thousand dollars, dead or alive. That was a tidy sum. He knew a dozen men who would kill without ruth for it.

But not this girl. Surely not this girl with the strong lissom body and the resilient step. She was a wild young cub, untamed, unlicked until today. A red-hot devil of temper could look out of her defiant eyes. And yet there was something in her clean courage that would not reconcile with the callousness of an assassin. Besides, it was not possible that from the ridge she could have recognized his face as the one on the posters.

She had taken him for another man. What man? An enemy to her people. That much she had as good as told him. He did not ask point-blank for information. The life he had passed through had given him a capacity for patience. One of the lessons taught by the wilderness is the futility of haste. In good time he would find out what it was all about.

"How long is a blizzard likely to last at this time of year?" he asked.

"You know as well as I do. Maybe a day, maybe a week."

"We can't stay here long without food and with very little fuel. How far are we from a ranch?"

"About five miles from our place. That's the nearest, except for a cabin our riders use. It's two miles farther up the creek."

"Stocked with food and fuel?"

"Yes. One of the boys is likely there now."

"Well have to break through to it as soon as there's a letdown in the storm," he said. "That won't be tonight. We'll have to make the best of this now. You hungry?"

"Yes."

He skinned the rabbit he had killed earlier in the day, prepared it for stewing, and found some salt and a couple of onions in his saddle-bags. Molly watched the stew while he produced from the gunny-sack two tin plates, a knife, and some tin spoons. Although she hated the man, with a youthful feminine ferocity untempered by tolerance, she could not withhold reluctant admiration. He was cold and hard, but he was strong and competent. There would be heard no whine from him if the cards turned against him in the game of life he was playing.

Oddly enough, she felt a curious lift of the spirit. For the moment they had shaved disaster and come to precarious safety. The threat of it still howled at them as the storm lashed at the cabin. Tomorrow was an unknown quantity. But in her throat was the prickle of excitement adventure brings.

CHAPTER 3
Concerning Katherine and Petruchio

Youth is not consistent. Its emotions are intermittent. Molly had abhorred Clem Oakland for years as a matter of family duty. He was an enemy with no redeeming virtue, a bad man whose evil reputation had run far. She realized that her meeting with him today would probably shift the basis for her dislike of him without mitigating it. Her hate had become personal and was no longer only a clan loyalty. A fire of shame burned in her bosom when her aching flesh reminded her of how he had laid violent hands on her body and thrashed it till the torture had become intolerable and she had begged for mercy.

But for this hour they were partners in a desperate adventure, one in which the stakes were life or death. Outside in the gray darkness raged the blizzard from which they had found temporary refuge by no great margin of safety. It separated them from others as effectively as a thousand miles of stormy sea. What lay ahead was uncertain. The only sure thing was that the universe had contracted to a space twelve by fifteen, that for the time they were as much cut off from the busy world as though they had been Adam and Eve in the garden.

It was a strange, exciting companionship, and it carried with it a reluctant *camaraderie.* They were like soldiers of opposing armies meeting for a short truce on a common no man's land.

Before the open fire they ate the rabbit stew and found it savory.

"I never liked rabbit until tonight," Molly said "You must be a good cook."

"Hunger makes a good sauce," he suggested.

"Maybe that's it. Anyhow, it's good. Arctic travelers always name their camps. Shall we call this Fort Safety?"

"It may be Fort Starvation before we're through," he said grimly.

"With a stocked cabin only two miles from here?" she asked, a note of derision in her voice.

"Two miles are as far as two hundred on a night like this."

"The blizzard won't last forever."

"It may last longer than our firewood."

"By morning it will clear up and we'll break through to Seven-Mile Camp." She added an explanation: "The cabin is seven miles from the ranch. That's how it gets its name."

She had risen to put her empty plate on the table. His sardonic eyes moved up and down her slender gracious figure. Shoulders and hips were in a straight line vertically. The long slim legs moved rhythmically. He thought of a spirited young race-horse. Perfect health and the free life of the outdoors had probably done that for her.

"You're going to look on the bright side, aren't you?" he jeered.

"Why not?" she flashed. "There's a bright-side even in being here with you. It will be such a relief afterward to be away from you."

A touch of angry color breathed in her cheeks. Served her right, she thought, for having shown him a moment of toleration.

"You haven't got rid of me yet," he reminded.

"Not yet, but I will."

"After our little account is settled." In the slow drawl there was no softness.

The girl glanced at him, startled. What did he mean? Was this a threat?

"How settled?" she asked, and a pulse of fury beat in her throat. "Do you expect to whip me again?"

He rose and walked across the room to her. Feet apart, hands in pockets, he looked down unabashed into her flashing eyes. The fine defiant poise of the small head, the insolence of her gallant youth, did not move him. He saw her as a spoiled child in spirit, advancing into womanhood dangerously self-willed.

"If you need it," he said coolly, his steel-gray eyes hard on hers. "Why not? Are you claiming to be a lady now? Come late in the day for that, ain't it, you damned little vixen?"

His words took her breath. No man had ever talked to her so before. That the attack was not in the least savage, that it was given in a low modulated voice, made it the more stinging.

"You're that kind of a man," she said scornfully.

"That kind exactly. A kind you've never met before, I reckon. Nobody has had the nerve to tell you the truth about yourself, missie. Well, you'll listen to it now. We'll take it for granted to start with that I'm no gentleman, so I can say what I think."

"I've heard of men like you. They enjoy bullying women, don't they?"

He ignored that as though she had not spoken. "It will do you good to get it straight for once. All your life you've been spoiled. You've indulged your temper, and folks have side-stepped it. Likely you've got the Indian sign on them because you're pretty. So you've got worse and worse, figuring you can get away with murder. You're as dangerous as a lunatic. Who gave you a license to ride around shooting at strangers and sticking knives in them? I reckon you think I ought to say, 'Thank you kindly, ma'am,' then you pull your devil tricks on me. Guess again. When you monkey with this buzzsaw you get hurt. Understand?

"I have to wear you out with my quirt again, your yelps don't mean a thing to me but evidence you're getting what's coming to you."

"If you hurt or insult me, you'll pay for it," she cried.

"Will I?" He lifted his shoulders carelessly in a gesture of complete indifference. "I'd advise you not to give that thought any weight as to how you behave. I'm kinda fed up with Katherine the Curst stuff."

Even in the cross-fire of the quarrel this reference surprised Molly, but instantly she picked it up.

"That's it, is it? You'd like to be Petruchio — and I'm to be your meek squaw. You forget I'm not married to you."

"Thank God for that," he said fervently.

"He doesn't hear you, Clem Oakland. You're too far away from Him for your thanks to reach God. Since you're going in for gratitude, better turn to the Devil you have served so well all your life."

"Did you say Clem Oakland?"

"You heard me."

"When did you recognize me?" he asked, intent on getting information.

There was a moment of hesitation before she answered evasively. "Everybody knows that big sorrel with the bald face and the white stockings."

"Oh, it was the horse you knew — a hundred and fifty yards away, or maybe more." His gaze clamped fast to hers. This was important. "You must have good eyes."

"I had field-glasses," she answered. Her manner was both reluctant and sullen.

"And it's always an open season for you on Clem Oakland?"

"You've got a nerve to say that. Why shouldn't it be. I'm not afraid of you because you're a killer and a bully and a thief."

"So I'm all that."

"All that, and more."

The girl's eyes blazed. The accumulated hatred of years fed by fresh fuel, was in her passionate challenge.

"You couldn't be wrong?"

"No, I couldn't. Do you think I forget my cousin Jim Haley? Or what you did to my father?"

"What did I do to him?"

Abruptly she turned away. She was not going to discuss with the enemy of her house the wrongs he had done it.

On one of the stools she sat down before the fire and looked moodily into it. The excitement

31

of the adventure had died down in her. She felt depressed and worried. At times she had to push fear into the hinterland of her mind. If Clem Oakland was all rumor reported him to be, there might be a dreadful hour ahead of her. Yet, strangely, in spite of his reputation, she could not wholly believe it. In those cool hard eyes, in the man's poised force, she read a denial of such baseness. That he was a hardy villain she did not doubt, but there was a small voice of reassurance in her that gave guarantee he was a clean and wholesome one.

He did not for long interrupt her thoughts. When the fire began to die down, he broke the frame of the bedstead for fuel and then the table. The wind at times fell away, only to break out again in renewed fury, as though it had been gathering strength for another attack on the cabin. The little building shook with the violence of the gale.

"Our stools will have to go next," he said, as he piled the last of the table on the coals.

"And after that?" she asked, breaking an obstinate silence that had lasted for several hours.

"You do the guessing," he said evenly.

Day broke at last gloomily, but for the time the wind had stilled. The leaden sky threatened more snow. Probably the blizzard would begin to howl again soon.

"We'd better start for Seven-Mile Camp," the man said.

Molly had just come in from a short tramp around the house. She had noticed sun dogs in the sky, a warning of more bad weather. Two false suns had been swimming in small perpendicular segments of a circle of prismatic color, and two others just below, all of them surrounding the true sun so as to form a cross of five orbs.

"Yes," she agreed. "Its going to be a lot colder — soon. No time to lose."

They traveled with no baggage. Even the saddle blankets were left behind so that nothing would hamper them. The man broke trail through the deep snow. It was hard going. The brittle crust gave beneath his weight, and they had to plow a path as they advanced.

Before the first quarter of a mile had been covered, their feet dragged heavily.

Molly's prediction was true. It had grown much colder already and the wind was whipping sleet into their faces.

"All right?" he asked, looking back.

"All right," she answered valiantly.

The progress made was slow. Molly began to count the steps she took. When she reached a hundred, she would begin again. Sometimes she sank down from sheer inability to lift her weary legs high enough in the heavy snow. She would get up, set her teeth, and start counting doggedly once more. One time he saw her on the ground and came back.

"All in?" he asked, dragging her to her feet.

"I slipped. Don't worry about me."

She saw that his beard was frozen solid from his breath.

"There's a cutbank just ahead. We'll stop there and rest awhile," he said.

They reached it and crouched under the bank, sheltering themselves from the wind. The cold was too intense to permit of staying long. He plunged out from it into the deep drifts and the girl followed him. She had made no complaint, though he knew she was in a bad way. He gave her good for that. She had sand in her craw.

Molly staggered drunkenly. Each step was an effort, to be undertaken individually by conscious volition. Immense weights dragged at the muscles of her legs. The storm increased. It drove into her face whips of stinging sleet more violent. She stumbled into a snowdrift and lay there.

The trail-breaker returned to her. "You've got to keep moving," he told her harshly.

"I can't. I'm through. Go on and leave me."

He did not argue, but pulled her up from the snowbed. "You're going on," he told her.

Obediently she reeled after him for another

hundred tottering steps before she once more collapsed.

"No use," she said piteously when he looked down at her.

His voice was rough. "Like to quit, would you? Nothing doing. You're going with me to that cabin."

He got her to her feet.

"I'm done," she murmured sleepily.

"Don't be a fool," he snapped, and slapped her face, not at all gently.

A momentary anger flared into her eyes. It gave her resolution to sway along the trail for another stretch. When her knees jack-knifed under her, they were in the lee of a cutbank above the creek.

"What's the use?" she begged. "I'm freezing anyhow."

"It can't be far now," he promised. "It's on the right bank of the creek, you said?"

"Yes." Her voice was faint.

He rubbed her face with snow, then held her body close to his to protect her from the wind-driven sleet. That she had reached her limit he knew. He would have to drag or carry her.

Sometimes he did one, sometimes the other. She was only semi-conscious. Once she begged him to leave her and save himself. His legs buckled under him. The path he made was as zigzag as that of a sailor returning from shore leave. He was down and up and down again a dozen times. But he floundered on with teeth clenched. His strength was gone. Only a relentless will drove the tortured flesh forward.

The wall of the cabin rose at last like a shadow out of the storm. He tugged and hauled his burden through the snowcomb hanging over the creek-bank and from there around the house to the door. His shoulder plunged at the framework like a battering-ram as he stumbled against it. The door gave way, and he staggered across the threshold like one helpless with drink.

How long he lay there he did not know. He wanted to sink into a stupor, but he knew that would be fatal. A fire must be lit. The girl must be looked after. The voices that told him so seemed to come from a great distance, to have little urge behind them. If he could sleep, only a little while . . .

His will reasserted itself. It made his muscles drag him from the floor, spurred him to work the numbness out of his fingers, to light a fire after many fumbling efforts. Presently it was roaring.

The girl's Levis, wet by the snow, were frozen stiff. He lifted her so that her body lay stretched in front of the fire. From her feet he pulled the high-heeled boots.

While a blanket from one of the bunks was

being heated, he unbuttoned the Mackinaw and slipped it from her body. As the Levis thawed, he slipped them from her legs. The woolen union suit below was wet, but he ignored that for the present, wrapping her tightly in the warm blanket. A second blanket he tucked about her.

He noticed that her eyes had opened and were following him as he moved about the room. His mind was inventorying the supplies.

CHAPTER 4
Fort Comfort

"You got through," she said in a weak voice, drowsily.

"By the skin of my teeth."

He threw off his slicker and moved across the room to examine the clothing hanging from nails in the wall. There were overalls, wool-covered chaps, a leather coat lined with wool, and a slicker. In a box he found shirts and underwear.

"First off, I'll get into some dry clothes," he said, by way of a hint to the blue eyes resting on him.

The eyes behaved themselves at once. They went back to the fire. It was perhaps the blaze that made the cheeks so flushed.

He changed from the skin out, swiftly and with no wasted motion. Only the bandage on the shoulder remained. The wet slops he had taken off he tossed into a corner. They could be dried later.

Beside her he dropped a suit of underwear and a pair of German socks he had found.

"They'll be too large for you," he said, matter-of-factly, "but I reckon you can make 'em do."

"Yes," she answered obediently.

"I'll light the cook-stove and look the grub situation over," he told her. "Make a complete change. I noticed your underwear is wet. We don't want any pneumonia from our snow trek."

And again she said "No" meekly, with unusual timidity. But she could not bring herself to make a start, not with this stranger in the room, the man who had saved her life, the man whom she hated. Though he had turned his back on her, she felt that every rustle of the garments would be a whispering confession of the intimacy into which Fate had thrust them.

"Get busy," he ordered curtly, without turning his head.

She did as be bade her, trying to still the sound of her movements. The noise he made rattling stove lids and breaking kindling was comforting. It told her cheerfully that her shyness was unnecessary, since he obviously considered it of no importance that a girl was undressing in the same room with him. Yet she remembered that he had stripped the Levis from her legs while she was still unconscious, and this troubled her modesty. As she hurried into the heavy woolens, she felt she was one huge blush from the toes she slid into the drawers to the roots of the fiery hair that had come tumbling down about her shoulders. Not until she had wrapped the blankets about her body did she feel relieved.

The blush was of her imagination, as far at least as her body and limbs were concerned. They were still blue with cold, though the returning circulation was beginning to send shoots of pain through her fingers and toes. She massaged her hands and legs vigorously. More than once she wanted to give expression to the sharp pain.

She thought the man must be psychic, for he turned from putting coffee into a pot to grin wryly at her.

"Hurts some about now, eh?" he asked.

"Yes. You, too?"

"Some. We're in luck. If our hands and feet were not stinging now, we'd have quit feeling for good and all."

"Yes." Then, in a low voice, "I reckon you made our luck," she said.

"You didn't do so badly yourself," he conceded.

"Even though you had to slap me to keep me from quitting?"

"Did the work, didn't it?"

"Yes. It's too bad you had left your quirt at the other shack."

It was strange that she said things she did not mean to say. Just now, at least, she wanted to forget their enmity, but something in her seemed to drive her to resentment. She knew she was not fair to him. He had saved her life. He had behaved very well since. Nobody could have shown more consideration than he. And like a spoiled and petty child she was seizing on an imaginary affront.

He met her on the ground she chose. "I wouldn't be surprised if I can find one here," he said. "A stirrup leather is pretty good."

It had been on the tip of her tongue to tell him she was sorry for what she had said, but his words froze the impulse. If he was as hard and callous as that, he did not deserve an apology. The situation was odious to her. Clem Oakland had no right to save her life, not after what he had done to her family. There should be nothing but hatred between her and him. It was better he whip her – though every time she thought of it anger flooded her – than that she should be under any kind of obligation to him. All her pride revolted at it.

"My father will pay you for any trouble you've taken for me," she said stiffly.

"I'll not trouble your father for my pay," he said coolly.

What did he mean by that, she wondered? Was he serving notice that he had claims he meant to enforce upon her personally? He had a bad reputation with women. She had always heard that. And yet, in his grim hard strength she could find nothing wolfish. More than once she had met men whose possessive eyes undressed women they admired. There was nothing of this in his stony bitter look. Hateful though he was, to be alone with him was not degrading.

The shed adjoining the cabin was filled with firewood. On the shelves of the cupboard built into the wall were canned goods, bacon, coffee, sugar, corn meal, and flour. If the blizzard lasted a week, they could make out very comfortably. What they had to do was to adjust their mental attitudes to their circumstances.

Molly realized this. Neither of them could leave. There was no room in Seven-Mile Camp for enmity. They were tied together, man and woman, conventions obliterated and they must make the best of it. Anger was a dangerously explosive compound which might lead to disaster. She was in no position to let her temper rule her judgment. The girl knew she had been foolish. It would he better to conciliate, to develop comradeship. Yet she had deliberately insulted him by suggesting pay for saving her life.

She made a swift about-face. "If you'll throw me the overalls hanging on that nail, I'll make breakfast," she said, in a tone of voice that surprised him. It was neither sulky nor unfriendly.

He tossed her the Levis. "Better rest. I'll take care of breakfast. You'll have chance enough to cook before we get away from here, looks like."

Presently she joined him at the stove. She was wearing moccasins. The blue trousers had been tucked up about four inches at the bottom. The mass of wavy red hair — though it was not red, he decided, but a tawny gold shot through with copper — had been done up in a knot at the back of her neck. Despite the difficulties of toilet, she had contrived to make herself sweet and clean.

"Are you making biscuits?" she said. "What can I do? Let me help." She sniffed the coffee avidly.

"Set the table," he told her. He was suspicious of this too sudden change of front. His accurate guess was that she had decided to try on him the effect of charm instead of temper.

During breakfast he smiled sardonically more than once. She was staging an act, and doing it rather well. It was impossible to deny her vivid good looks. Her small provocative face was mobile, her vivacious movements full of quick animal grace. He was not sure what her purpose was, but he was aware her friendliness was a mask.

Yet it was not wholly so. She was by nature amiable except when crossed. Within the hour she had escaped from death to the safety of warmth and good food. She was a healthy young creature, and the satisfaction of her hunger was a pleasure. The biscuits were delicious, the bacon savory, the coffee hot. Moreover, this hard tough man opposite her, enemy though he was, had an arresting personality.

His beard and his haggard wasted look had deceived her. He was younger than she had thought, probably not more than thirty. Recklessness was written on his intensely masculine face, but surprisingly she could find no baseness there. The bitter incredulous smile was unexpected. It did not seem to fit with Clem Oakland's reputation for smug conceit and bullying dominance.

He interested her, perhaps because he was unlike the men she knew. They were obvious people, quite understandable. She was not left guessing by them. But this man, with the sunken eyes like half-scabbarded steel, with the reticent strength so self-contained, gave her the feeling that she could not penetrate the defenses of his soul. It was annoying. She would have liked to feel that she could despise him, and this was impossible.

Molly was scattering the word "we" through her talk. They had become partners in the adventure. Before they had finished breakfast she said so in as many words.

"We're here. We can't help ourselves. No use quarreling. Let's declare a truce until the blockade is broken. We ought to work together, don't you think?"

"No more shooting, no more knifing?" he asked, with obvious sarcasm. "The beginning of a long dear friendship?"

"I didn't say that. But I don't see why we should always be at each other's throats. I've heard of friendly enemies, or at least neutral ones."

He found the idea rather amusing. "All right. We'll bury the hatchet, if your fancy turns to hatchets next time. You can play at being a lady, and I'll forget I'm a killer and a bully and a thief, not to mention a few other kinds of skunk you didn't find time to get around to when you were labeling me."

"I don't think that's a very good way to begin," she protested. "You'll have to meet me halfway if we're to be decent to each other."

"That's right," he admitted. "Got to put my best foot forward. I'll start in by shaving. There's a razor on the shelf."

It was surprising how different he looked after he had got rid of his three-weeks' beard. He had a good strong jaw and a mouth that suggested humor. Before he rebuttoned his shirt, she noticed how the muscles of his well set shoulders rippled beneath the skin as they

45

ran into the fine neck column. He carried his weight as lightly as a schoolgirl.

The wind still roared down from the divide driving before it great scudding clouds heavily laden with sleety snow. When Molly stepped out into it for a few minutes the gale shrieked down the gulch with an amazing fury. It lasted all day. With the early coming of darkness there was no sign of abatement.

After they had washed the supper dishes, Molly brought out a greasy deck of cards and a cribbage-board from a box under a bunk. They played for hours. The girl's mind was not wholly on the game. There would have to come a time, no matter how long she postponed it, when she would have to face the embarrassment of turning in to one of the two beds in the room, knowing that a strange man was in the other. The thought was terrifying. It made her stomach muscles tighten. He was not only a stranger, but one whose morals and character she had heard maligned for years. Fear grew on her. She could not push it away.

And he swept it out of her mind with a yawn, a direct level look, and a matter-of-fact word.

"I'm tired. Bucking snowdrifts is no easy job. Bed for me. Good night."

He used a bootjack to draw off his high-heeled boots, tossed coat and vest on a chair, and slid in between the blankets of one of the beds. Three minutes later, the deep even breathing of sleep came to Molly from his bunk.

Her preparations for the night were not much more extended than his. She had expected to lie awake worrying about him. Instead, her eyes closed almost at once.

When she awoke it was morning. He was looking after the fire.

CHAPTER 5

Rescue

During the night the wind had shifted. It no longer came from due north, but swept along the slope of the divide. By daylight its violence had diminished sensibly, though heavy clouds still obscured the mountains and were buffeted from one invisible peak to another.

Molly watched her storm-bound companion, at first drowsily, sleep still heavy on her eyelids, then more actively as she came to fuller consciousness. She must get up and help him, she told herself. But it was so warm and comfortable between the blankets. Body and mind were still in the state of relaxed languor following long and sound slumber. She stretched her legs and arms as a cat does, with the pleasurable sense of profound well-being.

The tension of her legs disturbed somewhat the sensory content. Each muscle sent its aching protest to her brain. From heel to thigh the fibers were stiff and sore from the unusual strain she had put upon them yesterday. Also, when her fingers massaged gently the twinging thighs, the tips of them could trace the welts made by a quirt.

"Take it easy," the man advised. "Better not get up till the room is warm. Then breakfast will be ready for you."

She procrastinated, though his suggestion was not in accord with the program she had laid out. Her idea was to do nothing that would stress sex. It could not be entirely obliterated for them, but it could be minimized.

"The storm is dying down, isn't it?" she asked.

"It's taking a rest for a while. We're going to have more of it."

Molly slipped out of the bed and slid her feet into the moccasins. She was already in the blue overalls. After a hurried toilet she joined him at the stove. It was characteristic of the new note in their relationship that without comment he had poured hot water into the tin washpan for her.

"I'm going to make flapjacks," she told him.

"Good," he assented.

She made a grimace at the dirty frying-pan. "Our riders aren't very clean housekeepers."

"You can wait till I'm through with the other one," he said.

"No, I'll clean this."

After breakfast he told her that he was going to take advantage of the break in the storm to

49

get in more fuel from the hillside back of the cabin. He had found an axe and a shovel in the woodshed.

"We don't know how long we're going to be snowbound, so we've got to be prepared for the worst," he explained. "I'm going out to wrestle in a few loads."

"Shall I go with you?" she asked.

"No. You'll be housekeeper."

Molly took the appointment seriously. She belonged to the ranch country and was not unduly fastidious. But dirt in a house she resented. Now she swept the floor, washed and wiped every dish in the place, cleaned the ashes out of the choked stove, and made the beds. By which time the day was well along and she could think of dinner.

Through the grimy window she could see her companion working on the hillside. His axe was swinging with rhythmic regularity. On the snow beside him a pile of wood was growing.

She found herself singing as she busied herself making dinner preparations. This was all good fun when she did not stop to think that the situation was shockingly improper and that she hated this particular man above all men. Presently gossip would race through the settlement. She had always been a bit careless of conventions, because she was Molly Prescott and not to be bothered with silly little rules.

But this was different. The tabby cats would do a lot of smirking and whispering. Well, she could not help it. Since she was in for it she might as well laugh as cry.

And there was something clean and fine about the adventure. She did not care what folks said about Clem Oakland. She was not afraid of him. Bad man though he was, he had the standard of the outdoor West. He would do her no harm.

Not that she recanted a word of what she had flung out to him about his evil qualities. He was all she had said. Well, perhaps not quite all. For she had called him a bully. It was on her uneasy conscience that she had ridden the high horse more than he. In her own way a woman could be domineering as any man.

When it was dinner time she plowed up the hillside to him. The drifts where he had broken trail were deep. It was snowing again.

"I'm the dinner bell," she called to him.

"Already?"

"It's not so early. I'll take a load of wood down with me."

He half-filled a gunny-sack and put it on her back. Presently he followed her down, carrying a pack he had roped together.

"We're in for more snow," he told her.

"Yes. I don't believe they'll reach us today."

"Will they know where to look for you?"

51

"No. But they know I was riding in this general direction." Her explanation, it struck him, was not quite frank. She was holding back something.

He glanced at the heavy sky. "Not today. Maybe not tomorrow."

"Dad will start looking for me soon as he can. He'll be worried awf'ly."

Dinner finished, he went back to his wood-chopping. The wind was rising again, and he wanted an ample supply of fuel in the lean-to. Before the afternoon drew to an early close, he tramped down the trail several times packing a jag of pine limbs.

In front of his bunk he stretched a blanket and behind this changed from his wet clothes. He could hear the girl humming a tune as she moved about her work.

While she set the table he smoked a pipe before the fire. He did not look directly at her, but he was very much aware of her presence. His impassive face did not betray the excitement he felt at being flung so intimately with this vital young thing. She moved across the floor as though life, the mere living, sang a song in her veins. With the unconscious insolence of youth she was dancing on the quicksands of the future. Some day she would be old and wrinkled. The thought was tragic. That beauty, keenly tempered like a knife-blade, would lose its edge. The light would go out of her face as the flame does from a blown candle.

That was absurd. With a sardonic grin he knocked the ashes out of his pipe and moved to the supper table. What did it matter to him how soon the little devil came to grips with the harshness of life? He had himself given her sharp notice that she was not exempt from its penalties.

It is strange, he reflected, how soon people adjust themselves to new conditions. Last night this girl had been flushed, shy, and fearful. Deep in her heart she had been afraid of him, full of dread lest the possessive male grow clamorous. Now she bubbled with careless chatter, as sure of him as though he had been her father.

She would not let him help her with the dishes. He had been working hard all day, and she was not the least bit tired, she insisted. When the super things had been cleared away, she brought out the greasy cards again. This time she had two decks and wanted to play Russian Bank.

"Don't know the game," he said.

"Then I'll teach you," she told him gayly.

She did. He learned easily, for he had card sense and had played a great deal. After losing the first two games, he surprised her by taking the third.

Abruptly he rose and pushed his chair from the table.

"I'll rest on my laurels. Time to turn in, anyhow."

Before he went to his bunk he contrived a screen to shut off the corner of the room where she slept.

Meekly she said "Thank you." Her gayety was a little subdued by the brusqueness with which he had risen from the table. Had she offended him somehow? She could not think of anything she said that might have annoyed him. Or was he just bored with her? That was possible, though not flattering. One of the stimulating irritants about him was that one could never tell what he was thinking behind that poker face of his.

During the night she was awakened by the slamming of the outer door of the lean-to. She could hear soft padding footsteps. Her heart fluttered. Almost she cried out for reassurance.

A low voice spoke gently. "If you're awake, don't worry. I've been closing the door."

It was amazing what comfort the words gave. They promised safety, made ridiculous the fear that had leaped to her throat.

By next morning the storm had entirely cleared. The snow flung back a million sparkles of sunshine. No breath of wind was in the air, no threat in the blue sky. Nature denied smilingly that she had ever been otherwise than kind.

It was close to noon when Molly called excitedly to her companion. "Look!"

She pointed down the valley to five slowly moving specks still a long way off. The man came down from his woodchopping. He would not need to lay in a further supply of fuel.

"I'd better make a big dinner. They'll be here in an hour or so," she said. "And they'll be hungry as wolves."

He assented, with no enthusiasm. The coming of these men meant more human contacts, and in these there was danger for him. They would want to know who he was, what he was doing in these barren snow wastes, though they would not at first put these questions into words since the outdoor West subdues its curiosity. What they might ask him, very bluntly, as soon as Molly had told her story, was how he came to be riding the bald-faced sorrel with the white stockings. To that query he had no answer that would satisfy. Nor did he care to tell them how he came to have a bullet wound in the shoulder.

Molly knew she ought to be happy at the prospect of relief and felt instead an unexpected heaviness of heart. As she moved swiftly about the room making preparations for dinner, the imminence of rescue brought no joy. Fate had snatched her into a brave adventure, dangerous and harsh but thrilling. Now she must go back to humdrum existence. There would be no high spots to mark the hours, no quick excitement of peril, no song of lifted spirit. The days and nights would again be proper and dull.

One thing she had to tell this man. It was not easy to say, for fear he might misunderstand. He might think her explanation personal, that she was trying to make friends with him. And that was absurd, since she hated him traditionally and personally. The reason she had to let him know this was that she owed it to herself.

With sleeves rolled back from the strong slim forearms, face flushed from the heat of the stove, she made a charming picture of engaging youth. Her companion did not need to look directly at her to know this. The flow and rhythm of her movements were inescapable.

A lock of wavy hair, about the tint of sunburst Tokay had escaped and fallen in front of her eyes. Because her hands were covered with flour, she brushed it back, using a wrist instead of fingers, when she turned to fling at him her shy explanation.

"About the knife . . . when I cut you. It just happened to be in my hand as I started for my horse. I had been getting a willow switch. And when you caught hold of me I was frightened

56

and struck out. It wasn't that I wanted to hurt you."

The words tumbled out at him in a small voice. He could take them as an apology if he wished.

His cool hard eyes bored into her.

"And your rifle. It just happened to be in your hand, I reckon, and just happened to go off in my direction."

The sarcastic retort struck her dumb. For the moment she had forgotten the rifle, and she had no answer ready. But he had rejected her little overture of self-justification. That was enough. Wounded pride poured hotly through her. A quick intake of breath betrayed her anger.

"I think you're the most hateful man I've ever met," she flamed. "I'll never speak to you again. Thank God, I'll be through with you as soon as my friends come."

"You'll be back again with the kind of yes-guys you can use as doormats," he said. "But don't be too sure about never speaking to me again. Some day I'll be asking you a question or two about that lead pill you sent to my address."

"After all you've done to us, you've got a nerve to say that. You deserve to be shot a dozen times."

"Once would be enough, if you'd be more

thorough," he jeered. "You're too soft to be a reliable killer. It takes nerve. You should have stayed on the rimrock and kept plugging at me. Instead, you got scared and ran. That's why you had to take a quirting that still makes you wince when you sit down. Killers have to be thorough, my dear."

"I never tried to kill you," she broke out.

"No? Just a little friendly salute in honor of my arrival."

"I don't care what you think. The opinion of Clem Oakland is of no importance to me."

She turned her back on him and began cutting biscuits savagely out of the dough she had rolled. Her folks were right. He was hard and callous and cruel. What a fool she had been to try to explain to him! A man such as he was would not have the decent instincts to understand. A passionate resentment against him flamed in her heart. Why of all the men in the world did he have to be the one who had dragged her to safety out of the blizzard?

CHAPTER 6
"W for Jeb and B for Taylor"

A trim, well-set-up young man led the rescuers. He swung from the saddle and advanced to meet the two waiting in front of the cabin.

His brown hand went out to Molly. "Good morning. Dr. Livingstone, I presume," he grinned.

The girl had read Stanley's story of the search for the great African explorer and she laughed as she shook hands. "Will you write a book about it?" she asked.

"No can do. I see you're all right. That's fine." His gaze shifted inquiringly to the man standing beside her.

"Mr. Oakland," she said, her voice a trifle chilly. "I supposed you knew him."

"Oakland?" he repeated.

"Mr. Clem Oakland." Then, stiffly, without looking at the companion of her adventure, she completed the introduction. "Sheriff Walsh."

"But this isn't Clem Oakland," Walsh corrected.

The other man smiled sardonically. "So I told her, but she wouldn't believe me. Jeb Taylor is the name."

Molly stared at him, the color mounting in her cheeks. Her thoughts churned furiously. Who was he, then? How did he come by the big sorrel horse? Why had he not explained himself instead of letting her think he was Oakland?

Walsh looked from one to the other. There was something here he did not understand, but that could wait.

"Glad you're both all right. We've been worried, Molly. This will be good news for your father. He's leading a party below Paddy Burns's prong. Figured you might have taken the south fork."

"I knew he would be terribly worried," the girl cried. "But what could I do? The storm came on so fast. We reached the old Berry cabin and next day during the lull broke through to this one."

The other men were grouped about them. All of them Molly had known for years. They voiced pleasure at her escape, but she detected embarrassment. Mr. Jeb Taylor's place in the picture was not clear to them. Ought they to discuss it or ignore it?

"I met Mr. Taylor in the blizzard," she explained, still flushed. "We made for shelter together. Lucky for me we did. I couldn't have reached this cabin without him. He had to drag me part of the way."

"Three loud cheers," Walsh said cheerfully, and shook hands with the man who called himself Taylor. "It's fine your luck stood up, Molly."

"Yes, Steve. We did have a narrow shave, but it's all right now." Molly passed to a topic less personal. "Dinner is ready, boys."

"And we're sure enough ready for it," answered one of her father's riders, a young brick-red Hercules named Peters with a head as bald as a billiard ball

"Oh, lady, lead us to it," another begged. "If you think bucking snowdrifts is no work, ask Slim Hodges. I'm here to tell the world different."

Molly beckoned the sheriff aside. "Who is with Dad on that search party?" she asked.

"Let me see. Your brother Bob — and Tom Maloney —"

"My cousin Jim?"

"Yes."

"You're sure? You saw him go?"

"Yes."

It seemed to him that she drew a breath of relief. He wondered why. What vital interest could she have in the assurance that Jim Haley was one of the party? Was it possible that she had given her heart to scapegrace Jim? That would be a fool thing for Molly to do. But girls were that way. They fell in love with handsome scamps and lived to regret it.

The rescuers ate incredible quantities of food. Beans, biscuits, bacon, rice pudding, salt pork, and coffee vanished into the caverns that led to their stomachs. They shoveled in supplies as though they never again expected to sit down at a table. Taylor observed that the sheriff was less voracious than the others. His table manners were above criticism.

He had, it appeared, been caught by the storm at the Prescott place while on a business trip. The talk moved more easily with him to keep it going, and he saw to it tactfully that the subjects were not ones that would embarrass Molly. The theme of the adventures of two snowbound in a small cabin was one close to the surface of all their minds, but when it pushed through to the air, he was casually matter-of-fact about it.

Taylor studied him with some interest, not only because he was sheriff, but because he was an unusual one. Steve Walsh was a slender black-haired youth, lean-flanked and clean limbed. His vitality was noticeable. The muscles of his legs and shoulders rippled when he moved. Attractive brown eyes were rather widely set in a good-looking tanned face the lines of which broke often to mirth. The head was small, and covered with close-cropped curls. Its owner carried it with careless grace.

After he had shown a right appreciation of Molly's cooking, Slim Hodges flung a question in one word at Taylor.

"Stranger?" he asked, his mouth full of rice pudding.

Taylor slanted one appraising look at the cowpuncher. It told him all he wanted to know. Slim was towheaded, snubnosed, and thick-lipped. There was a dumb, lost-dog look about his face. That he was anybody's fool could be safely guessed.

"Yes," the traveler said curtly.

"On business?"

"Looking for a winter resort."

Peters snorted. Slim did not quite know what to make of the answer but he tried to be helpful. "You won't find it up thisaway, friend."

"If you're sure of that, I'll quit looking."

"Stands to reason, don't it? With all this snow —"

The grins of his companions could not be missed. Slim stopped. He guessed vaguely that he was making himself the goat again.

Outside, a little later, he recurred resentfully to the matter of the stranger's presence. "This fellow Taylor. What does he claim he's doing here, anyhow? Howcome he to be here with

63

Miss Molly? Why, doggone it, if they met up when the blizzard started —"

He hesitated. Steve Walsh had appeared in the doorway and was lounging toward him.

"Tell us all about it, Slim. Then we'll know," the sheriff suggested.

"I was just saying —"

"You always are. My vote sure goes to you, Slim, for president of the old ladies' knitting society."

"That's all right, but if old man Prescott knew this guy Taylor had —"

"Did be appoint you his rep, Slim?"

Hodges opened his mouth to reply, but he did not get that far. The sheriff's feet slipped from under him and he caught wildly at Slim. They went down together, the cowpuncher underneath, into a deep drift beside the path. The weight of the officer jammed the other's face into the snow. Slim heaved spasmodically to free himself. Walsh clawed his way to the surface, slipped again, and sent the cowboy down just as he was finding his feet. The two wallowed furiously, arms and legs thrashing.

From deep down in the drift a smothered protest rose.

"Doggone it, Sheriff —"

That was all. Walsh's flailing arm swept a handful of snow into the other man's open mouth. The sheriff seemed to find it almost impossible to get a foothold that would allow him to rise.

When at last the two men emerged from the drift, the rest of the party rocked with laughter.

"Kinda slick under foot, Sheriff," Peters said, with a wink.

"I reckon I was awkward," Walsh admitted. "We've certainly had an elegant sufficiency of snow-baths for a while. You and I both, eh, Slim?"

Slim looked at him reproachfully. "If I didn't know better, I'd 'most say you were acting thataway on purpose, Sheriff," he complained. "Seems like a fellow couldn't hardly be that teetery on his feet. Soon as I started to get up, you kept slamming me down."

The sheriff brushed snow solicitously from the disheveled puncher. "Too bad, Slim. I certainly did some skating. Most of it on your anatomy. Hope I didn't injure any of your geography permanently."

"I'll bet I et a gallon of snow."

"Wouldn't think you would have been that hungry after ruining Miss Molly's dinner the way you did," Peters grinned.

"I didn't eat any more dinner than you did, fellow," Slim protested indignantly. "An' I wasn't hungry. You don't get the idea. Every time I opened my mouth to yell, seemed like Steve here was jamming snow into it."

Though Walsh had stopped Slim's chatter for the moment, he knew there would be a certain amount of tongue-buzzing about Molly and the stranger. This was inevitable, though the two had been flung together unavoidably. In a thinly settled country like this, all the inhabitants knew everybody else's business. Molly had held her head high. A good many would be glad to snigger over this episode. That the girl was innocent of any wrong would not prevent gossip.

Steve Walsh admitted a curiosity of his own, both as her friend and as the sheriff. It was plain to him that she was snubbing this man Taylor, though according to her own story he had saved her life. Something had occurred between them she resented. What was it? Taylor had not insulted her modesty. From her attitude Steve was almost sure of that. But for some reason she was holding a grudge at him.

As an officer of the law, Steve wanted to know more about this man who was wandering in the snow wastes with no apparent reason. The fellow's face was vaguely familiar to him. He had seen it somewhere recently, but his memory refused to say definitely where. The association was too elusive for coördination at present. One of these days, perhaps this very hour, the connecting link would pop into his mind.

Walsh went back into the house. "Soon as you're ready we'll hit the trail, Molly. We'll have to hump to make the ranch by supper time. I'm sending Frank on ahead to get word to your father that you are safe."

"I'm ready now."

"Good. We brought a spare horse for you. The rest of us will have to take turns spelling Mr. Taylor in walking."

"I'll try not to impose on you," Taylor said.

The sheriff picked up from a bunk a Stetson hat and put it on. He took it off and looked inside. The hat didn't fit. He had taken Taylor's instead of his own.

"Queer," he murmured.

"What's queer?" Molly asked.

"Oh, nothing. Things a fellow notices."

Molly took the hat from him, a little abruptly. The initials stamped by a cutting-machine in the sweat-band of the hat were W B.

The girl laughed, not pleasantly. "W for Jeb and B for Taylor," she said.

Walsh made no comment. He looked, with the ghost of a smile in his eyes, at the man who said his name was Jeb Taylor and had the letters W B in his hat.

"A little mistake," Taylor said coolly, meeting with no apparent confusion the steady regard of the sheriff.

"Probably they never taught spelling at the school where Mr. Taylor attended," Molly suggested.

"Made by a fellow in a restaurant where I ate," Taylor went on, as though she had not spoken.

"Did he eat with his knife?" the girl asked acidly. "Was that the mistake?"

The owner of the hat carried on easily, to the sheriff still. "He took my hat off the hook and left his own."

"It has been done," Walsh admitted.

"Yes. You just now started to wear this one away."

It did not seem well to the officer to mention that he had picked up the hat on the chance it might have a story to tell.

"That's so," he agreed. "Well, you got a good hat in exchange. That's one compensation."

"It would be interesting to know what name this W. B. stands for, wouldn't it?" Molly asked, looking at Taylor with insolent eyes. "The man who owns it may be an outlaw or a horsethief for all we know."

"A regular scalawag," the stranger said, his unwinking gaze on her. "We know he's a hat-thief. Maybe he's a killer and a bully, too. Who knows?"

The girl knew her thrust had got home, though he gave no sign of it. She had told him that he had stolen a horse belonging to Clem Oakland and he had answered by tossing back to her the epithets she had spat at him. He was a cool customer, whatever else he was, or he would not have had the nerve to fling such a challenge at her. In effect he had asked her why she did not tell the sheriff he had been riding a C O horse.

Walsh realized there was a clash between them, though he did not know what it was about. Molly was making an accusation, and the man was not taking the trouble to defend himself. Of what was she accusing him? And why had she mistaken him for Clem Oakland? Something significant had taken place between these two, something that had left a residue of bitterness. He could read it in the sharp hostility of the girl, in the sardonic mockery of the man. In time, no doubt, he would discover the reason.

The officer led the way out of the cabin. "All aboard for the Prescott ranch," he called cheerfully.

Molly swung to a saddle on a rough, round-bellied bay and Walsh adjusted the stirrup to the length she required.

"I had to turn Gypsy loose when we reached the Berry cabin," she told him. "Do you know whether he got home?"

"He made it to the ranch late that first night.

Buck was at the stable and let him in."

"That's good. I was afraid he wouldn't find his way."

"He was pretty badly petered out."

Molly leaned down a little to ask the next question. In spite of herself, she lowered her voice. "Was there another horse, too?"

"Yes, he had company." The brown eyes of the sheriff raised to meet those of the girl, seemed to her to hold something in reserve.

"A big sorrel with a bald face and white stockings?" she asked.

"Carrying a CO brand," he added.

She nodded, apparently having no more to say. But he had another word.

"Taylor was riding that sorrel, of course."

It was a statement, not a question. Molly looked around, to make sure none of the others could hear.

"Do you think he's one of the Oakland gang?" she whispered.

He gave her a dry Yankee answer. "What do you think?"

Into her voice flamed a swift feminine ferocity. "That's what I think. I never met a man so — so —"

She broke off, rejecting the adjectives that came to mind.

Walsh smiled. "I gather you don't approve of him."

"He's the hardest man I ever met," she cried in a low voice. "An automobile engine is soft compared to his heart."

"No news," the sheriff said briefly.

What he wanted to know was the character back of that iron will.

CHAPTER 7
Aunt Jane Wants to Know

The ride to the Quarter-Circle X Y, as the Prescott place was called on account of its brand, taxed the cow-ponies to the limit. After having already broken seven miles of trail through deep drifts, the animals were stiff and weary before they started on the home journey.

Steve Walsh led the way on his own buckskin, a tough and wiry animal which showed less signs of fatigue than any of the others. There had been some discussion the night before in the bunk-house about the staying qualities of horses. Dug Peters in particular had insisted that those of solid colors, especially roans and sorrels, would outlast other mounts. The sheriff had offered to match his buckskin against any other horse they cared to name for a five-hundred-mile ride. That was why he looked around more than once and grinned derisively at Peters, whose roan was dragging very perceptibly.

"Don't let that broomtail quit on you, Dug," he called. "Remember that there are no other broncs like roans. They've got the stamina for a long trail."

"This horse is carrying fifty pounds more than any other in the outfit," Peters protested. "With a fair break it would make that buckskin of yours look like thirty cents."

They crossed the creek and followed the opposite bank. Even though the trail had been broken, the deep snow made heavy going. Steadily they plowed forward, mile after mile, floundering into draws and clambering up rises.

The men took turns at walking during the first miles. As they drew near the ranch, most of them were on foot leading their horses. The ponies were worn out. A dozen times one or another of them had stumbled and gone down.

Walsh had Molly on his buckskin, though she protested she was quite able to walk. She had insisted on traveling part of the way on foot like the others

"Buck is fresh as a daisy," Walsh explained, not quite truthfully. "I want him to show up Dug's roan and that sorrel Hank claims is a world's wonder. I'd let you walk if it was necessary, Molly."

"After such a good day's work don't you think we could favor Buck a little, Steve? I truly am able to walk."

"Sure. But there's no need of it."

He looked back. The procession was strung out for more than half a mile. Taylor was trudging at the sheriff's heels. Hank was two hundred yards behind, far ahead of the other punchers. The cow-ponies dragged at the end of the bridle-reins.

Already the short day was giving place to dusk. The sun had dropped behind a cow-backed hill and the shadows had climbed far up the slopes so that only the tips of them were in shine. Soon it would be dark.

But they were close to the Quarter-Circle X Y. The smoke from its chimneys rose into the clear air. The barking of a dog could be heard.

"I never knew it was so far from the creek up to the house," Molly said, smiling at Steve. "I can remember when I thought it was less than a quarter of a mile."

Her head was drooping with fatigue. "Soon now," he promised. "You can go to bed after supper and sleep for a week."

Molly slid from the saddle in front of the porch, but as she reached the ground, her knees buckled under her weight. Someone caught her as she was going down. She looked up, into Taylor's sardonic face.

She straightened and freed herself at once. Without looking at the man again, she went up the steps of the porch into the arms of her Aunt Jane.

"Praise God!" the older woman said, with a sob in her voice. "We thought — we were afraid —"

"I know," Molly agreed, and wept a little with her.

"When Jim came home without you — and the Gypsy —"

"Is Dad back yet?"

"No. As soon as we heard you were safe, we sent word to him."

They walked into the house and were followed by the two men. Walsh introduced the stranger, adding an explanation.

"Mr. Taylor found Molly in the storm and got her to a place of safety."

"It was rather the other way," Taylor corrected. "She found me and took me to the cabin. I was lost and she fired a shot to attract my attention. Some day I hope to be able to pay my debt to Miss Prescott." He tacked an ironic rider to the wish. "It has been a pleasure to me to pay a slight installment on account."

The angry eyes of the girl raked him contemptuously. "You can discuss that with my father or my brother." Abruptly she turned to her aunt. "First thing, I'm going to take a hot bath."

She walked out of the room.

"I expect you would like a bath, too, Mr. Taylor," the older woman suggested.

"There's nothing in the world I'd like more," he told her promptly.

After Taylor had been taken care of, Jane Macmillan went to the room of her niece. There were questions she wanted to ask. Molly lay in the tub, luxuriating in the contact of clean water as hot as her flesh could bear. From the bedroom adjoining, Jane put her queries.

"Who is this man, Molly?"

"Says his name's Jeb Taylor. I don't believe it."

"Why don't you believe it?"

"Because. He as good as told me it wasn't."

"Then why does he say it is?"

"I s'pose he doesn't want to tell his real name. His initials are W B."

"How do you know that?"

"Saw them in his hat"

"He talks like a Southerner, with a drawl."

"Yes."

"Don't you know *anything* about him?"

"What would you like to know, Aunt Jane? If you're interested, we could give him a questionnaire to answer."

"Why shouldn't I be interested?" Miss Macmillan demanded tartly. "The story I hear is that he saved the life of my niece and spent three days and nights alone with her in a cabin. So I gathered from Frank when he got here. If I'm wrong, please correct me."

"You're absolutely right."

"I don't suppose you were both dumb all that time. Who is he? Where does he come from? How did he treat you?"

"I don't know who he is or where he comes from. I think he's one of Clem Oakland's men. He treated me rotten."

"How did he treat you badly?"

"He's a brute."

"You mean he —"

"No, I don't mean that at all." Molly soaped a washcloth prodigally. "You needn't worry, my dear. His caveman instincts don't run to sex. It was all just as proper as though Dad had been with me. You may heave a long sigh of relief, as they do in books. Your niece returns to you as pure as —"

"That will do, Molly. You needn't be vulgar. And I don't see what you have to complain of, since he saved your life and treated you as a perfect gentleman would."

"Did I say that's how he treated me?" A little ripple of sarcastic laughter came to Jane Macmillan. "He told me quite early in our acquaintance that he was no gentleman. He needn't have taken the trouble. I'd already found it out."

"Just what do you mean? Was he insulting?"

"It depends on what you call insulting."

"Did he . . . make advances?"

"He did not." Molly was a good sport and intended to give the devil his due. "No man could possibly have been more considerate that way."

"You ought to be very thankful he's that kind of man."

"Do you know what kind he is?" the girl asked. "I don't."

"But you don't like him."

"I detest him," Molly flung out with energy.

"He didn't run around and fetch and carry for you I presume."

"His idea is that a woman is inferior to the great god-man, and that she ought to stay in the kitchen except when she is having babies for her lord and master."

"Molly!" reproved Jane severely.

"Excuse me, Aunt. I forgot the stork brought babies."

Miss Jane, still old-fashioned in a modern world, threw up protestant hands. "If I didn't know you I'd think you common, Molly. Why do you say such things?"

"He'd like to be a modern Petruchio."

"How do you know? Did he say so? Did he do anything to make you think so?"

Molly had no intention of going into details. What had passed between her and Taylor was their own private and personal business. She felt competent to fight her own battles.

"One gets impressions. What does it matter? I don't like him. Let it go at that. The important thing is what Dad is going to say when he finds one of the Oakland gang here."

"He won't like it," Jane admitted. "But I don't see that he can do anything. If the man saved you from the storm, your father will have to be decent to him while he's here. I don't suppose it will be for long."

"No." Molly agreed. "It's awkward, though. Dad will feel that he's here spying things out." She added, viciously. "I dare say he is, too. There's something mysterious about him. Why doesn't he come right out and tell who he is and what's his business?"

"We must be civil to him, no matter what we think. After all, he did help you reach Seven-Mile Camp."

"He dragged me there through the drifts after I had become helpless and part of the time unconscious," Molly said. "It's just my luck that it had to be one of the Oakland crowd who did it. Dad will get as much pleasure out of it as I do – and I hate it."

"What must be must, so we'll all have to make the best of it," Jane summed up. "Would you like me to bring your supper up? Then you wouldn't have to dress."

"No, I'll come down."

Jane took the splashing of water as a hint that she was delaying proceedings. "Supper in about half an hour," she called back as she left.

CHAPTER 8
Mostly About
Mr. Jeb Taylor

Clint Prescott frowned at the sheriff, puffing at a corncob pipe. "Who is this fellow Taylor, Steve? What's he doing here? By jacks, I don't like it."

"He's brought you luck so far," Walsh said quietly. "Molly admits she couldn't have reached Seven-Mile Camp without him. Bite on that first of all, Clint. Say he's one of Oakland's men. Say he came here on some of Clem's dirty business. You've still got a big percentage in your favor. I'd say kinda ease him out of here when the roads open."

The ranchman slammed a big brown fist on the table. "I don't want to be under any obligations of any kind whatever to Clem Oakland or any of his damned outfit. And I'd like to tell this fellow so, too."

"Why not?" Walsh asked. "Why not let him know you're so stubborn that you'd rather lose your daughter than have her saved by a guy you don't like?"

81

"I didn't say that. Not by a jugful. What I say is that it's a bitter pill for me to accept a favor from any of those scalawags." He ripped out an explosive oath. "The only way I want to meet Clem or his warriors is with my gun smoking. That outfit has run on me too long. It's war."

"I'm supposed to be sheriff of this county, Clint," young Walsh said amiably, but with crisp decision. "Don't make a mistake. I don't aim to let either you, or Clem run hog-wild. You'll stay inside the law, both of you."

"Go tell him that, boy," Prescott flung back angrily. "What's the sense in you talking like that skunk and I are on a par? Did I start this thing? Did I shoot down his riders? Did I horn in on his range? Did I pull dirty tricks with the Forest Service to cheat him out of the grass he owned? What's eating you, Steve? D'you think I'm going to sit like a buzzard on a cottonwood limb while that crook steals me blind? To hell with your law when it can't protect honest men."

"No way to talk, Clint. The State of Montana is bigger than any citizen in it. You can't set back the clock thirty years. I'm telling you. You've got to remember that a private war with the Oakland outfit don't go unless you do your fighting with modern weapons before a judge and jury. Be reasonable. As an individual, Steve Walsh I'm for you every time against Clem and his gang, but as sheriff, he's playing no favorites. Might as well know that right now."

The young man smiled, a warm and friendly smile that took some of the sting out of the blunt words. He liked the Prescotts and he did not like the Oaklands. Clint did not need to be told that.

Nor did he need to be told that this gay youth had iron in his blood. He had given proof, as far as Clem Oakland was concerned, by arresting his brother Russ after a gun-battle in which the new sheriff had wounded the man. That there might be no doubt as to the supremacy of law, Steve had ridden alone into one of Clem's cow-camps and dragged back to Tincup a C O puncher wanted for murder. The fellow had killed at the instigation of his employer, and Clem had sworn an oath of vengeance against this fool officer to whose head a little power had gone.

No, Clint had no complaint to make of Walsh as sheriff. The trouble was that the case of the owner of the Quarter Circle X Y was one that had got outside the law. Clem intended to ruin him, and was on the way to do it. There was not room for both of them in the county.

"I'm going to protect myself," the ranchman said doggedly. "You can bet your last dollar on that. The law ought to back any play I make. I'm straight. I never blotted a brand in my life.

This fellow is a thief and a killer. But he's twisted around so that the law protects *him* in a lot of his skulduggery. I'm the one to blame because he's stirred up trouble for a dozen years undermining my rights! I'm the one who is outside the law. Hell! If this country was what it used to be, that fellow would be strung to a cottonwood inside of twenty-four hours."

"You can't quarrel with me about that," Walsh said. "Listen, Clint. I know well as you do what a bad outfit Clem is. My advice is to let him run on the rope and hang himself. One of these days – soon, too – he's going to make his big mistake. Then we'll blow him off the map. He thinks he's got the world by the tail for a downhill pull. He's all swelled up like a bladder. If you only have a little patience, we'll prod a gad into Mr. Clem Oakland and watch him go plunk."

"You don't know what you're talking about, boy. This fellow is a fox as well as a wolf. If I don't fight, I'll be out of business inside of two years. So it's going to be me or him."

Taylor walked into the living-room and stopped near the door. "Private conversation, gentlemen?" he asked by way of offering to leave.

The ranchman's salient jaw jutted out toward him. "No, sir," he said harshly. "I was just telling Sheriff Walsh where I stand with Oakland and his gang."

"Afraid I don't know them," Taylor said.

"Don't you?" Prescott's keen eyes challenged the statement. "Well, there's nothing private about my views. Anybody is welcome to them. I think Clem is a liar, a thief, and a murderer, and the knot-heads who follow him are a bunch of yapping coyotes."

"Mr. Prescott believes in plain speaking," Walsh suggested with a smile.

"I gather so."

Taylor's hard eyes took in at length the owner of the Quarter-Circle X Y. He was a large man, heavily built, bullnecked and strong-jawed. Hands and face were darkly tanned. Criss-cross wrinkles made diamond-shaped patterns on the back of the leathery neck. The resolute eyes, the close-shut lips, spoke of a dominant will. In a gray flannel shin and corduroy trousers thrust into the tops of high-heeled boots, he looked the old-timer he was. His guest judged him to be both imperious and explosive. He would fight at the drop of a hat to defend what he regarded as his rights.

"If you should meet up with Clem, Mr. Taylor, you can tell him I'll be waiting at the gate for him any time he gives the word," Prescott told him bluntly.

"And you can tell him I said," added Walsh, "that anybody gets hell in the neck and starts trouble, I'll finish it for him."

"Am I likely to meet him?" Taylor asked blandly.

"That's what I'd like to know. Are you?" demanded Prescott. The eyes under the beetling gray brows were like live coals.

"A fellow can't sometimes always tell who he's going to meet," Taylor said coolly.

A second time the big brown fist of the ranchman crashed down on the table. "Knew it! Knew it all the time! You're one of his damned litter."

"Since you're sure of that, where do we go from here?" the stranger asked.

Walsh interposed. "Just a moment, gentlemen. Let's know how the cards lie. Were you headed for this ranch when the blizzard caught you, Mr. Taylor?"

"No." The word fell after a scarcely perceptible hesitation.

"Didn't come into this country to spy on the Quarter-Circle X Y?"

"Not at all." The answer was pat and prompt, but the smile that went with it was enigmatic.

"Or to do any of Clem Oakland's dirty work?" the sheriff asked, the gay smile robbing the words of much of the offense.

"How could I, when I don't know him?"

"If you don't know him, how come you to be on that bald-face sorrel that's down there in the

86

barn?" Prescott broke in savagely.

The cool and flinty gaze of Taylor shifted to his host. "That's a real long story," he said evenly. "I don't reckon I'll go into that right now, sir. I'll just mention that everyone who rides a C O horse doesn't have to be a C O man. If a cat had kittens in an oven, they wouldn't be biscuits, would they?"

"That kind of talk gets nowhere with me, fellow," Clint stormed. "You're one of the Oakland outfit or you ain't. Which is it? If you've got nothing to hide, why don't you come clean?"

The muscles in the lean face of the Southerner went taut. "I don't reckon I quite get the idea, Mr. Prescott," he said, his low voice almost a drawling purr. "Are you God Almighty in this neck of the woods? Do I have to give my pedigree and show a passport? I've told you I don't know this man Oakland. Why should I keep on saying so?"

"You haven't told me how you come to be riding his horse."

"That's only half of it," Taylor said quietly, looking straight at him. "I'm not going to tell you. Maybe you're the high muck-a-muck around here, but that doesn't buy you a thing with me. I'm not on the witness stand, and I don't allow you can hector and bully-puss me into saying this and that. Maybe I borrowed the

87

horse. Maybe I bought it. Maybe I stole it."

Molly appeared in the doorway. "Did I leave my book here?" she asked of nobody in particular, glancing first at her father and then at Taylor. The former was flushed, she observed, the latter coldly hostile.

"I dunno, honey," Clint said impatiently, anger still in his voice. "You'll find it around somewhere if you did."

"Just have a pleasant chat?" she asked airily.

Walsh grinned. "Something like that."

"I suppose Dad is thanking Mr. Taylor for all his kindness to me."

"You run along, girl," her father ordered curtly.

Molly's decorous smile did not wholly conceal mockery. "Am I to go to bed?"

She was the one person who could banter Clint Prescott and escape without a blast of anger. She was dearer to him than anybody else in the world, and from the time when she had learned to put words together she had given him persiflage and affectionate derision.

" 'Course you've got to have the last word. You always had. If I had you to bring up over again, I'd see what a strap would do for you. Of all the sassy young squirts —"

He stopped, in despair of doing the subject justice.

"Mr. Taylor thinks it isn't too late

yet," she said primly.

"What's that?" her father rasped.

The girl looked at the Southerner, and as their eyes fastened she felt once more the drums of adventure beat in her heart, a sense of suddenly stilled pulses followed by a clamor of the blood.

"He gave me his ideas about women," she explained. "They are to be treated rough. It's the only way to keep them in their place."

Walsh was interested and curious. He had caught that battle of the eyes. A deeper crimson was not streaming through her cheeks for nothing. He decided to do a little probing.

"What is a woman's place, according to Mr. Taylor?" he asked.

"You would probably call his views a little old-fashioned. She is property, and naturally she is to do as she is told. She is to be polite and proper. When she is called she is to come."

"Is she to go away when she is told?" her father wanted to know.

Molly smiled in appreciation of the hit. "Oh, yes, Dad. And I think she is to curtsey when she is given orders. I'm not sure about that." She turned to Taylor, her eyebrows lifted in a question.

He understood that she did not intend to make her indictment specific. She was not going to tell what had taken place between them. Perhaps her pride influenced her. She might want him to know that she could fight her own wars without calling in others to aid her.

"Don't ask me," he said with a grim little smile. "I can't recognize this man you're telling about."

"No?" she said, scornfully incredulous.

"Do you happen to be a married man, Mr. Taylor?" the sheriff asked with a grin.

"I do not. Why?"

"I've noticed that makes a difference. It's the unmarried men that know how to bring up a wife in the ways she should go. Later, our ideas are changed for us."

Molly found her book and departed. Taylor followed the girl from the room.

The owner of the Quarter-Circle X Y went back instantly to the previous question. "You noticed how he ducked out of giving any explanation of himself, Steve. When he claimed he didn't know Clem, he had his tongue in his cheek. By jacks, he 'most laughed in my face."

"I'm not so sure, Clint," the younger man demurred.

"You're easy satisfied if you think that fellow is here on legitimate business. An honest man doesn't have to hide information about himself."

"I didn't say he was an honest man."

"What d'you mean?"

"Nothing definite. I'm asking myself questions, Clint. I've seen that man somewhere, but I can't place him. Funny, too. He's not the kind you'd forget easily."

"You've probably seen him with Clem Oakland."

"I don't think so. I'd remember that. It's the association I don't get." Walsh looked with narrowed reflective eyes out of the window into a white world. His mind was searching for a clue that just escaped him.

"What's the sense in making a mystery out of him, boy? He comes on my range riding a C O horse. He can't tell where he got it or what he's doing here. So he just throws a bluff that it's none of my damn business."

Walsh shook his head. "So that proves him one of Clem's men. No, Clint. I don't reckon it's as simple as that. For one thing, he's riding Clem's own personal horse. I've seen it a dozen times, always with Clem in the saddle. Take your Black Bart. Do you let any of your boys take him on a long trip?"

"No, sir. Neither on a long nor a short one."

"Clem wouldn't turn over his sorrel to someone else any more than you would Black Bart."

"Then how did he get the horse?" Prescott asked impatiently.

"He gave us three guesses, that he borrowed, bought, or stole it. It's a cinch he didn't borrow or buy it."

The cattleman's thick body straightened. "You think he stole it?"

"I don't know. He's no common horsethief. There's more to the man than that. I haven't got him pegged, Clint. He may be one bad *hombre.* He's hard as nails. But he is strong and game. I'd pick him out of a thousand to ride the river with. That's one reason I can't feature him playing second fiddle to Clem Oakland or any other man. He's got all the earmarks of a leader."

"You're riding around in circles, Steve. He bought the sorrel, it was loaned to him, or he stole it. You're trying to tell me he didn't do any one of the three. All right. How did he get it?"

"That's what I'm going to find out. But it will take time."

"Personally I'm satisfied he's one of Oakland's warriors. Soon as the roads open I'll expect him to *vamos.* Until then he's a guest of the ranch, but I'm not going to be a liar and pretend he's a welcome one."

Prescott rose, walked to the fireplace, and knocked the ashes out of his pipe. He had made up his mind. Since he was a stubborn man, Walsh did not attempt to change his

opinion. Besides, there was always a chance
that Clint was right. Taylor might be a C O
rider.

CHAPTER 9
Jim Haley Explains

Taylor found Molly on the porch.

She was looking across the valley at the white hills which ran back to the Haystack Range. Except for the perpendicular face of Black Buttes, the whole country was covered with a blanket of snow.

"So we're going to keep our little secret, you and I," he said mockingly.

She turned and looked at him. "Do you think I want my father arrested for murder?"

He raised his eyebrows in polite doubt "Would it be as bad as that if we put our cards on the table? A shot from ambush, a knife-slash, and a whole flurry of kicks and fist jabs! If we set them against a quirting, wouldn't they count for anything?"

"I'm not going to risk it." The blue eyes blazed at him. "Did you come out here to taunt me because I have to keep to myself how hateful you are? Don't you understand that I speak to you only while you're our guest? After that, you'll go your way and I'll go mine."

He felt less sure of himself than he had at Seven-Mile Camp. She was in a dress bought a few months earlier in San Francisco. It was an expensive gown of black velvet, trimmed with fur, and it fitted her slender body as though she had been poured into it. A delicate penetrating fragrance was wafted to his nostrils. Clothes had transformed her. She was no longer a boylike hoyden in Levis and high-heeled boots. The poised disdainful lift of the chin, the hot defiant eyes, the streamlike line of the body, confounded his sense of cool superiority. In her superb insolence she looked so untouchable. It was amazing to recall that his knees had clamped down roughly the gracious torso, that the marks of his whip still discolored the firm white flesh of her limbs.

"Why waste all this chat on me, since it turns out I'm not Clem Oakland? Am I worth it?" he asked.

"Don't flatter yourself I hate you," she told him, a soft breathing color in her cheeks. "I despise you."

"No, you don't," he corrected. "That's what you'd like to do, because you're furious at me. But you can't make a go of it. Before you can despise anyone, you have to feel he is base."

"And you're not?" she challenged.

"What do you think?" he drawled derisively.

"Can you deny that you're either a spy of

Clem Oakland's or a horsethief?"

A whimsical and bitter smile twitched at his lips. "Let's not go into that. I'm like the Prince of Wales when he travels as Mr. Windsor. Since I'm incog, some questions embarrass me."

"I suppose so. But they wouldn't embarrass an honest man."

"You're passing judgment without waiting for the evidence," he mentioned.

"I'm ready to hear the evidence."

"But I'm not ready to offer it."

The sardonic derision rebuffed her. She became aware, through the acute disappointment that spurred her anger, how much she had wanted him to justify himself. Yet even now her feeling bore out his claim that she did not despise him, at least with no complete assurance. Something in him more potent than external evidence spoke in his behalf. He was hard. He might be lawless – a criminal even. But he was not base.

This was an absurd reaction to rest upon, she realized, and did not let it escape from her to him.

"Suits me. I'm not interested anyhow," she said carelessly.

Her unconcern was a fraud. The man had occupied her thoughts day and night since they had met. She had cherished her hatred and searched for reasons to be scornful of him.

He laughed, hardily. "Not interested, eh? Let me tell you something, Mistress Katherine. You've spent hours figuring on how to get even with me. I'd not care to say how often you've clinched those pretty white teeth when anger boiled up in you. Tell me you hate the sight of me, and I'll believe you. But don't try to tell me you're indifferent after I've treated you the way I did. Not you."

The accuracy of his intuition surprised Molly. She flung away pretense. When she spoke a vibrant wire strummed in her voice.

"All right. I hate you. Let it go at that. There isn't anything more to be said, is there? Unless you are still presumptuous enough to think you can play Petruchio to me."

She turned on her heel and walked back into the house. A quarter of an hour later, someone knocked on the door of the little sewing-room where she and her aunt often worked. In answer to her "Come in," a young man stood hesitantly on the threshold, still holding to the doorknob. He did not seem quite sure whether he was welcome.

"Oh, it's you," Molly said coldly.

He was a rather small, neatly built youth, very good looking if one did not object to a weak mouth and indefinite chin. His hair was dark and curly. In his face was a suggestion of sulkiness.

"Haven't had a chance to see you alone since —"

"— since you ran away," she interrupted acidly.

"You haven't got the right of that, Molly," he explained. "How did I know you weren't right there at my heels?"

"I see. You didn't run away. You just left,"

"Have it your own way," he said petulantly. "You will, anyhow. I never did see such a bossy girl in my life. After I found you weren't with me, I came back. But you'd gone."

"That makes it all right, then," she told him, with obvious sarcasm.

"Everyone acts like I lost you on purpose," Jim Haley complained angrily. "All the boys down at the bunkhouse jumped me. I kept telling 'em you got lost in the storm. Honest, I was scared of your father, he got so wild. And Bob —"

He stopped, and for a moment his fingers caressed a cut cheek. A vain youth, he did not care to go into particulars as to what Bob Prescott had done to him.

Molly observed a black eye and an abrasion on the chin. She regarded them with a certain amount of satisfaction. "So Bob objected, did he, because you left his sister alone in a blizzard? Seems unreasonable."

"He's bigger than I am," Jim said sullenly.

"And I keep telling you I didn't leave you. I went back to look for you."

"Bob's eighteen and you're twenty-three. It's too bad he whipped you. Did you come to me for sympathy?"

"You know why I came, Molly. I want to fix it up. I want you to get it right. If you tell folks I wasn't to blame, they won't all act like I was some kind of a skunk that had drifted in. I don't know what you've got to blame me for. Naturally I lit out. I figured you were foggin' at my heels. When I found out different, I turned around and hunted you."

"But by that time Mr. Taylor and I were on our way," she jeered.

"Did he — act mean?"

Molly looked at her second cousin. There was something unfathomable in that contemptuous regard, but he got perfectly the sharp sarcasm of her words.

"Oh, no. Said he liked being shot at. Said he was pleased to meet me, and it was too bad I wasn't a better shot."

"As the old saying goes, all's well that ends well. He looked after you well as I could have done. I'm the one that gets the worst of it."

"Yes, I had a delightful time. I ought to be grateful to you for running away. Excuse me, I mean for leaving."

99

"Did you — say anything to this Taylor about —?"

"No, I didn't. Neither to him nor to anybody else. You needn't worry about that."

"I didn't say I was worrying. I'm not scared of him or anybody else. If he didn't treat you right, all you've got to do is tell me and I'll have a run-in with him."

"I'm afraid you'd be too far away to hear. If I have any complaints, I'll make them to Dad — or to Bob." She added the last three words with a malicious smile.

That smile was a whiplash to his self-esteem. He had not behaved well, and he knew it. But he wanted to convince her that he had taken the only course possible. Once more he plunged into an explanation of his conduct.

"If you're satisfied with yourself, why talk so much about it?" she asked when he stopped for breath.

"Because folks have got me wrong. They're acting like I quit on you, Molly. I'm entitled to fair play like anyone else," he pouted.

"I think you're getting a little better than fair play, Jim, if you want my opinion," she said bluntly.

"Now, looky here, Molly. You know how I feel about you. You know ever since I've been a kid I —"

She broke in, sharply. "That's enough about

that, Jim. I don't ever want to hear another word of that kind out of you. Not ever. I won't listen to it. I'm just not going to be annoyed."

"It didn't used to annoy you," he reminded her peevishly.

"I used to like all-day suckers, but I don't care for them now. So please remember. Make eyes at some other girl. I won't be bothered with you. I've told you this before. Cut it out."

There was exasperation in her voice. She was ashamed for him and for herself that he could show himself a poltroon and expect to talk to her of love. His stupidity seemed to stress the unmanly thing he had done. Molly had been brought up in that outdoors which is still close enough to the frontier to demand of its dwellers courage as the first virtue. To have pluck was no special merit. Not to have it was a fatal lack.

He covered his retreat with dignity. "All right. If that's the way you're going to act," he said loftily.

"That's exactly how I'm going to act."

"When a fellow comes and explains —"

"Don't be an idiot, Jim. There are some things that can't be explained."

"Some day you'll be sorry —"

"Yes, I know. When I see you making another girl happy with your attentions. But I'll try to bear up and hide my breaking heart."

"You always were high-hat, like you were the

Queen of Sheba or something," he accused resentfully.

"Was she that way, too?" Molly asked guilelessly.

He flung out of the room in a pet, dignity forgotten.

CHAPTER 10
"This Is Station —"

The living-room of the Quarter-Circle X Y ranchhouse was a pleasant place to rest. Molly had furnished it herself. She had consulted with a Denver interior decorator and had achieved a happy result. The subdued homelike warmth of the drapes blended excellently with the furniture and the dominating fireplace at one end of the big room.

Jane Macmillan sat in an armchair knitting a sweater. She had an old-fashioned conscience which felt easier when her hands kept busy. Walsh was at a card-table playing solitaire, Taylor at one side of the open fire reading a book. The fourth person present was Molly. She moved about restlessly, now fiddling with the radio, now looking over the shoulder of the card-player.

"You can move that queen," she told him.

"So I can." He made the move and uncovered a seven of spades. Presently he said: "We're leaving tomorrow morning, Mr. Taylor and I."

"Sure you can break through, Steve?"

"Think so. A lot of snow melted today, and they'll be opening the road from King City. Somewhere near the head of the divide, we'll meet the workers."

"Why don't you play that eight?"

Someone was advertising over the radio the merits of bathing powder. Molly cut him off, turned the dial, and tuned in on another station.

Taylor did not look at her, but he was acutely aware of her presence. The girl's vividness filled the room. She carried her healthy vigorous body with the lightness of a wood sprite. Her step was almost resilient. So Mary Queen of Scots, he thought, must have trod the halls of Holyrood when she bewitched Chastelard. After which flight of fancy he smiled sardonically. His interest in her was annoying. He did not like the girl. Her attitude toward life he thoroughly disapproved She was selfish, spoiled, willful. Yet it was fascinating to find so hard a mental finish, such a cool and flinty decision, encased so beautifully in the warm softness of young flesh. There was an urge in him to break down the arrogant pride, so far least as he was concerned. He had not the least intention of falling in love with her. She was the last woman in the world he would want to marry, and that was saying a good deal, since women played no important part in his life.

But she stimulated opposition in him. A struggle had been going on between them ever since their first meeting. He could feel the clash of minds, just as one feels the grinding of steel on steel in a fencing match.

It was absurd, he told himself. He was taking a small thing far too seriously. For him, women were out for always. He had definitely closed the door to the normal life of other men. It was imperative that he live hard and warily as hunted beasts do. What this pert young whipper-snapper of a girl thought had no validity as far as he was concerned. Why waste energy letting himself be irritated by her?

Molly picked up another station on the radio. She moved across to the piano, sat down, struck a chord or two, and rose abruptly.

"My gracious, child, why don't you sit down and read?" Miss Macmillan suggested

"I don't want to read."

Over the radio a man from some Southern State was broadcasting the news of the day. He finished describing the recent floods and took up a new topic. His words induced a momentary silence in the room of that snowbound ranch hundreds of miles from the speaker.

"It is curious how quickly the news of the day is displaced by more recent happenings. Not long since we in this section could think of nothing else except the Somerton Bank robbery, in which President W. V. Baker of the First National, and Assistant Teller Manlove were killed by bandits, two of whom were shot down in the chase. It will be recalled that the other two outlaws separated and escaped capture."

The lean muscles of one of the four in the living-room had suddenly grown rigid, his nerves taut. He had become alert in every fiber. Yet he was so wholly master of himself that his eyes did not lift from the page of the book he was reading.

The voice of the broadcaster rolled out unctuously.

"The leader of the robbers, Webb Barnett, wounded in the battle at the bank, was pursued by posses through three States, narrowly escaping the officers several times by shrewdly outguessing them. When last seen he was in Wyoming, pushing hard for the border. It is believed that by this time he has crossed into Canada."

The number of those in the room greatly interested in what was being said had increased from one to three. Steve Walsh sat motionless at the table, a card still in his hand. Molly stared at Taylor, lips parted, a queer sense of suffocation in her bosom. Webb Barnett! And the initials in the hat were W B.

She caught once more the voice of the man

at the microphone.

". . . describe him for the benefit of officers in the north who may chance to be listening. This desperate bandit Webb Barnett is twenty-eight years old and weighs about one hundred and seventy-five pounds. He is very strong and is built as symmetrically as a Greek god. Eyes steel-gray and deep-set. Face strongly masculine. Walks as lightly as a prize-fighter and gives an effect of slenderness. Will probably not allow himself to be taken without a savage battle, as . . ."

That was all. Molly had crossed the room and tuned out.

"I don't suppose we want any more of that," she said in a voice that was stifled in spite of an attempt at lightness.

"No," agreed her aunt placidly. "I don't see why they put crime on the air. We read enough of it in the newspapers without that."

Walsh played the card in his hand and examined the layout of those on the table. "Looks like I'm stumped," he said, and added, as though carelessly: "What station talking, Molly?"

"I don't know," she answered

"Rather interesting, don't you think?" he went on. "It would be strange if some officer did happen to be listening in and then bumped into this Webb Barnett later." He looked at

Taylor. In spite of himself his eyes were beaming with excitement.

Taylor glanced up from his book. "Not likely," he said negligently.

"Why not?" Walsh asked. "This Barnett can't be more than three hundred miles from us right now, putting it the highest figure. He might be within twenty-five miles. There's a chance he's even nearer."

"Goodness, I hope not," Miss Macmillan said, in her gentle voice. "You think of the most disturbing things, Steve. Why in the world would this terrible man come around this neighborhood?"

"I didn't say this neighborhood, Miss Macmillan," the sheriff answered easily. "The point is that he isn't going in a straight line for whatever point he's aiming at. He's twisting here and there, ducking towns, touching settlements only when he has to have food. Probably he has had a heck of a time of it. He has to go where he's driven. Don't you think that's likely, Mr. Taylor?"

"Sounds reasonable," Taylor agreed evenly. "Well, the sooner he is captured, the earlier honest folks will sleep in peace."

"You think so," the sheriff said.

"Don't you?"

The eyes of the two met in a long challenge. Those of Taylor did not give way a

108

fraction of an inch.

"Why do men like this Barnett take to crime?" Miss Macmillan asked plaintively. "He must be an able man. Surely he could do well in some field of honest endeavor. I can understand how scum of the city, brought up with no standards of decency, can do dreadful things like this. But this Webb Barnett, if he is like the description that broadcaster gives of him —"

"Probably he isn't," Taylor said, with his cynical smile. "We've got to make allowances for oratory. The man we've just heard likes the sound of his own voice."

"I have a photograph of Barnett at my office," Walsh said, his cool gaze on the other man. "Not a good picture but good enough to tell me he's a fine-looking chap. I'll pay you a two-edged compliment, Mr. Taylor. He reminded me of you."

"Then I don't see how such a man can fling away all his opportunities to do such a thing," Jane puzzled.

"The study of why men go bad is always interesting," the officer admitted. "We've had a large class of outlaws in the West who seem to have gone bad out of sheer perversity. They had lots of the characteristics of good citizens, and then — something happened to them. I can't explain it. Maybe Mr. Taylor can."

Walsh made the suggestion with a little smile that had a touch of debonair impudence.

"Who knows?" Taylor shrugged. "Poor home training — lack of moral fiber — muddy brains — drink — bad companions — and in a few cases innate viciousness. Chances are, when you see this Burney, if you ever do —"

"Barnett is the name," Walsh corrected.

"Barnett, then. If you ever see him, you'll find he has a weak chin or a wavering eye and other signs of inferiority."

"I've an idea, on the other hand," differed Walsh in a gentle voice, "that we'll find him a mighty tough and competent proposition."

"Fortunately, he isn't any of your business. He didn't commit his crime in your territory," Molly said to Walsh.

The sheriff did not lift his gaze from Taylor. In his brown eyes there was a glitter Molly had never seen before. For a long time Steve had been her friend. She was aware that some day he might be more. To her there had always been something very attractive in the gay gallantry of this graceful young fellow. He was the only person she had ever met whose smile could be almost feminine in its charm without impairing the masculine virility of its owner. Walsh was the most popular man in the county. His friendliness endeared him. His dashing courage won him admiration.

But at this moment he had no time for friendship. His mind was full of the job he had to do. Molly realized it, with dread. He did not even take the trouble to answer her foolish suggestion.

She did not understand why her voice had trembled when she had spoken or why such a tumult stirred in her heart. It was silly to be so swept away by the drama of this situation. It was idiotic to find herself fluttering with alarm. Steve could look out for himself. He was a match even for this hardy villain with no regard for human life, this outlaw who had probably for years traveled a long crooked trail and was now come to the beginning of the last crooked mile of it.

Why was she so distressed? Why this queer cold drench of despair?

Aunt Jane folded up her knitting, gathered her belongings, and prepared to leave. She was quite unaware that a duel was being fought in the living-room that very likely would end in tragedy.

"Are you going with me, Molly?" she asked placidly.

"Not . . . just yet," the girl answered.

"Then I'll say good-night. Pleasant dreams all."

After the door had closed behind her, Walsh spoke first. He did not lift his voice, but Molly felt as though steel grated in it.

"Well talk business now, Mr. Webb Barnett. You understand that you're my prisoner?"

"I've been figuring that you think so," the other man answered grimly.

Through Molly's mind there flashed a sentence used by the broadcaster – "Will probably not allow himself to be taken without a savage battle."

"Do you have to do this, Steve?" she begged, in a sudden panic.

"I have to do it, Molly," her friend answered, not lifting his eyes from the man whose hat was stamped with the initials W B.

"Montana expects every sheriff to do his duty, Miss Prescott," said Taylor cynically.

"I've been dumb," Walsh told the other man. "It stuck in my mind I knew you, but I couldn't somehow get the connection. It was that photograph of you in my office, of course. But I'll say one thing for myself. The likeness isn't good."

"You insist I'm Webb Barnett?"

"I'm going to take a chance on it."

"And the C O horse I was riding? What about that?"

"My notion is, Mr. Barnett, that you were being pressed pretty closely and that your own mount was worn out. You were likely down in the Picket Wire country, maybe in Clem's own town Summit. So you grabbed the nearest horse and lit out. It happened to be Clem's sorrel. How will that do for a rough guess?"

Taylor turned his bitter sardonic smile on Molly.

"Your friend agrees with you that I'm a horsethief as well as those other names you called me," he said.

"It's about bedtime, Molly," Steve said quietly. "How about good-night?"

Though he spoke to the girl, his eyes still watched narrowly the man he meant to make prisoner.

"What are you going to do?" Molly cried, looking from one to the other and back again. "Both of you."

The color had washed out of her cheeks. Fear filled her bosom and stifled her. Why did Steve want her out of the room? Would she hear the sound of roaring guns as soon as she had closed the door? She could not leave them. She could not walk away and let this dreadful thing happen. Her imagination envisaged red tragedy. One or both of these men, so vital, so full of supple splendid life, before her heart had beat a hundred times, might lie slack and crumpled on the floor.

Steve smiled, but there was no comfort for her in that smile. It seemed to Molly to hold a chill and wintry threat.

"I can speak for one of us," he said. "I've declared myself."

"I'll speak for the other," Taylor replied quietly, with just a touch of the Southland drawl. "If Mr. Walsh has a warrant for my arrest, I'll surrender, as any honest man would."

"I don't need a warrant," the sheriff answered curtly. "The law doesn't require it."

"In that case I'll surrender, of course, without one," Taylor said.

Molly stared at him, surprised and relieved. Did he mean it? If so, why? It was impossible to associate fear with that strong bony face, with the steel-trap mouth, with the hard mocking eyes. After having ridden so far and so hard for his freedom, surely he would not tamely submit to be dragged back to the scene of his crime.

It was the sheriff, not Taylor, who made explanation to Molly.

"Mr. Barnett accepts facts. He is in an enemy country, surrounded by deep snow. Even if he killed me and got away from the ranch, he would be caught inside of a few hours."

"He forgets, too, my deep respect for law," the fugitive added, with his bitter smile.

CHAPTER 11

Molly Goes into Battle

Molly found her father in the little room he used as an office. He was working on some accounts. At her entrance he looked up.

" 'Lo, Tiddlywinks," he said.

"Steve wants to see you in the living-room," she said.

Something in the girl's voice and face startled him.

"What about?" he asked.

"We've found out who that man Taylor is," she answered.

That she had captured his interest Molly knew. Silently he waited – chair tiptilted, strong teeth biting on a cigar – for her to go on.

"D'you remember that bank robbery at So-merton, Texas, where the president and a teller were killed and two of the bandits were shot down by posses later? There was a lot about it in the papers. Well, this Taylor is the leader of the outlaws."

"By jacks!" After the first astonished moment

115

of grasping the fact, he flung a question at the girl. "How do you know?"

"It came in over the radio — a description of him and his name. He just calls himself Taylor. His real name is Webb Barnett. He must have been making for Canada when the storm caught him."

"Then he isn't one of Clem Oakland's men?"

"No."

"Howcome he to be riding that C O sorrel?"

"Steve thinks he was hard pressed in the Pickett Wire country and just picked it up."

"By jacks!" the ranchman exclaimed again.

"Steve has arrested him."

"It will be a feather in his cap."

"If you let him do it."

Clint Prescott turned a long inquiring look on his daughter. He wasted no words. Soon enough she would let him know what was on her mind.

"He saved my life. He's your guest. Are you going to let Steve walk off with him as though you had no rights?" she continued.

Clint knew her of old. She was trying to repress an intense excitement.

"What do you want me to do, honey?" he asked.

"It doesn't matter how much a villain this man is," she urged. "We're under a heavy obligation to him. At least I am, and you are if —"

"Sure I am," her father interrupted. "What you want me to do? Talk to Steve?"

"Talking to him won't do any good. You know Steve. He's sheriff, and he'll bull through — unless you prevent him."

"How can I prevent him? Like you say, he's the sheriff. Want me to buck the law?"

"You've bucked it for yourself, haven't you? In this fight with Clem Oakland. When it wasn't with you, I reckon you've ridden over it often enough."

"That's different, girl. I can't step in between Steve and a prisoner he has arrested."

"Not even though the prisoner risked his life to save mine?" she flamed.

"We got to be reasonable, Molly. This fellow is an outlaw and a killer, unless you and Steve are barking up the wrong tree. If he's been caught, that's the break of the game. He wouldn't ask me to go to the pen to save him from the penalty of his crimes. Not if he's a game guy, he wouldn't. And this fellow is. I'll do anything for him I can, but —"

"Except the one thing that will help him," she broke in swiftly. "You'll aid him if it doesn't cost you anything. That doesn't sound like Clint Prescott, unless all these years I've been wrong about him. I've been proud of my father, because I thought he was a good friend."

"Is this Taylor my friend?"

"I'd think, if you care anything about me —"

"What's the use of talking foolishness, girl?" he interrupted roughly.

"Well, then, since you do —"

"Thought you didn't like this man Taylor?"

"I don't. He's detestable. What's that got to do with it? I've got to pay my debts all the more when I owe them to someone I dislike. Don't you see I can't desert him? He dragged me out of the blizzard when I was unconscious. He wouldn't leave me to die, though he could hardly lift one leg in front of the other. Now you want me to turn my back on him. I won't do it."

Her voice broke on a sob.

Prescott rose, abruptly. "I'll go see Steve. It won't do any good, but I'll talk to him."

She followed him into the hall. "Steve can't take him away if you won't let him."

The ranchman went fuming into the living-room.

"What's the big idea of arresting one of my guests, Steve?" he demanded

"Call him a guest of the storm, Clint. You didn't invite him here, did you?"

"He's here, ain't he? I don't like your coming to my house and arresting my friends."

The sheriff asked exactly the same question Prescott had put to his daughter a few minutes earlier. "Is he your friend? How long have you known him? This man is Webb Barnett, wanted in Texas for bank robbery. That's why I'm arresting him. I don't reckon you have any objections."

"How do you know he's Webb Barnett? Does he admit it?"

"Not necessary. It's written in his hat."

"What is?"

"The initials W B."

Prescott turned to Taylor. "Is your name Webb Barnett?"

"My name is Jeb Taylor. I've mentioned that several times, but Mr. Walsh seems hard of hearing," the prisoner said.

"Take a look at the band of his hat, Clint," the sheriff advised.

Taylor reached down and picked up the hat beside the chair in which he sat. He tossed it to his host. Prescott looked at the band.

"I don't find any initials here," he said.

"No? May I look at it, Clint?" Walsh asked. A moment later, after one glance at the hatband, he laughed cynically. "I see Mr. Barnett doesn't make the same mistake twice."

Molly, too, examined the hat. The part of the band with the telltale initials had been ripped out.

"Mr. Taylor doesn't want to be known as Webb Barnett, but he is a little too late," the sheriff continued. "Both Molly and I saw the hat before he got busy with it."

The ranchman turned to his daughter. "Did you see the letters W B in the hat?"

The girl's answer was prompt. "I saw some initials. The first was a W or an M. Depends on which way you looked at it."

Walsh grinned. "I see my witness has gone back on me. Never mind. I'm satisfied it was a W, and that is all that matters."

"You don't want to make a mistake, Steve," said Prescott. "If I was in your place, I'd go kinda slow."

"Would you think that way about it if you didn't feel under an obligation to this man?" the sheriff asked, cocking an eye jauntily at his friend. "Seems to me I heard you singing another tune last night. Makes a difference whose ox is gored, eh? When you thought he was one of Clem Oakland's men, you were ready to throw him out on his ear."

Clint declined to make an issue of his change of front.

"This man doesn't look to me like a bank robber. I'd say he was a straight-up rider a fellow could take the river with."

"That's an opinion. I'm dealing with facts, Clint," the officer said.

Prescott turned impatiently to the other man. "Hadn't you better spill your story, Taylor? This boy is all filled up with a fixed idea. Can

120

you pry it out of his mind?"

"I doubt it," Taylor said derisively. "I'm no bank robber, but I don't carry around with me affidavits to prove an alibi."

"You're Webb Barnett," charged Walsh, looking directly at Taylor.

The arrested man, coolly on guard, met his gaze with a mocking smile. No muscle twitched in the thin brown face. Whatever else he was, Clint thought, the fellow was a hardy devil who feared neither God nor man.

"Taylor is the name," the prisoner drawled. "Jeb Taylor."

"Have it your own way," Walsh said crisply. "But Taylor or Barnett, you're going to Tincup with me."

Molly broke in, her eyes hot and defiant. "Mr. Steve Walsh, sitting to himself for a portrait of a brave and fearless officer," she challenged.

Walsh laughed. There was this about Molly, that when she came into action it was with flags flying.

"Maybe so," he admitted gayly.

"Playing to the gallery for a renomination," she went on.

"And after that there's the governorship," he grinned. "And someone has to be president."

Angrily Molly turned and walked out of the room.

CHAPTER 12
Molly Plays a Lone Hand

Molly did not understand the keenness of her emotional disturbance. The basis for it was not entirely her desire to pay a debt. She was profoundly shocked to learn that her rescuer was an outlaw and a murderer. To hold a grudge at him because of his bitter harshness and callous indifference was one thing. To recoil from the knowledge that he had set his face toward ways wholly evil was quite another.

Not for a moment did she doubt that he was Webb Barnett. Steve Walsh himself could not have been more sure of it. She did not blame Steve. He was only doing his duty. If he had given way to her wishes, she would later have despised him for it.

But her own position was different. She had a debt to pay and meant to discharge it if she possibly could. Infamous though this prisoner was, she had to find a way of freedom for him. If she could do that, she would be through with him. It would not matter then if he were recaptured later.

After leaving the living-room Molly had talked with her father again. She had upbraided him for deserting her cause, passionately and with bitter words. Prescott had tried to explain that he had gone as far as he could, and when she would not see it, had exploded angrily and driven her from the room. He would give her no more help. She knew that. Whatever she did would have to be done on her own. Moreover, it must be something that involved no harm to Steve. For she did not intend to sacrifice his life in assisting a criminal to escape.

Impatiently she paced the floor. Back and forth, back and forth. There must be some way, if she could think of it. Steve was a good officer. He would be hard to fool, for he would watch his prisoner as a cat does a mouse. But she had as good brains as he and ought to be able to outwit him.

The sheriff and his prisoner were in her brother Bob's room. The boy had moved out to the bunk-house to make a place for Taylor, and now Steve had joined the other man. He was to sleep on a cot carried in for the night. Molly had heard him tell Taylor he would be obliged to tie him to the bed, and the Southerner had advised him ironically not to trust a rope.

The girl did not understand even yet why the bank robber had surrendered so tamely. If he let himself be taken back to Texas, he was lost.

She would have guessed him one to go down fighting rather than to submit to such a fate.

But that was just now an academic question. Since he had not fought to save himself, she must fight for him.

In the next room Steve was moving to and fro making his preparations for the night. The muffled sound of voices reached her. Presently the window was thrown up. She listened to the creaking of the sheriff's cot as he settled in it. After that there was silence.

That open window! From it Molly's plan germinated fast. It might not work. Steve was a light sleeper. She had heard him say so. If he woke too soon, it would mean failure. But she had to take a long chance.

Swiftly Molly slipped out of her dress and into a pair of Levis. She put on a flannel shirt and soft-soled moccasins. From a drawer of her dressing-table she took a sharp-bladed pocket-knife. Impatiently she looked at her wrist watch. She must allow time for everybody to settle down to sleep.

Half an hour later, she stole from her room and downstairs. She opened the front door and crossed to the stable. Buck Timmins would be sleeping in the little bedroom adjoining the hayloft, but it was not likely she would waken him. The difficulty of arousing him was a family joke.

124

The bald-faced sorrel was in the third stall. His bridle was on the wall back of it. She dared not light a lantern and had to put the bridle on in the darkness, feeling her way along the animal's head and nose with deft fingers. Then she found a blanket and saddle. More than once, before she tightened the cinch, she stopped to make sure Buck was not stirring.

The crunch of the snow beneath the horse's hoofs as she led the sorrel to the willows back of the root-house set her heart fluttering. She could see no lights either in the bunkhouse or in the big ranch-house, but she felt as though the enveloping shadows were alive with watchers. With a slip knot she tied the C O horse to a young tree.

Noiselessly she slipped through the darkness to the cottonwood in front of Bob's room. It had been years since she had climbed it, but in the old days she had often used the tree as a ladder to reach the window. Since then the branches had been trimmed, but she believed she could still swing across to the ledge.

The cottonwood was a short-trunked one with spreading limbs. She threw the end of a rope over the lowest branch, went up it hand over hand, and swung a leg lithely up to get support. From one bough to another she moved carefully, edging far out on the one leading to the house. Gingerly she reached for the ledge with one hand and a knee. A moment later she was crouched on it, scarce daring to breathe as she listened through the open window.

Molly lowered her head to let it pass under the casement and sent one foot out to explore for a landing-place. Her toes touched the floor and she very cautiously transferred part of her weight to them. An inch at a time, with infinite precaution, her body passed into the room.

She waited by the window what seemed to her a long time. It was necessary to creep forward silently. If she pushed against a chair her enterprise was doomed. Very gently hands and feet groped in the darkness. A floor board sounded. She stopped, in a panic of fear. An outstretched hand touched a blanket.

If the prisoner should cry out or speak! That she had to risk. Her fingers traveled along the blanket and came to a chin. One of them, the forefinger, dropped warningly, on the lips above. The head nodded understanding.

That gesture thrilled her. He was awake and knew what she was trying to do. Once more they were partners in a desperate adventure.

From a pocket of her Levis she drew the knife and slowly opened it. Her hand searched beneath the blankets and found a rope. She severed it. Presently she had cut hands and feet free.

The man on the cot stirred restlessly. Molly

waited, terror in her throat. He settled back to stillness.

Taylor's hand felt for the knife. She gave it to him and was aware of his movements as he worked with it on the rope. Slowly he drew back the blanket and raised his body. The bed creaked.

A sharp voice from the cot made staccato demand. "What are you doing?"

To Molly it seemed that the Southerner's body uncoiled like a released spring. It plunged across the room and hurled back the sheriff as he was rising from the cot. The girl heard the sounds of deep breathing, of bodies threshing in struggle, of a crash of heavy bodies.

A voice ordered harshly, "Turn on the light."

Molly did so. Walsh lay lax on the floor. The other man released him and rose. Both were fully dressed except for coats and shoes.

"I'll have to tie him," the Texan said. "And gag him."

"You haven't killed him?" Molly asked, horror in her eyes.

"No. Don't think so. He struck his head as he went down." Then, as he was tying the officer's hands, Taylor added: "He never had chance. I was on him before he could get set."

"If he's dead —"

"He isn't. See. His eyes are fluttering. I'll have to stop him from calling for help." Taylor drew a handkerchief from his pocket, folded it, and fitted it into the mouth of the sheriff as a gag. With a piece of rope he tied this into place so that it could not easily be worked out.

After he had secured the feet of the officer, Taylor rose. He put on his coat and boots. "Where from here?" he asked Molly.

"I'll show you," the girl said "This way."

She stopped before reaching the door. The eyes of the sheriff had opened and were watching her.

"Can you breathe all right, Steve?" she asked in a low voice, kneeling beside him.

He nodded.

"I'm awf'ly sorry you got hurt," she told him.

A ghost of a smile flitted into the brown eyes. It was the smile sarcastic. If he had been able to speak, he would have told her that such solicitude was touching. She understood, and was distressed. For she felt she was in a false position. Steve was her friend. He stood for law, and was entirely in the right. This Barnett was an outlaw and a killer, personally hateful to her. Yet circumstances had conspired to drive her to his side and make her a criminal too.

"I'll see you're freed just as soon as I dare," she promised, and she put her handkerchief beneath the back of his head where the blood was trickling through the curls.

Even this did not satisfy her. She went to the

water pitcher, dipped the end of a towel into it, and bathed the wound with soft and gentle touch.

"We'll have to tie up his head," she said to the Texan.

Taylor brought another towel and they applied first aid.

This done, she led the way into the passage and downstairs.

CHAPTER 13

"I'll Never Forget"

Through the snow the escaping man followed Molly to the root-house. She was in Levis again, he saw, as she had been during those memorable days and nights when they had been alone, one man and one woman, in a universe of white solitude. Into his veins an eager uncurbed exultation poured.

She had saved him. Strangely, that was what lifted his spirits, the fact that it was through her he had won free. The freedom itself was a lesser cause for gladness.

Back of the root-house she stopped. "Here's your horse," she said in a kind of still cold voice. "You'd better go to Seven-Mile Camp. There's nobody there now. You can help yourself to food. After that —"

"— I can go to the devil my own way," he interrupted.

"For all I care," she answered.

She was such a slim clean-limbed young thing, and in her eyes there was such a passion of contempt for him. Beneath the stars he saw the rise and fall of her slender bosom, and he knew she was emotionally keyed up. He guessed that she hated herself for what she had done for him, that she was daring him to believe there could be any reason for it other than the obligation of the debt she had felt impelled to pay.

"You can despise me now, since you find I am base, after all," he told her cynically. "It wouldn't be any use, would it, to tell you I've had a bad break and am not as bad as I seem? You'd know I was lying."

"No use," she flung back fiercely. "I know what you are. Thank God, I'll never have to see you again after tonight."

It burst from her almost like a cry. But it did not sound like one of thanksgiving.

"Since all debts are paid," he suggested.

"Yes."

"Except what you'll have to pay for freeing me. Have you thought of that?"

"Don't think I'm not ashamed," she countered, and her voice quivered.

"But you had to do it."

"Because I'm a fool," she admitted in a wail. "Because I couldn't let Steve arrest you when I owed you so much."

For a long moment he said nothing. He did not move. His eyes burned into hers. In her bosom a hot excitement kindled. Something

131

wild and primitive fluttered in her heart.

"So that's all," he said.

Her answer came, dry as a whisper. "Yes."

A wave of emotion crashed through him. He said, with his bitter sardonic smile, "I'm a man beyond the pale – if I'm a man at all to you, and not just a hunted wild beast."

"An outlaw and a killer," she reminded him in bleak despair.

"Not even human."

She shivered, not speaking, since she didn't dare to trust her voice. All the passionate resentment had died and passed out of her. In every fiber of her being she longed to have him draw her into his arms, and yet within her a faint bell rang a protesting warning. She mustn't stay here. She must go – now. Before . . .

And then they were in each other's arms. Her lips trembled to his. Body clung to body in a mad sweet intimacy. Their pressed emotions of many hours fused for one pulsing minute.

She pushed herself from him, savagely. "Go – go!" she cried.

The fugitive swung to the saddle and held a tight rein as the horse protested. He guided the animal close to her and looked down.

"I'll never forget," he said hoarsely. "Never."

And with that he was gone.

A stricken young thing, she turned unhappily toward the house. Summer, which had sung in her heart a moment, sang no more.

She stumbled through the snow in a mist of tears, whipping herself with her own self-scorn. So she was that kind of girl. All the time she had been lying, to herself, to her father, to Steve, to the prisoner. She had pretended, had even made herself believe that some tie of honor bound her to the man and that to do less than save him would be ingratitude. Whereas, what she had wanted, in her wild and wicked heart, was to help him because she had fallen in love with him.

What reason had he ever given her to induce such folly? From the first he had trampled down her self-respect and pride. Yet he had probably known for days what a fool she was and had laughed up his sleeve at her. To have flung herself at any man would have been bad enough, but at such a one as this was without excuse. He had said it himself. He was beyond the pale. Probably the only women he knew were those who like himself were outlawed.

Wanton! That was the word for her. She had disgraced herself and her family. She had gone with keen-edged passion into the arms of a man whom she knew to be a villain. The thought of it was a revelation to her. She had not known she was like that. There had been in her no faintest guess that a wave of emotion could crash through her and sweep her so violently from the anchors of her conventional upbringing. One thing at least she could be thankful for – that she had been blind to her feeling until after those days at Seven-Mile camp.

Yet, even while she lashed herself for her folly, she knew that she did not regret saving him. If it had been necessary to do it over again, she would have done the same.

Quietly she slipped upstairs and into the room where she had left the sheriff. To attract attention he was drumming with his feet on the floor. At sight of her he stopped.

First she removed the gag, then cut his bonds.

"Are you much hurt?"she asked.

"I'll have a headache for a while. That's all. I suppose our friend has lit out?"

Color streamed into her cheeks. "Is he your friend? He isn't mine," she said.

He looked at her, curiously. "Like to have you for my enemy sometime," he said, with a short laugh.

"I hope I'll never see him again," she cried passionately.

"I hope I do," he differed dryly.

"If you do, I'll never interfere again."

"I'll take care of that," he assured her.

"I've evened the score with him," she explained, and passed to another subject. "Shall I look at your head, Steve?"

"Why not?" he said whimsically. "Since your friend who isn't a friend broke it, after you had butted in on other folks' business, it's only fair you should mend it."

"It didn't bleed much," Molly said.

"Reckon it was the shock put me out. It will be all right after it's washed. By the way, you didn't mention what has become of Mr. Taylor, *alias* Barnett."

"He's gone. I'm going to wash this and bathe it with an antiseptic. Then I'm going to tie a towel around your head. I hope you'll be able to sleep."

"I never could sleep much on horseback," he laughed.

"Can't you wait till morning, Steve?"

"No. I forgot to mention to you that I'm sheriff of this county and a prisoner of mine has escaped. I'll be right busy tying to recapture him."

"There's no use going out now — in the night," she urged. "I'm not thinking about him, Steve. Truly I'm not. He's got away, for the present, anyhow. I'm thinking about you."

She was busy making preparations to take care of his head. His eyes followed her, with no resentment in them, but rather a kind of quizzical bewilderment. She had gone a long way to save this outlaw Barnett. He did not know many women who would have had the courage to do as much, even for a man they loved. And Molly did not love the outlaw. She detested him. So at least she had repeatedly said. Not three minutes ago she had reiterated her feeling, with a good deal of heat. Perhaps too much. What a woman said about a man was not always what she thought.

"You ought to rest tonight," she continued. "You oughtn't to go out in the cold. Can you lean forward a little more, please?"

Very gently she washed the wound. The touch of her fingers was like velvet.

"Did he mention which way he meant to go?" her patient asked experimentally, knowing well enough that if she gave him any information, it would not be accurate.

"I thought I'd better not ask him," she answered.

"The beggar took my gun with him," Steve said, grinning ruefully. "I'll have to borrow one from Clint. This is going to give my rep an awful jolt, Molly. That portrait of a brave and fearless officer will look smudged."

"I oughtn't to have said that," she admitted impetuously. "You were doing right, Steve. I knew that all the time. It's pretty rough on you, to lose your prisoner and get a broken head, too. Excuse me a minute. I want to go to my room for some iodine."

She was not gone half a minute, but when she returned, her father was in the room with Walsh.

"Thought I heard a noise up here, like someone drumming," Prescott was saying, his keen eyes sweeping the room.

"Where's your prisoner — under the bed?"

Before the sheriff answered, he stooped, picked up a pocket-knife, closed it, and put it carelessly in his pocket. "He's taking a *pasear* Clint."

The ranchman read sign: a blood-stained towel, bits of cut rope, a wadded handkerchief that had been a gag.

"He knocked you cold and lit out?"

"Right, first grab out of the bag." By way of explanation Walsh added: "Molly heard the row and came to the rescue, in time to give me first aid."

The girl's father looked at her, then back at the sheriff. "You were some careless, Steve, looks like."

"I'll say I was," he agreed, with emphasis.

There was a good deal about this Prescott did not understand, but he meant to find out.

"I'm surprised. Doesn't seem like you, Steve, to let a prisoner slip one over on you like that."

"We all make our mistakes. I thought I had the fellow tied good and tight. Even had a rope with one end tied to him and the other to my

137

foot, so that if he moved much, he'd wake me."

The ranchman watched his daughter dab the wound with iodine. When she had finished pinning a towel around the head, he shot a question at her.

"How come you to be wearing Levis and a flannel shirt, Molly?"

"I s'pose they were handy," she said.

"Handier than a dressing-gown?" he demanded brusquely.

"I hadn't gone to bed yet. I was just trying on things."

"When you heard a noise in this room, why didn't you call me?"

"She probably thought we were just dropping our boots," Walsh suggested easily. "Getting ready for bed."

"I didn't ask you, Steve. I asked Molly."

"No use, Steve," the girl said quietly. "We'll have to tell Dad."

"I'm not a plumb fool," the owner of the Quarter-Circle X Y announced. "That story of yours wouldn't get by with a tenderfoot. I aim to know the facts."

Molly looked at her father, chin up. Into her cheeks the hot color poured.

"I did it," she explained. "I came in by the window and cut the rope that tied this Taylor."

"You damned little wildcat!" her father roared. "Haven't you got any sense a-tall?"

"I told you I'd help him if you wouldn't," she defended.

Prescott slammed down on the table a fist that made it dance. "I never saw your beat for butting into other folks' business. If you were a boy I'd wear you to a frazzle with a willow. You act like you're crazy. Before you get through, you'll have this whole country talking about you. By jacks, you dumb idiot, Steve can put you in jail if he's a mind to do it."

He stopped, from the sheer inadequacy of words.

"I'm through now, Dad," the girl said, in a small contrite voice. "I just thought, since he had done so much for me —"

"*You* thought!" interrupted her father scornfully. "Like its important what you think. Always got to have your own way. Can't let me decide what's best. Go ram-stamming ahead spite of hell and high water."

"I'll do as you tell me now," she promised humbly.

Her meekness was born of the discovery that had come to her back of the root-house. She had no fight left in her.

"After you've done the mischief. Don't you know that this whole country is going to talk about it? You've laid yourself open to common gossip."

"Hold your horses, Clint," advised Walsh

calmly. "Who's going to know that Molly was in this unless you go and shout it out to everybody? In the first place, nobody outside of us three knows I had arrested Barnett. So they can't know he escaped unless you want to broadcast it. There's no great harm done."

"Except that you've got a broken head and lost a prisoner who would have brought you a lot of glory."

"My broken head will mend, and I haven't lost a prisoner, but mislaid him for a while."

"You're a white man, Steve. I'll say that." Prescott spoke with fervor. "It's more than this little fool deserves."

Walsh glanced at Molly and smiled. "How do we know what she deserves, Clint? You don't reckon she enjoyed climbing up here and doing what she did. In the dark I might have shot her. It took nerve to do it. She figured she owed it to this man. We all make mistakes, but we don't all make ours on the side of generosity."

"I think you're a peach, Steve!" Molly cried, and bit her lip to keep back tears. "I dare say I was a fool. I know I was."

"Where's this fellow now?" Prescott asked his daughter abruptly.

"I don't know. I had that C O horse waiting for him back of the root-house. He rode away."

"Without saying where he was heading for?"

"I didn't care where he went." Molly felt the

hot blood burning her cheeks as she thought of that passionate parting. "I don't ever expect to see him again. I just wanted him away from here."

"Hmp! I'll bet the fellow never stopped to say thank you."

"I didn't want his thanks, Dad. It just seemed as though I had to help him, and so I did. Maybe I'm crazy, like you said."

"I've got work to do, Clint," the sheriff said briskly. "Before any of your boys get up in the morning and mill all over his tracks, I want to find out which way he went. Can you get one of the boys to saddle my Buck? But first off, we want to agree on our story. How would this do? We heard a description of Webb Barnett over the radio. Later on, it came to me that this fellow Taylor was the guy they were advertising for. I started to arrest him, but he saw me coming, slammed me on the bean with the barrel of his gun, and lit a shuck out of here. Does that look reasonable?"

"I don't see anything wrong with it," Prescott admitted.

"Steve ought not to go out tonight," Molly insisted. "He might catch cold and get pneumonia or something."

"You're getting mighty considerate of him," her father said, with heavy sarcasm. "After giving this bird Barnett a chance to kill him while he was making his getaway. But you're right at that. Tell you what I'll do, Steve. I'll slap a saddle on Black Bart and have a look-see my own self, instead of you. It won't be easy to find which way this fellow went, because the boys have been breaking trail all day in about forty directions looking after our stock. But I'll do my best."

"It's up to me, Clint," his friend said. "I'm sheriff."

"Molly is right, boy. You got no business going out. I'll be your deputy for tonight. I reckon I can cut trail about as well as you."

"Better," Walsh admitted. "But that's no reason —"

"Then you stay here. After we know where he's heading for, if we find out, I'll drop out and let you carry on. That's fair enough."

Walsh knew that what Prescott said was good sense. The blow on the head had left him pretty wobbly on his feet.

"All right. I'll go to bed if you'll report to me as soon as you find out anything," he consented.

The ranchman went to his room and dressed. Molly met him as he came out into the hall.

"Let me go with you, please, Dad," she begged.

"What for?"

"You need someone for company. The boys

142

are all tired, and I can't sleep anyhow. I'm too excited and nervous. I'd love to ride with you. Maybe I could help."

He guessed that this was her gesture of repentance and his heart softened to her. "I reckon you better go to bed, honey," he said.

"What for? Just to toss around? I'd like to get tired, and then I'd sleep."

"Are you dressed warmly?" he asked abruptly.

"Yes."

"All right. Come along. You can turn back and come home when you've had enough."

Prescott put a flashlight in his pocket. They walked to the stable and he saddled two horses.

"Chances are this fellow will strike for a main-traveled road, figuring he may be able to get out of the country now the telephone wires are down," the ranchman said. "I'd guess he's heading for Tincup or Meridian. Which way did he start?"

"I didn't see him go," Molly answered, hating herself for playing the rôle into which she had been forced.

It was the habit of her life to tell the truth, to be frank, to have no shameful secrets. She had none of the sinuous indirections that mark the course of many women of more complex existence. Even when she had been away at boarding school in the East, she had retained a simplicity some

143

of the other girls thought naïve.

Molly did not choose soft words to palliate the thing she was doing. In order to protect this villain in his flight from justice, she was deliberately lying to her father; in effect, at least, if not in so many words. She had promised not to interfere again, to do as she was told. Yet she had come along to make sure Clint took the wrong trail and to blot out, if possible, the right one.

"Just where did you leave him?" Prescott asked.

"Must have been about here," she said.

His flashlight showed him the snow cut up by the tracks of a dozen horses and men. Nothing could be learned here.

"We'll push toward the main road," he decided. "Farther we get from the ranch the fewer tracks there will be. We'll ride along the road, see where he strikes it, and find out whether he's turned toward Tincup or toward Meridian. If he's aiming for Meridian, Steve and I can take the Fisher's Prong cut-off and get there first."

"Yes," assented Molly.

Early she lagged. Twice her father turned to rejoin her.

"No sense in your going along if you're fagged, Molly," he told her.

"I guess I am, Dad," she admitted. "Gypsy

doesn't want to follow you and I haven't enough pep to make him."

"Shag along home, girl, and get to bed."

"Do you mind if I do?"

" 'Course not. Don't bother to unsaddle Gypsy. Leave him in the stall and I'll take care of him."

"I reckon I'm a quitter," she confessed. "Good-night."

"Good-night," her father said. "You go to sleep and forget your worries, child."

He was a little surprised. It was not like Molly to give up so readily any undertaking she had started. He would have been astonished to see how instantly the weariness disappeared as soon as the darkness had swallowed her.

Gypsy discovered that his mistress was full of energy. He moved down the hill at a fast road gait.

Molly churned up the tracks back of the root-house and crossed to the trail to Seven-Mile Camp made by Steve Walsh's rescue party. There had been a good deal of wind at night and the snow was disappearing rapidly. There were spots so bare that an individual track could be picked up without difficulty. Several times she rode back and forth between the house and the creek, to make sure the prints of the C O horse were obliterated. This done, she crossed the stream and followed the path that had been plowed up the slope. She held Gypsy to the rut of travel. For more than a mile the pony wound back and forth along the twisting brook. Molly had done all she could, since she had to reach the stable before her father. She turned and headed for home.

At the stable she unsaddled, glad to know that her father had not yet arrived. She slipped unnoticed into the dark house and up to her own room.

Without turning on the light, she undressed and went to bed. As she nestled to the pillow, she realized that one thing she had told her father was true now even if it had not been then. She was tired.

But her mind was still active. She did not find it easy to go to sleep. Vagrant thoughts chased one another through her mind.

She despised herself for having broken trust with her father and with Steve after she had promised in good faith not to interfere again. Why had she done it? Was she so lost to any sense of decency that nothing counted but her unbridled feeling for this scoundrel?

It puzzled her to recognize in this new Molly Prescott the girl she used to know. She was traveling uncharted ways. No doubt she would have been very scornful of another girl as weak as she had been. To tell the truth, to do right had always been so simple. But when she had been put to a test, one that involved her own emotions, it had not been so easy.

Well, she was through now. She would never see this hunted bandit again. He would be out of her life and out of her thoughts. She would discipline herself. She would not let her mind dwell on him. To begin with, she would count sheep and go to sleep.

One . . . two . . . three . . . four . . . five . . . How under the stars with a little rustling sound her body had swayed toward his and she had found herself . . . No . . . No . . . six . . . seven . . . eight . . . nine . . . ten . . . He was out of her life . . . His kisses stung her lips. She felt her body clinging to his in an embrace tumultuously rapturous.

Molly groaned. What was the use of saying he was out of her life since her thoughts, whenever she unleashed them, turned to him like steel filings to a magnet?

She had often, in days past, given an impersonal consideration to this thing called love. It had never touched her intimately. She fancied mildly for a time one lad or another. Recently she had thought much about Steve, wondering if he might be the man. That love might be a devastating and destructive force she had not conceived. That it could pour though her trembling body and burn like fire came as a revelation.

It was a revelation in which she exulted even while it shocked. A few hours ago she had been a child in understanding. Now she was a woman. For life, she thought, is written in experience and not in years.

He had said he would never forget. The words had come from him as though driven by some inner compulsion. Surely he had meant them. Evil though he was, there was in him a kind of stark sincerity. Even bad men could not be all bad. Once he had said to her, in his bitter ironical way, that he might not be as bad as she thought, and she had denied him a chance of explanation.

It was strange, but even now, when she knew what he had done, some queer insurgent corner of her brain refused wholly to condemn him. The crime he had committed seemed so inconsistent with the quality of the man. He had himself defined the causes in a man that led him to go bad. Poor home training – lack of moral fiber – weakness preyed upon by drink or bad companionship – innate viciousness: none of these would explain him, unless it was the last. He was strong. One could not get away from the force in him. Master of his impulses, he would walk the road he had chosen. Was it possible, then, that of deliberate choice he had elected to follow crooked and evil trails?

Molly could not believe it. The look in a man's eyes, the way he carried himself, the impression he made: they could not all be lies. There burned in this Webb Barnett who called himself Jeb Taylor the dynamic spark of self-respect that denied complete baseness. Truth abode in him somewhere.

And he had promised never to forget. Neither would she. Not ever. With youth's lack of perspective, with its failure to realize how obliterative are the marching years, Molly was convinced that the emotions so vivid in her now would endure as long as she lived.

CHAPTER 14

Taylor Talks Himself Out of a Jam

Taylor did not know how long a start he had. It would depend upon how soon Walsh picked up his trail. The sheriff would probably expect him to strike for a main road and head north, on the theory that he would try to get out of the country before the telephone wires were up again. This would be a long shot. Within twenty-four hours at most trouble-hunters might be expected to have the lines repaired. If so, a man wanted by the officers could not easily slip past them.

The hunch of the fugitive was to cut back south for fifty miles or more, then push west into Idaho. He had an impression that not so far north the storm had been much less severe, in which case travel ought to be easier.

At Seven-Mile Camp he stocked up with provisions. He was likely to be for some days in a thinly settled country, and he wanted to see as few of the inhabitants as possible. His best chance of escape was to disappear in the wilderness and leave no witnesses to his going.

Particularly, he wanted to swing wide of Summit. To meet Clem Oakland or any of his friends just now would be awkward. Around the country of the C O ranch he could not defend his title to the bald-faced sorrel.

As the cow-pony plowed through the snow, Taylor gave its owner good on one count. He knew horses. This one had both speed and stamina.

His guess about the storm had been a good one. The depth of the snow decreased as the sorrel left the miles behind him. He came to a country where only patches of it showed.

After a few hours, Taylor made camp in a draw dotted with pine trees. He picketed the sorrel, lit a fire, and rolled up in his blankets. When he awakened, the sun was up.

He cooked and ate breakfast, saddled, packed, and was on his way.

Swinging out from the draw into the open, Taylor came face to face with two men. They were moving toward him, but were still fifty or sixty yards distant. His first thought was that Walsh had trailed him down already. A moment later, he dismissed this fear. Neither of these men bore any resemblance to the sheriff. As they came closer, he took stock of them.

One was a big rangy fellow in the costume of a cowman. He had a hard, gross face both rapacious and cruel. It told of dissipation, but not of weakness. The opaque eyes were cold and black as jade.

His companion was of medium height and so thin that the hardpacked flesh of his body made a scant covering for the bones. The chalky eyes were shallow and shifty, the chin weak, the teeth broken and soiled.

Before the men pulled up their mounts, Taylor knew this meeting was significant. The strangers did not have the manner of casual good will customary in those who come upon another traveler in the wide-open spaces. With no word yet spoken, the Texan knew himself threatened. He observed that the big man shifted his hands on the rifle lying across the saddle in front of him so that it would be ready for instant action. The heavy body, which had sagged laxly to adjust itself to the motion of the horse, straightened and grew rigid.

"Got you!" the thin man yelped jubilantly with an oath, at the same time flashing a revolver. "Stick up yore hands!"

Taylor let his two hands rest on the horn of the saddle. "I don't get the idea, gentlemen. Is this a hold-up?" he inquired quietly.

"Don't make any break, fellow, unless you want to get pumped full of lead," the big man scowled, with an ugly rasp to his voice.

"Wouldn't think of it," the Southerner replied. "Maybe after a while you'll let me know what it's all about."

"You know damn well what it's about," the rangy cowman said savagely. "Frisk him, Ed. Get his guns from him."

"Just a moment," Taylor interposed mildly. "What d'you want? Who do you think I am?"

"We don't care who in Mexico you are. If you lift either of those hands, I'll blow you to hell."

"Where did you get that horse?" Ed asked, shallow eyes gleaming with triumph.

"Oh, this horse," the fugitive answered, with a manner of relief. "I'll tell you about that."

"You tell us after Ed has collected your hardware," the man with the rifle said dogmatically. "Don't forget I've got you covered. If you bat an eye —"

Taylor sat motionlessly while the smaller man relieved him of his revolver.

"Only one gun, Clem," the searcher announced.

So this was Clem Oakland and one of his gang. No wonder Clint Prescott did not like them. If both of these men were not ruffians, they were entitled to sue their faces for heavy damages and get a verdict. That he was in a jam Taylor knew. He had to talk himself out of his predicament. For these customers were more likely to drygulch him than wait for the law to punish.

"He called you Clem," Taylor said "Are you Clem Oakland?"

"You've said it."

"And I'm Ed Flannigan," the smaller man said, with an evil grin. "If that means anything to you."

Taylor spoke to Oakland quietly. "You're the man I was looking for."

"Yeah?" Oakland laughed, a ring of cruelty in his mirth. "Then you've found me."

"I was heading for the Picket Wire country."

"I'm to believe that, am I? Probably bringing back the horse you stole. Is that the story?"

"The horse another fellow stole, Mr. Oakland." Taylor threw one leg across the horn of the saddle to rest more easily as he talked. "The sheriff, Steve Walsh, arrested the man that stole it. He had him at the Quarter-Circle X Y Ranch."

"At the Quarter-Circle X Y, eh?"

"Yes. Owned by a big bully-puss fellow named Prescott. There's been a blizzard up in that country. It came up sudden. I had to hotfoot it to the ranch for shelter."

"Go on. You're doing fine," Oakland jeered.

"I reckon I'll have to come clean, gentlemen. I'd got my tail in a crack over a little trouble I had at Ten Sleep, over in Wyoming. The word was out to look for me. This busy sheriff of yours recognized and arrested me."

"What kind of trouble?" demanded the cow-man harshly.

Taylor hesitated, as one does who is being driven to say more than he would wish. "Well, I — fact is, I had to gun a fellow and make a swift getaway. He happened to be a deputy sheriff. It kinda got crowded on me."

"What had you done?"

"The claim is I robbed a post-office. Nothing to that. They got me mixed with another fellow."

"I expect so. What post-office?"

"At Basin."

"And after he'd arrested you, Walsh saw what a good citizen you were and turned you loose?" Oakland asked, with heavy sarcasm.

The fugitive grinned sheepishly. "It wasn't quite thataway. He got just a leetle mite careless for two seconds and I knocked him cold with the loaded end of a quirt. Then I helped myself to his six-gun, grabbed this sorrel and lit out in the night."

There was a gleam of satisfaction in Oakland's cold jade eyes. This story of the discomfiture of Walsh he would like to believe. The fellow told it glibly. Of course, he might be a colossal liar. He was in trouble up to his neck right now and naturally would say anything that might help him.

"Don't believe a word of your story," Oakland

said suspiciously. "You know what we do to horsethieves in this country, fellow, and you're pulling this one for your skin."

"How far are we from where this horse was stolen?"

"About twelve miles. Maybe fifteen. Why?"

"When was it taken?"

"You know when. Friday morning. What's that got to do with it?"

"And this is Wednesday. Five days to travel fifteen miles. I certainly must have been making good time if I was trying for a getaway."

Taylor had scored heavily. He knew it. It would be difficult for anyone to imagine a reason why a horsethief should hang around the scene of his crime five days waiting to be detected. He expected to score again presently, as soon as Flannigan made a certain little discovery. The prisoner could help him make it, but it would be more effective if the chalk-eyed man stumbled on it by chance.

"What's your name?" Oakland rapped out.

"Jeb Taylor."

"Live at Ten Sleep?"

"Not exactly. I kinda drifted there. You might say I live in Colorado."

"I've only got your say-so for all this."

"That's right. I'm a stranger here." Taylor's glance shifted to Flannigan for an instant and he gathered confidence from what he saw. The gaunt man was staring at the butt of the revolver he had taken from the captive. He was in process of making the expected discovery. "It's too doggoned bad I met you here. In a couple of hours more I would have been at your ranch with the horse, Mr. Oakland. I'd say I didn't have very good luck."

"Say Clem," broke out Flannigan, "there's an S W cut on the handle of this gun."

"Lemme see," the other man ordered curtly.

Flannigan passed the gun to his leader.

"You claim you took this from Walsh after you had knocked him out? That what you're asking me to swallow?" the big man said presently.

"That's the fact, Mr. Oakland"

"Did the other fellow escape too — the horse-thief?"

"No, sir, he didn't. The fellow wasn't in the room at the time. The sheriff was grilling me about this and that when I saw my chance. It was look out for the number one. I burned the wind away from there."

"I don't know whether you're lying or telling the truth," Oakland admitted bluntly. "Sounds like a fairy tale to me."

"Why does it? How can you explain my being here with that gun of Walsh any other way?"

"Maybe it's not his gun," Flannigan said.

157

"Maybe I had his initials carved on my gun six or seven months ago expecting to meet up with you gents this morning," Taylor suggested sarcastically. "Maybe I stuck around here a week or so to see if I couldn't steal another horse."

"You might have lost your way," the chalk-eyed man advanced weakly.

"With the sun riding up there in the sky to tell me which is south and which north. You'll have to guess again on that one." Taylor turned to the cowman. "I'll tell you straight, Mr. Oakland, that I figured you and I might do business. I've told you how it is with me. I'm in a jam, like I said. Need some place to hole up for a while. Maybe some day you could use a man like me. *Quien sabe?*"

"You're from Colorado, you say?"

Taylor's eyes narrowed slightly. There was a wary glitter in them. "Colorado will do. I may have come from two or three places."

"A few jumps ahead of a sheriff?"

"I've heard folks don't ask too many questions out this way, Mr. Oakland."

"That depends. When I find a stranger with my horse, I'm entitled to ask plenty. Don't think anything else for a minute, fellow."

"I ain't making a complaint. All I'm saying is that if I've got a mothworn secret or two up my sleeve, they wouldn't interest you."

"What does Steve Walsh look like?" Oakland demanded abruptly.

"He's a curly-headed guy, brown eyes, kinda athletic in build. I reckon a girl would call him good-looking. That ain't the way I'd put it. I'd say he was one of these slick, smart, know-it-all cusses who get all swelled up on themselves."

Taylor spoke with a touch of venom. During the past few minutes not only his manner but his appearance had changed. He had taken on the furtive slack-jawed look of a second-rate bad man. His speech was less incisive, not so well chosen.

"Describe Clint Prescott."

The description Taylor gave was accurate but not favorable.

"How many kids has he got?"

"I saw two, a boy about eighteen and a girl maybe a year or two older."

"Names?"

"Lemme see. The boy they called Bob. Seems to me the girl was Molly."

"On which side of the creek is the house?"

"West."

Oakland gave up. "All right, fellow, I'll accept your story for the present. If you've lied to me, God help you. But you'll stick around. Make a break to get away and you'll get about ten feet. Understand?"

"Y'betcha! Do I get my gun back?"

"You do not. I'll take good care of it for you. Slide off that horse. You can ride this one."

They exchanged mounts.

Oakland headed toward the north. After they had traveled steadily for about an hour, the prisoner murmured a reminder.

"I don't want to be fussy, boss, but I'm getting kinda nervous. Looks to me like we're going straight back to the Quarter-Circle X Y country. I'd hate to bump into Sheriff Walsh."

"You'll go where I say. But I'll tell you one thing. I'm not going to turn you over to Walsh, not unless you've been lying to me," Oakland growled.

Flannigan's splenetic laughter came in as a kind of chorus. "And not even then," he added, menace in his shifty eyes.

"Where are we going?" Taylor asked.

"You'll know when we get there," the cowman snapped. "If questions are necessary, I'll ask them."

They rode for hours over the hilltops. It was past noon when Taylor looked down on a valley which he recognized. Below them, not more than a mile away, lay Seven-Mile Camp.

CHAPTER 15
Walsh Qualifies as an Expert

Clint Prescott came back to the house after his scouting expedition, frankly puzzled. If Taylor had reached the main road, he had not been able to discover any evidence of it. There ought to have been a break in the snow where his horse had plowed up to it from below.

The ranchman did not wake the sheriff to tell him what he had not found. Steve needed the rest, and nothing could be done till daylight, anyhow.

At breakfast Walsh listened to his story. The rest of the Prescott family were present, including Miss Macmillan and Jim Haley.

"I can hardly believe even now that this Mr. Taylor is a criminal," Jane said, wide-eyed at what she had been told. "Why, he seemed such a gentleman. His manners are very good."

"His company manners," Molly amended.

"So he wiped you over the head with the barrel of his gun, Sheriff," Jim commented, with scarcely concealed satisfaction. He was jealous of Walsh for more reasons than one.

"As already mentioned," the officer admitted ruefully.

"And then lit out?"

"With my six-gun and Mr. Clem Oakland's horse. I wish you'd been around to head him off, Jim." Walsh dropped the last so innocently that Jim was not sure whether it was meant as a sarcastic dig or not.

"I'm glad he wasn't," Jane said, with emphasis. "It's lucky we weren't all murdered in our beds."

Bob was as excited as his aunt, but not so shocked. "I don't reckon he goes around bumping people off promiscuous. Say, Steve, where do you go from here? If you're looking for a posse-man, I'll sashay along with you to round up this bird."

"You'll stay at home and 'tend to your own business," Molly said promptly; and as an afterthought added, "won't he, Dad?"

"I won't either, not if Steve calls on me," the boy flung back.

"First, I have to find out which way he's heading," Walsh said, helping himself to bacon. "Then I'll take out after him, probably with one other fellow. You're a mite young yet, Bob. Now Jim is just the right age."

"I don't know as I've lost any outlaws," Jim replied. "Besides, I'm busy."

"I'm not," Clint said. "How would I do, Steve?"

"You'd do fine, if I find I need anyone. Soon as the telephone is working, I'll have to do some long-distance calling. We'll cut him off in every direction."

"I hope you bring him back here," Bob said.

"I hope you don't," his aunt differed fervently.

From the window of her room Molly watched her father and the sheriff as they rode out trying to pick up the trail of the escaped prisoner. They vanished behind a hill, moving in the direction of the main road. It was two hours before she saw them again. The two men stood and talked for a few minutes in front of the house. Her father came in. Steve moved toward the creek.

The sheriff stopped his horse on the trail his party had made coming back from Seven-Mile Camp. He swung from the saddle and scrutinized something that held his attention.

The girl watching him felt the stomach muscles beneath her heart give way. She knew that he was about to start toward a discovery.

He slowly followed the path to the creek, crossed the stream, and rode up the slope beyond. At the top of the hill he disappeared. Half an hour later, she saw him again. His horse was loping up the trail to the house.

Prescott had gone to look after some stock. Molly went downstairs. She was pretty sure Walsh would want to see her.

He did.

"Let's go to your father's office where we can be alone," he said.

She led the way. Steve closed the door after they had entered and looked at her. His smile derided and yet admired.

Molly had perched herself on her father's desk. She was swinging a slim silk-clad leg jauntily.

"You're pretty good," he told her.

"Aren't I, as they say in English novels?"

"But not quite good enough."

"Will you have me put in jail?" she asked him saucily.

"Clint told me you went out with him last night and got tired."

"So I did."

"Before you got home I'll bet you were." His quizzical grin was not unfriendly. "I don't get you, young lady. Last night you told your father you were through helping this fellow. You said you would do as Clint told you from then on. And you went right out and fooled him to a fare-you-well. So as to save this criminal again."

The light went out of her face as the flame does from a blown candle. "Yes," she admitted bleakly.

"Why?"

"Why what?"

"Why did you do it? I've known Molly Prescott since she was so high." His hand measured a space from the ground. "This doesn't seem like the Molly I know. You'd helped this fellow escape. You'd paid your debt in full — if you owed him any. So you said yourself. Then you went out and did it all over again. Broke your word to do it."

He could see the color mounting beneath her steadfast eyes. Only once before, for a moment or two last night, had he seen that shamed look on her face. It had been of the essence of her keen-edged youth that she should be sure of herself even to the point of unconscious insolence.

"You're too polite, Steve," she told him bitterly. "Why don't you tell me I'm a dirty little liar?"

"You're not. I've never known you tell a lie. You think straight too." His narrowed eyes gave her a long scrutiny. "There's something in this I don't understand, unless —"

"Maybe I'm possessed by a devil, the way folks used to be," she suggested moodily.

Yet underneath her saturnine despondency was alarm. It was like the game she used to play as a child when one looked for a hidden object

165

and was warm or cold, depending upon the distance from it. Steve's mind was treading very close to her secret.

"Unless you're in love with Taylor," he continued.

To hear her ignominy put into words sent the blood pouring into her face. She was so distressingly aware of it that she felt she must be hot to the touch. The naked heart ought to be as sacredly guarded from ruthless eyes as the nude body. So she thought, and yet realized he was within his rights. If he was probing her feeling, it was because she had interfered with the performance of his duty.

"You use your imagination, Steve," she said, with a scornful tilt of the chin.

"Not as much as you do, perhaps," he answered, his appraising eyes watching her steadily. "A girl might become interested in him, if she was thrown a lot with him . . . alone."

"You ought to write stories," she advised derisively, sure that he knew her ridicule was a fraud.

"She wouldn't know at first he was a blackguard," he went on evenly. "What she would see would be his strength, the masculine vigor of him."

"You understand women perfectly. There's one little thing you've forgotten, though. I thought he was Clem Oakland, the man who wounded my cousin, who tried to kill my father, who wants to ruin us all. It would be so natural for me to fall in love with someone I hate, wouldn't it?"

"That would keep you from being indifferent to him, and maybe you fell in love after you found he wasn't Clem."

"I'll tell you something I've never told a soul, Steve," she broke out impulsively, in a fury of scorn at herself, as one bites on a sore tooth in protest at the pain. "He whipped me when we first met — with a quirt, brutally."

"Whipped you?" repeated Walsh, incredulously amazed.

"As some men whip a dog that has tried to bite them. The purple marks are on my legs now."

"But, good Heaven, why?" he cried.

Already she could have bitten her tongue for telling, but she had to go through. "I was in Levis. He took me for a boy and thought I had shot at him."

"What made him think you'd shot at him? And how could he mistake you for a boy?"

"I didn't mean to tell you, Steve," she pleaded. "I don't know why I did, unless it was to make you see how impossible it is I could like this man. You promise me never to tell . . . never . . . not anybody."

"Of course I won't tell, if you don't want me

to." He was aware of a passionate desire to take hold of this ruffian Barnett and beat the life out of him with his naked hands. "But I don't understand – I don't see –"

"Not even if you think it would be best to tell – for my sake," she urged, desperately. "I don't see why I said anything about it. I meant never to tell anyone."

"You can forget that you told me, Molly."

"The storm had started and Jim and I were hurrying home when we saw him on the C O sorrel. Jim thought he was Clem Oakland and shot at him."

"Shot at him?" Walsh said, surprised.

"Yes. Why not, if you come to that? Clem had wounded him once, when he didn't have a chance. He had tried to kill my father."

"And Barnett thought you were the one who had shot at him?"

"He didn't see Jim at all. I ran for Gypsy and didn't make it. I had been cutting a switch and had a knife in my hand. So when he laid hands on me, I struck out at him, not thinking about cutting him. But the blade went into his shoulder. So he whipped me, till he found out I was a girl."

"Where was Jim all this time?" her friend asked harshly.

"Jim had ridden away. He thought I was coming right after him."

"I see," Walsh commented, with grim dryness.

"He came back afterward, but we had gone then."

"Says he came back, eh? Couldn't we get him a Carnegie medal?"

"That's all done with now," she said. "Mr. Taylor, or whatever his name is, fought hard to get me to shelter. After he had saved me, he treated me with as much consideration as even you could have done. I want to be fair to him."

"Even though you hate him."

A pulse throbbed in her throat. He read in the blue eyes what he was not meant to see.

"Or love him," he added.

"Could any right-minded girl . . . care for him . . . knowing what he is?" she asked.

"I reckon," he said gently. "Love's a queer thing. I've seen many a good woman care for a man who wasn't worth a barrel of shucks. And sometimes the other way about."

"After he'd treated me the way he did? Wouldn't I have some decent pride?" she demanded, in self-scorn.

"This love business isn't always reasonable. It doesn't go by merit like a civil-service examination. But I hope you don't care much for him. It couldn't bring you any happiness."

"I know that as well as you do. I'm a fool, Steve — just a plumb fool."

"Maybe you're just a little bit romantic," he suggested, with a cheerfulness that declined to take the matter too seriously. "I've had a case on a girl one week and the next was clear over it. You'd be surprised how quickly the human heart recovers from a solar plexus wallop."

She smiled a little ruefully. "Lessons in love. Apply to Steve Walsh, expert."

"Did I claim all that?" he grinned.

"Do I have to take anything? Or do I recover automatically?"

"The best way to forget is to get interested in another fellow."

"Who, for choice?" she asked, playing up to his friendly attempt at diversion. "The best friend I have — nicest man I am acquainted with — knows what an idiot I've made of myself, so he's out of the question."

"Don't be so sure of that," he differed gayly. "It's human nature to want what you can't get. If I'm that nicest man, I'll probably begin losing sleep over you right off. You'd be a real sweet girl if you had a better disposition."

"Thank you, kind sir," she said, curtsying.

"I might do a lot worse than you, though I'd hate to swap a good friend for a wife."

"Couldn't she be both?" Molly asked. "That's a general question, Doctor Walsh. I'm not going to hold you to any rash answer you may make."

"She might be both — if she was Molly Prescott before she became Molly Walsh."

"Aren't you paying me a compliment?" she said doubtfully. "You don't have to do that while you're treating my case."

"I don't do it because I have to. I think I'm starting to slip already. Help, help!"

She shook a small, finely modeled head of wavy copper. "You don't need any help. I can look through to that decorously concealed grin of yours."

"In revenge for that I'll go hunt down my rival. *Adios, carissima.*"

"Is Dad really going with you?"

"So he said. I'll talk it over with him."

"I wish he wouldn't, Steve. Couldn't you take one of the boys?"

"Maybe so. I'll see."

He had cleared the atmosphere for her, momentarily at least. She had told him what was in her heart. He had made her smile. That was something. After looking at the situation through his viewpoint, she had discovered that her fault was not so dreadful.

In spite of his gay friendliness there was nothing soft about Steve Walsh. He had never had to go hunting his heart among the young women he knew. It was a well-regulated organ that stayed at home. Molly had always been to him a charming willful girl with whom it was

171

fun to exchange badinage. Now she had become a fascinating problem. To be regarded objectively, he reminded himself.

Walsh found Prescott superintending the loading of a sled with hay. It was necessary to get feed to stock cut off from the home ranch.

"Still of the same mind about going with me, Clint?" the sheriff asked.

"Are you just guessing? Or have you a trail to follow?"

"I've cut sign. My bird flew to Seven-Mile Camp last night."

"By jacks, I'll bet your guess is good. Figured he could outfit himself there with grub, though there can't be much left."

"I'm not guessing. He won't be there now, of course. I'll have to take a pack-horse. Liable to be out several days. I'd think you would hate to leave your stock right now."

"I do. Fact is, I want to boss this job of looking after them. You can have one of the boys."

"Suits me. Which one?"

"Dug Peters is good, if he wants to go."

The bald-headed young Hercules jumped at the chance. Prescott gave him instructions about packing a lead horse with supplies. This the puncher did while the sheriff tried again, as he had unsuccessfully done several times before, to reach either Tincup

172

or Meridian over the wire.

"I've got Tincup," Steve said to Molly, who was in the room. He was very pleased at making the connection.

His deputy, Owen Martin, answered the call. Walsh explained how he had been held up by the blizzard and then gave an edited version of his news. He instructed Martin to establish contact with every town in a radius of a hundred miles and to spread the information that Webb Barnett, Somerton, Texas, bank robber, had been seen at the Quarter-Circle X Y ranch, but had escaped.

"I'm going after him myself with one of the ranch boys," he concluded. "Don't know when I'll get back. If you learn anything important, call up Clint Prescott and tell him. Good-bye."

"Maybe I'll be here instead of Dad when Mr. Martin calls," Molly said, a spark of quizzical impudence dancing in her blue eyes.

"In which case I may or may not get Owen's message," Steve said calmly. "It won't matter much, anyhow, as I expect to get Mr. Barnett myself."

"You feel quite sure?"

"Not so sure," he confessed. "But if I don't get him, someone else likely will. He is nobody's fool, but he doesn't know the country."

"When you bring him back, if you do —"

"When I bring him back, if I do, a certain

173

young lady I know won't get a chance to gum up the law's machinery again. I'll be watching her the way a cat does a mouse-hole."

"Wouldn't it be better to watch your prisoner, as you did last time?"

"I'll watch him, too. You'd be surprised."

"I see you don't trust me."

"No farther than I can throw a yearling by the tail, young woman."

She watched him walk lightly out of the room, with the smooth flow of muscles that seemed to set a rippling through his body. The graceful poise of the small curly head, the jocund gayety bubbling so near the surface, the sudden warm smile, all contributed to a picture of charming *insouciance*. As her perplexed gaze followed him, she frowned, half-whimsically, half in dismay. How perverse is the human heart! Here was a hero all ready for her to spend her girlish admiration upon. Instead, her eyes must wander toward one far more villain than hero.

Because her heart was engaged in this enterprise of manhunting. Molly's feet took her to the porch. Peters had brought three horses to the house. Two of them, saddled, he had tied to a snubbing-post. The third carried a pack on a cross-buck. It had been tied on with a thirty-foot lash rope.

Steve was examining the job. He turned to

174

Peters with manifest respect.

"So you can throw a diamond hitch, Dug," he said, "Not many can nowadays."

"I'm the only waddy on the place can do it, not counting the boss," he boasted. "Punchers don't know nothing any more. Just a bunch of brakemen. No more sense than to put their tin plates after they've et on the chuck-box lid instead of in the pan. Don't know sic' 'em."

"Dug is a pessimist," Molly explained.

Peters demurred. "No, ma'am, I'm a Presbyterian, though not practicing much right now."

The sheriff swung to the saddle of his Buck and waved a hand in farewell to Molly.

CHAPTER 16

Taylor Fixes
the Sheriff's Clock

That Clem Oakland had come here for no good, Taylor did not doubt. Evil had plowed its seams in that hard gross face. In his youth the fellow had probably been handsome, though with something wolfish in the eyes. But with the years deterioration had set in. The evidences of unbridled passion were written on him.

It was a fair guess that the man had come into Quarter-Circle X Y territory to do harm to his enemy. In what way Taylor could not guess. Presently he would find out.

Just now Oakland lay sprawled at ease on a cot in the cabin at Seven-Mile Camp. He did not take the trouble to keep his muddy boots from soiling the blankets. That was characteristic of him, Taylor soon discovered. He was clear neither in body nor mind.

To Flannigan he told a story of how he had treated a woman and her young spineless husband. The tale certified him for what he was, a bully and a brute. Nobody with the least decency of feeling could have done such a thing or could have told it afterward. The broken-toothed man with shifty eyes grinned appreciation.

"I'll bet that held 'em," he said.

His boss dismissed in a sentence the subjects of his story. "The galoot had no guts and the Jane no jingle."

If Taylor was a scoundrel, at least he was a clean one. The ruffian on the bed would have been surprised at the murderous impulses churning through the brain back of the prisoner's slack-jawed grinning face. But Clem Oakland was no psychologist. He did not care what men thought. Only the overt act became important, and that not often. For like many shallow egotists he had a profound contempt for his fellowman.

Taylor gathered that they were in no hurry. Someone was to meet them here, and he would have a report that would probably precipitate action of some sort.

To miss the bitterness of Oakland's feeling toward Clinton Prescott was impossible. It expressed itself in almost every reference made. The two men had been enemies ever since the owner of the Quarter-Circle X Y had thwarted the ambition of the other to go to the State Senate. That had been the first clash. There had been many since. Clint had once forced an indictment of Oakland for cattle rustling and had nearly secured a conviction. The trial had inspired such bitter feeling that for weeks men had walked Tincup in fear of their lives.

Since then Oakland had taken on the importance that comes with power and large holding. Most men of his acquaintance, aware of the man's ungovernable temper, trod softly in his presence and took care not to oppose him openly. Clint Prescott alone had treated him with scornful contempt.

This attitude of Prescott had been a mistake. It had infuriated Clem without intimidating him. The man was dangerous. He had his sly ingratiating side, as well as his ruthless one. Somehow, by bribery Clint claimed, he had made himself solid with the office of the forest supervisor. The owner of the Quarter-Circle X Y brand was gradually being forced to the poor grazing of the dry lands.

He had spent a large sum building a dam to irrigate alfalfa lands, and, though he had gone through the necessary preliminary formalities to get permission to do this, Oakland was challenging his legal right. It began to look as though the challenge would be effective.

Most of this information Taylor picked up from the boastful and rancorous talk of Oakland. The fellow had no reserve. He hated, and he let his hatred boil out of him.

In one of his outbursts Clem told more than he meant to tell. His present visit had to do with the dam. They were waiting here for a man they called Dean, who had been up to the reservoir investigating it. From a jubilant threat flung out by Oakland, the Southerner gathered that he intended to ruin Prescott without waiting for the slow process of law.

"I'll put him out of business so quick he'll think the whole Missouri has flooded down on his damned Quarter-Circle X Y," the big man bragged.

"Go slow, Clem," the other C O man advised, speaking from a corner of his ugly mouth, with a quick look at Taylor. "What this guy doesn't know won't hurt us any."

"Don't mind me," the prisoner said, with a placating smile. "I aim to light out of this country *pronto*, gents. I ain't interfering with any hands you sit in to play. Live and let live, I say."

On one of his periodic trips to the door, Flannigan flung information over his shoulder. "Three fellows heading this way along the creek."

The big man got up from the bed and walked to the door.

"Two men and a pack-horse," he corrected.

"Looks like they're coming here," the chalk-eyed man said. "Maybe we better drift back into a draw until they've gone."

"When in doubt run," jeered Oakland. "That's your motto, Ed. Well, it ain't mine. We got here first. I'm comfortable where I am. Let's find out who these guys are before we light out."

He walked to his saddle-bags and got a pair of field-glasses.

Taylor leaned back in his tilted chair. He had not even glanced out of the window. "I can tell you who one of 'em is," he said coolly. "Mr. Steve Walsh, sheriff, on the trail of an escaped prisoner who wiped him on the bean last night with a gun-barrel."

"Correct," agreed Oakland, after a long look through the glasses. "I don't know as I recognize the second fellow. It's not Prescott."

The Texan brought the front legs of his chair to the floor and rose. "Time I got out of here," he said briskly.

"I'm not sure about that," Oakland demurred, his eyes narrowing. "Hold your horses, Mr. Taylor, if that's what you call yourself. Don't get on the prod. Plenty of time."

"Walsh will be here in twenty minutes."

"Maybe so. Maybe not." The voice of the big man had become almost a purr, his manner foxily sly. "Looks like you get a break. Are you a pretty good shot with a rifle, fellow?"

180

Taylor looked at him, startled. He did not need a diagram drawn of this man's meaning. At the Quarter-Circle X Y he had heard talk of Oakland's threats against the sheriff. Now Clem intended to use him as the instrument of his revenge. At the dictation of the cowman, Taylor's finger would pull the trigger. The fugitive would bear the blame. If necessary, the other two would have a very plausible story to tell of having been completely surprised by the outlaw's homicidal impulse. They might even kill him afterward, as evidence of good faith and because dead men do not tell tales. Yes, that would probably be the way of it, though very likely the big ruffian's mind had not traveled quite that far as yet.

That his captor was serving an ultimatum Taylor knew, though he was not certain just what the consequences of refusal might be. Either they would turn him over to the sheriff, or else they would get rid of him and the officers too.

"Not so good," he answered.

"Then you'd better be lucky," Oakland said, with a cruel smile. "If I was to lay this rifle down close to you, and if you grabbed it up quick, I wouldn't have time to prevent you from shooting Walsh with it, would I? But if you missed, naturally Ed and I would get over our surprise right off and pump bullets into you, the same as any good citizens would. Understand?"

Taylor flung out a gesture of protest. He looked frightened, the weak and impotent drifter before the law who had not nerve enough for murder.

"Listen, Mr. Oakland! I don't want to get into trouble gunning this fellow. He ain't done me any harm. Lemme jump a horse and beat it. I still got time," he urged.

"Don't make any mistake, fellow," the big man said ominously. "You'll do as I say. If you don't, Ed will bump off Walsh and I'll give you the works soon as he has done it. I'm boss here."

Oakland drew his revolver and let the barrel point toward the floor. He looked at the prisoner, his jade eyes gleaming.

"One or the other, Mr. Taylor," he went on, with suave menace. "Which is it to be?"

The Texan played for time. "Seeing as I'm druv to it, I'll have to do as you say. No two ways about that. Gimme the rifle. I hate to do it. I'm no killer." His voice was trembling. His hands shook.

"You claimed you gunned an officer in Wyoming. A deputy, you said. Go yourself one better and get you a sheriff in Montana. Be a sport." This from Flannigan, grinning an evil broken-toothed smile.

182

"I don't even know which one is Walsh," Taylor weakly demurred.

"You'll know in plenty of time," Oakland told him harshly; "They're not near enough yet. Listen. I'm doing you a favor. You gun this bird that's after you and light out of the country. What could be fairer?"

"I c-can't go around killing every officer I see."

"Up to you," Oakland answered cruelly. "I've told you how it will be."

"This fellow's got buck fever, Clem," the gaunt man said contemptuously. "He's scared of Walsh, when all he's got to do is draw a bead on him and blow the daylight out of him."

"I'm not scared either," Taylor protested, a thin bluff in his voice. "I'll show you. Lemme go out and tackle this fellow. It'll be him or me one."

"Why go out?" Oakland asked. "You'll have an easy shot from cover. Take your time. Point is: don't miss."

"W-what about the other man?"

"He'll pull his freight soon as you've got Walsh. Don't worry about him. Would a drink steady your nerves?"

"My nerves are all right," Taylor boasted. "If it's neck meat or nothing, I can get this man for you."

"Not for me. For yourself." The big man

grinned wolfishly.

"All right. Have it your own way. He's here at his own risk. I ain't to blame if he comes hunting trouble."

"Sure you're not," Flannigan said, and his furtive glance darted for an instant to his chief. "I was just a-funnin'. Knew all the time this Walsh didn't have you buffaloed."

The mind of the prisoner worked coolly and actively to find a way out. The weak front he had put up was a blind. They would keep him covered every moment, but their vigilance might relax if they thought of him as one with no courage. The only chance was to throw them off guard for long enough to take his forlorn hope.

"I didn't ask him to come here looking for me," Taylor went on, plainly working himself up to an edge for the crime. "He knew mighty well he wasn't going on any picnic. If I fight back, he's got no legitimate kick."

"I should say not," Flannigan cajoled, at the same time easing a revolver out of its holster.

Oakland stepped to the corner of the room and picked up one of the rifles leaning against the wall. He made sure that it was ready.

"I'll certainly get him," the Texan cried, excitement riding in the words. "He's through, that fellow is."

At the same time he was ransacking his brain

184

for a plan. All very well to look for a forlorn hope, but he might never get a chance to try one. No use attempting to turn his rifle on these men. Bullets from their revolvers would crash into him before he could make a move.

With his left hand Oakland passed the rifle to Taylor. A six-shooter was in the right. He gave instructions coldly.

"Stand behind the door there. Keep your back to us. I'll give the word when to let him have it."

Taylor peered through the partly open door-way. The men with the pack horse were not more than three hundreds yards away.

"He's the one in the lead, don't you reckon?" he asked.

"Yes. Don't push on the reins. I'll say when."

"If I don't get him first shot, I'll keep on fannin'," the man with the rifle promised. "I'll fix his clock. Don't you worry."

Oakland's malicious laughter snorted out. "Me worry? Fellow, you do the worrying – if you don't get him."

The riders had crossed the creek farther down and had started up the slope. The three horses were strung out on the trail, about a hundred and fifty yards from the house.

"Now, I reckon," Taylor said in a high excited falsetto.

"Wait."

"Doggone it, they're getting close."

Apparently the Texan's nervousness overcame him: He was squinting along the barrel of the gun as he took aim. The rifle roared.

Buck's feet went into the air. The crash of the weapon sounded again.

"I've got him, by gum!" Taylor shouted, and dashed out of the house to run down the slope. "He can't get away from me now."

So it appeared. With the flash of the second shot the body of the sheriff was lifted from the saddle. It lay sprawled on the ground a moment before Walsh made any attempt to save himself. Then the man rose and in an odd lurching fashion stumbled to the bank of the creek and plunged down. As he disappeared, a boom came from the house and a bullet hissed through the bushes.

The pack-horse was plunging wildly in the snow. Peters had got a revolver into action and was firing at Taylor. A moment later, his startled horse bolted and crashed through the cherries on the rockrim. The roan stumbled and flung the big puncher over its head into the creek.

The first shot from the house had missed Taylor. The bullet from the second tore through his forearm like a red-hot knife. He had been almost a ten-second man, years be-

186

fore. Now he raced through the snow with the long reaching stride which had carried him first to the tape in high-school days.

CHAPTER 17
Tough Luck

The branches of the young cherry trees whipped Taylor's face as he jumped through them from the rockrim to the creek. His right foot landed on a round stone and flung him into a snowbank when the ankle turned.

An almost buoyant greeting startled him. "Welcome to our city, Mr. Barnett."

A gay white-toothed smile flashed at him from the brown face of Steve Walsh. The eyes of the sheriff sparkled. That young man was enjoying the lift of spirit that high adventure brings.

Taylor's rifle lay on the edge of the stream six feet beyond his reach. He glanced at it and at the Colt's thirty-eight in the hand of the officer. Strategically an armistice seemed indicated.

"You're not hurt," he said.

Walsh pretended to misunderstand his meaning. "Hurt! Because you hurried so to join me? Not at all. I'm delighted."

"When you took that fall from the

saddle I was afraid —"

"Touching solicitude. Let me reassure you. That fall was sheer melodrama, though it seemed called for under the circumstances. By the way, if you're through borrowing my revolver, I think I'll have to reclaim it. No, don't trouble yourself. I'll get it."

"I haven't it here."

The sheriff assured himself that this was true. He did not quite understand this, so he asked a question.

"Are you a magician, Mr. Barnett? You had a six-shooter and no rifle. I find you with a rifle and without a revolver. Presto, change. How-come?"

A shout reached them. "Hello, there!"

"Dug Peters," the sheriff explained.

He picked up the rifle and started to climb the bank, still with an eye on the recaptured prisoner.

"Keep cool in the snowbank, Mr. Taylor," he advised cheerfully. "I'm not leaving you. As your host, I —"

Taylor interrupted, to call a startled warning. "Stop! For God's sake! Clem Oakland is —"

He was too late. A shot rang out. Walsh staggered, swayed on the rim, and pitched forward to the ground.

Taylor clambered up through the brush and stooped to pick up the fallen man. He heard the crash of guns, but paid no attention. With Walsh in his arms he stumbled down to the bed of the creek.

A second time he went up the short slope. From just above his head a small limb dropped, snipped off by a bullet. As he picked up the rifle which the sheriff had dropped, Taylor could see Oakland firing at him. He did not wait to locate Flannigan, but took the bluff in one sliding jump.

Yet only to climb back cautiously through the bushes. First of all, Oakland must be stopped. He must be taught, sharply, that danger waited for him here.

The big cowman was straddling down the hill confidently. Fifty yards back of him, not far from the house, Flannigan was crouched behind a cottonwood. Oddly enough, even in the heat of battle, the man recalled to Taylor's mind the sneer his chief had flung at him. "When in doubt run." The chalk-eyed man was remaining in a position where retreat would be possible if it seemed advisable.

The warning Taylor gave Oakland was in the form of a shot. It brought the man up in his stride. He turned and ran, parallel to the creek, for the cover of a small gully. Taylor took a swift aim at the speeding figure and missed a second time.

In another moment he was back in the creek.

A stone's throw farther up there was a bend in the stream that would offer a better defense position.

He staggered along the rough bed of the creek, sometimes on ice, sometimes in the shallow water strewn with slick boulders, carrying both Walsh and the rifle. The edge of the water was matted with young cherries through which he had to push a way. At last he reached the bend and under an overhanging ledge put the lax body of the sheriff.

From the screen of a brush tangle he searched the snow-field for his enemies. Neither of them was in sight. Motionless he waited, with the patience life in the open had developed. It was several minutes before a black mass crept out of a snow furrow and moved cautiously in his direction. Taylor recognized Oakland. Again he sent the man a sinister warning.

Clem stopped and aimed swiftly at the brush where the Texan was concealed. The man had fired at the smoke without seeing his target, but he had missed not more than a foot.

Taylor took a careful aim before his finger pulled the trigger. He saw the cowman stagger and drop his rifle. For a moment Clem stood helpless, as though dazed, then he stooped, recovered the weapon, and went lurching toward the house. He moved like a drunken man no longer master of his motor muscles.

From the stable Flannigan emerged, started to go to meet his companion, and thought better of it after Taylor had flung a bullet his way at random. Oakland passed into the stable.

Presently the two men came out. They were on horseback. Taylor noticed with a grim smile that Flannigan was on the side farthest from the creek. If anybody was going to be shot, he preferred it to be Clem. The third horse trotted after them.

They rode toward a low line of hills rising against the horizon. Taylor saw them disappear over a cowbacked rise, appear again silhouetted against the sky, and drop out of sight into a gulch formed by two spurs abutting the range.

He knew he would see no more of them. They were headed for home. Oakland was too busy with trouble of his own to have any pleasure in making it for others.

Taylor turned his attention to the wounded sheriff. Walsh had been shot in the side. The wound was not bleeding much externally, but it was impossible to tell from a casual examination whether any vital organs had been injured. The Texan did what he could in the way of first aid. Brought back to consciousness by the ice-cold water from the creek, the brown eyes of the officer rested upon the other man.

"You got me," Steve said faintly.

"I'm not going to do you any harm," Taylor assured him. "Listen. I'm going down the creek to find your friend. We've got to get you to a doctor."

The officer shut his eyes. He had not enough energy to take much interest in what was being done for him.

Rifle in hand, Taylor moved cautiously along the stream. He had no desire to stop an unexpected bullet. The one that had struck his arm had done enough damage.

Rounding a clump of bushes, Taylor came face to face with Dug Peters. The cowpuncher had evidently been working his way up the creek.

Dug threw up his arm swiftly. As Taylor dropped back of the brush, he heard the roar of the other's revolver.

"Don't shoot!" the Texan cried. "We've got to look after Walsh."

As evidence of good faith he tossed the rifle into the open.

There was a moment of tense silence before Peters ordered harshly, "Come outa there with your hands up."

Taylor did as told.

"Whaja mean, fellow, about Steve?" the lank bald-headed cowboy demanded.

"He's been hurt. You'll have to go to the ranch for help."

"You shot him," Dug charged.

Taylor did not try to set him right. There was no time for explanations or arguments.

"He can't travel on a horse. Tell Prescott to send a sled for him — and to get a doctor soon as he can."

"Where is Steve?"

"Come on. I'll show you."

Peters followed at the heels of the other.

"The point is for you to catch a horse and get back to the ranch soon as you can," Taylor went on. "I'll take care of Walsh while you're away."

"Why would you take care of him after shooting him?" the puncher asked suspiciously.

"I didn't shoot him. Clem Oakland did."

The Quarter-Circle X Y man had seen nothing of Oakland. He had pitched into the creek on his head and been knocked unconscious for a few minutes. This barefaced falsehood made him angry.

"What's the use of lying, fellow? I saw you come outa the house with your gun smoking. I saw you knock Steve off that Buck horse of his."

"All right. It doesn't matter now. We've got to do the best we can for him."

They had reached the bend. Peters knelt on one knee beside the sheriff, at the same time keeping an eye on his prisoner.

"How goes it, Steve?" he asked.

The wounded man did not open his eyes.

"He's dead! You've killed him!" the cowpuncher gasped.

The eyelids of the officer flickered. "No," he denied faintly.

"Listen to me," Taylor urged. "You've got to catch a horse and ride hell-for-leather to the ranch for help. Forget about who did this. I'll stay with him. The rest is up to you."

Peters was full of suspicions, but he could not think of a better plan. That the fugitive did not intend any further harm to the sheriff, he was convinced.

"What's the matter with you going to the ranch for help?" he wanted to know.

Taylor smiled, sardonically. "I'm supposed to be Webb Barnett, wanted for bank robbery in Texas. I wouldn't feel comfortable at the ranch."

"All right. All right." Peters surrendered abruptly. "I'll see if I can catch a horse. But if you do Steve any harm —"

"Don't be a fool. What would I do him harm for? Get started, man."

"Anything I can do for you, Steve?" the big puncher asked gently. "Before I go."

Walsh shook his head weakly.

From the bank Taylor watched Peters approach and mount his roan. The buckskin of the sheriff and the pack-horse had joined it on the edge of the creek a hundred yards below the house. After Peters struck the trail back toward the ranch, they started to follow more leisurely.

This did not suit the plans of Taylor. He took a short cut down the bed of the stream, hurrying as fast as he could through the snow and bushes. Presently he came panting from the creek to the trail in time to head off the buckskin and the pack-horse.

He caught Buck, swung to the saddle, and drove the other animal back to the bed where he had left his patient. Here he loosened the lash rope and put into a sack provisions, a frying-pan, and a coffee-pot. The sack he fastened to the back of the saddle on the buckskin. This done, he tied the sheriff's horse to a sapling.

Taylor had been too busy to attend to his own hurt until now. He stepped to a small sandbar and removed his coat. The shirt-sleeve he rolled up. The bullet had passed through the flesh of the forearm.

"A nice neat job, Mr. Oakland," he commented aloud. "Here's hoping you get as much pleasure out of the pill I sent you."

He washed the wound and bound it with a handkerchief. Barring the chance of blood-poisoning, healing ought to be only a matter of time. There would be some pain, and another wound was very annoying just after the one in his shoulder had ceased to trouble him. But he had been lucky at that. Half an hour or less ago he had been confronted with an imperative to murder, with the alternative of being shot down. He had done his best to save Walsh. It was not his fault that his best had not been good enough. There was a certain grim satisfaction in the knowledge that the villain Oakland had not escaped scot free.

Certainly he took the prize for bad luck, Taylor reflected somberly. He had risked his life to save Walsh, yet both the sheriff and Peters believed he had tried to kill him and that he had fired the shot which struck down the young officer. The cowpuncher evidently did not know Oakland was within a hundred miles of the scene. If Taylor was captured, there would be no way to clear himself of guilt. The outlook was an ugly one. In case Walsh died, there would be another murder charged to his account. The testimony of Peters, that he had seen him come out of the cabin firing at the sheriff, would be conclusive enough for any jury. The truth as a defense would be so unbelievable as to help convict him.

Well, they could not hang him twice, Taylor told himself bitterly. Either Montana or Texas would have to bear up under a disappointment.

The Southerner returned to his patient. Walsh lay with his eyes shut, breathing heavily. There was not much to be done for him. Taylor did what he could.

CHAPTER 18
On the Dodge

As Taylor waited out the hours beside the wounded sheriff, dark thoughts marched raggedly through his mind. He bathed the face of his patient. He climbed occasionally the little bluff above the creek, to make sure that Oakland was not slipping back to complete his vengeance and that the rescue party was not in sight. But all the time he brooded in fragmentary fashion on his problem. Ideas flitted through his brain. He made and discarded plans. But mostly it was Molly who filled his mental vision.

It was like a knife-thrust to him that she would be done with him now finally and completely. She would think that he had stayed at Seven-Mile to kill her friend. What else could she believe?

All her interest in him had been against her better judgment. There had been, he guessed, some glamour about their meeting. She was a flamy young thing, eager, warm, intense, and she had been caught in the sweep of their adventure. Even so, it had been with shy reluctant step that her spirit had come to its passionate and innocent surrender. He saw again the dark mystery of her eyes in the small vital face so provocatively disturbing to his peace of mind. He felt her hot tender lips lifted to his.

And he cursed the evil fate that had thrust them apart forever. She would hate him bitterly, implacably. That would be a necessary solace to her self-esteem, since he had been proved once more a villain.

Early winter dusk was falling over the white wilderness when he caught sight of a little cavalcade moving toward Seven-Mile Camp from the Quarter-Circle X Y. It was time for him to be gone.

He swung to the saddle and rode away in the growing darkness. To escape observation, he kept close to the creek for some distance. The wild cherry trees would conceal him from sight.

That a posse would pursue him at once seemed to him unlikely. Prescott would be concerned first with the safety of Walsh. But the fugitive knew that word would be got to Tincup and Meridian as soon as possible of the events at Seven-Mile. If the telephone was in order again, the officers of every county within a hundred miles had already been notified. The hunt would close in upon him before the next sunset.

Not twenty-four hours earlier, Taylor had left Seven-Mile with hope in his heart. A girl had inspired it. She had freed him, given him largess of her love, sent him on his way warm of soul as he had not been for many days. All that was changed. He had been wounded, thrust deeper into trouble, convicted of gross ingratitude. He had lost her sympathy. His chance of escape had dwindled almost to zero. He would be captured or shot down, he did not greatly care which.

He no longer had any expectation of escape, though he had to keep going because of the flinty will in him that would not quit. Odd how history repeated itself. After the Somerton business, he had been harried, a wounded man, for a thousand miles. Now he was starting again, once more wounded, with another murder marked against his record, new posses closing in on him as those others had done farther south.

Again he bore to the direction which led from Tincup and Meridian. The reasoning which had moved him then still seemed good. If he had any chance, it lay to the south and west.

His camp was on the bank of a good-sized stream. He lit a fire, cooked, and ate, not because he had much appetite, but because he had to keep up his strength. The wound in his arm pained a good deal. It throbbed continually, except when be got snatches of sleep.

As soon as day broke, he dressed the arm, making sure the bandage was not too tight. He drank some coffee, ate a little bread and bacon, and broke camp.

All morning he traveled without seeing anyone. About noon he got a scare. He was crossing a ridge back of a prong when he looked down into the valley below to see five men. They were on horseback and armed with rifles. He knew for whom they were looking.

Hurriedly he drew back from the ridge to the valley on the other side. Whether he had been seen or not, he was not sure. He put Buck to a lope along the shoulder of the hill and dipped into a draw. Above this he had to cut a wire fence or be driven down. When he reached the summit of the next hill without sighting the posse, he felt relieved. Apparently they had not seen him.

But the hunters had cut him off from the west, for the present at least. He had to bear eastward, to make sure of not running into them again, and every mile he took in that direction was lost ground which later would have to be retraced if he was not captured in the meantime.

Darkness found him still free. He picketed the buckskin in good grass. At a campfire he made coffee and heated a can of pork and beans from his store of supplies.

The wounded arm still pained a good deal. The wear and tear of the day's travel had left him fagged and irritable. But he slept well and awoke in the morning with a real appetite.

Early in the day he met a puncher riding a line fence. The man hailed him and Taylor stopped to chat. The fugitive gathered that the other had not been to his home ranch for three days. No news had reached him from the outside world. The Texan had a story to account for himself. His brother owned a ranch in Meagher County and he was heading that way for a visit. If he found a job, he would probably stay. From the local rider he got a verbal contour map of the adjoining country.

They said 'So-long' and went their different ways.

An hour later Taylor came on a mountain corral where three men were working stock. One of the men caught sight of him before he could retreat. He jogged on down to the enclosure and told again the story of a brother in Meagher County.

A long-jawed man with dead eyes brushed the perspiration from his face with the sleeve of a shirt. "What's your brother's name?" he asked.

Taylor looked at him indifferently. No apprehension was observable in the traveler's unshaven face. "Brown. Jack Brown," he said.

"Don't reckon I know him. I worked for an outfit in Meagher County last year. Where's your brother live?"

"Search me. I'm a stranger. Post-office is Cottonwood."

"Never heard of it. On the railroad?"

"No. Jack is no letter-writer. I haven't heard from him but once in three years."

They smoked cigarettes companionably and Taylor departed, having once more been given directions which he could not use. Naturally it was assumed he would want to head down into the populated valleys where main-traveled roads ran.

He had left the corral without stirring any suspicion, but the results of his little visit were unfortunate. Ten minutes after he had ridden out of sight, two others stopped for a word with the cowboys. One was a gangling boy, not yet out of his stringy teens. The second was in his late forties, a large bull-necked man, tanned, shaggy-browed, keen-eyed. He had the resolute look of an outdoor man who had lived forcefully on his own through turbulent days.

"Morning, gentlemen," the older of the two said crisply. "Seen anything of a fellow on a buckskin horse? A rather heavy-set fellow about thirty — gray eyes — good looking."

The lantern-jawed man stared at him. Both of these strangers were armed with rifles. That told the story.

"He went over that hill not five minutes ago."

The boy gave a little whoop.

One of the cowpunchers, his arms on the top rail of the fence, asked a question. "Who is he?"

"He's a criminal wanted by the law. We're after him," the big man answered.

"You a sheriff?"

"No. He wounded Steve Walsh, our sheriff — maybe killed him. I'm Clint Prescott, of the Quarter-Circle X Y. This is my boy Bob."

"Jiminy!" The lantern-jawed man was at bat again. "If we'd only known it! But I reckon we couldn't of stopped him without guns. What's he done, outside of wounding Walsh?"

"Robbed a bank in Texas. Killed two men while he was doing it. Did you get any line on where he is going?"

"Said to Meagher County. Claims he's got a brother living there named Jack Brown. Post-Office, Cottonwood. I reckon maybe he was stringing us."

"Let's go, Dad!" urged Bob excitedly. "He'll get away if we give him a chance."

Clint smiled grimly. "Right you are, son."

The two riders followed the fugitive over the

hill. From the summit they could see a long sweep of country. A wooded creek wound deviously into a valley.

"He's following it," Clint decided. "Must be. It's the only cover he could find on these bare hills. We'll push on down. Hope he doesn't see us."

They traveled fast, but warily. The man was a desperate character. What had happened to Steve Walsh might easily happen to one or both of them if they were not careful.

After they had followed the stream for a mile or more, they pulled up to make a decision. A small tributary had come down from a fold in the hills to join the creek. Had Barnett remained in the valley or taken the up trail along the brook?

At the junction horses had recently milled over the ground. It was impossible to read sign. There was only one way to make sure, and that was to follow both forks.

Clint thought the chances ten to one that Barnett had stayed in the valley. He made up his mind to let Bob scout the tributary.

"Be careful, boy," he urged. "If you see him, get under cover and fire a shot. Don't try to arrest him. I'll cut across and come a-running. Understand?"

"Yes, Dad."

"Keep your eyes skinned and move slow. If

you come to a place where he might be hidden, make sure before you go ahead."

Clint had misgivings about letting Bob go alone, but he was convinced the outlaw was sticking to the main stream where there was more brush for cover. He had sent the boy away partly to lessen his danger, for at any minute now they might jump the hunted man.

The ranchman rode slowly forward, his gaze sweeping along the stream to catch a glimpse of the buckskin horse. More than once his eyes searched the fringe of bushes bordering the upper fork.

One of these glances brought a lift to his heart. A man on a buckskin was riding out of the last clump of brush along the upper branch. He was making for the crease where the folded hills came together.

Prescott gave his horse the spur, let out the whoop of the hunter, and raced across the open.

CHAPTER 19
Bucked Out

When Taylor saw the two horsemen dropping down over the hill into the valley, he knew that trouble, overdue by several hours, was following him on a hot trail. He would have guessed it even if he had not caught the gleam of the sun on the rifle-barrels. These men had stopped at the corral. They had asked a question and been answered. Wherefore they were here.

The rifles established his deduction almost as a certainty. Wayfarers in Montana do not nowadays carry weapons. Revolvers are no longer a part of a citizen's daily dress. Winchesters have not been in since Indian days except on sporadic occasions when questions as to the ownership of calves became unusually acute.

Therefore it was a reasonable surmise that these rifles were being carried for a specific reason. Taylor thought he could name that reason. He recalled phrases of description used by the radio announcer whom they had heard at the Quarter-Circle X Y.

"This desperate bandit Webb Barnett . . . will probably not allow himself to be taken without a savage battle."

Since then he had become more of a bogyman by ambushing the sheriff who had tracked him down. Probably posses were combing the whole country for him. Rumor had no doubt been busy with his name until he was held as dangerous as Harry Tracy had been.

Taylor dared not trust to speed alone. This was open country, except for the wooded creeks, and he would soon be run down. He had to stick to the brush, at least until his pursuers had descended to the creek. At the junction of the streams he swung to the left, on the chance that those on his trail would take the more heavily timbered one in the valley.

From a brush screen he watched the two stop to consult. He saw them separate, one to take each fork.

The Texan's bitter grin flashed for a moment. His usual bad luck! There was no bush above him. He would have to fight or let himself be pushed into open country, unless he could persuade the man-hunters that the discretion of retreat would be wisdom.

A moment later he recognized Clint Prescott and knew this last hope was vain. The Quarter-Circle X Y man was hard as hammered iron. He would never quit and let his prey get away without a battle.

Prescott caught sight of him about the same time. The ranchman let out a shout and sent his horse pounding across the open hillside at a canter.

Already Taylor was crowding the buckskin toward the hill fold through which the little brook ran. A barbed-wire fence intervened. He swung sharply to the left up the hill. At the summit a cross-fence ran at a right angle to the first. Once more the Texan was driven to the left.

He was trapped. There was no time to stop and cut wire. If he turned back, he must face Prescott. If he kept going forward, he must meet the other man.

The shout of the ranchman came to him. "Look out, Bob!"

A bullet struck a rock in front of Taylor. Young Prescott had fired.

The Southerner pulled up his horse.

"You're bucked out, fellow," Clint called. "Reach for the sky or I'll drill you."

The ranchman had slipped to the ground. He held his rifle in both hands, ready to take aim if the outlaw made a move. What surprised him was that the fugitive had not once reached for the Winchester strapped beside the saddle. Now the man rested both hands on the horn in front of him. Even yet Clint could not believe he meant to give up without a struggle. If he was such a tough *hombre*, why had he not made a fight for his freedom as he had against Walsh? Was there some trick about it?

"Don't move!" Prescott ordered, and walked slowly toward his prisoner, watching him warily.

Bob's horse came up on the lope.

"We've got him, Dad!" the boy cried excitedly.

"Slide down from that horse," the ranchman snapped. "With your hands up. Don't you lower them, or I'll pump lead. That's right. Turn your back this way. Take any hardware he's got on him, Bob."

Young Prescott searched the Texan. His father tied the hands of the man behind him and fastened the other end of the lariat to the horn of Clint's saddle.

"I reckon Walsh or Dug Peters did this," the ranchman said, indicating the wound in the forearm.

"No."

"What you mean — no?" Clint demanded.

"You wouldn't believe me if I told you," Taylor said.

"I s'pose you shot yourself by accident," Bob said derisively.

"No. Clem Oakland shot me."

"Clem Oakland!" repeated Clint surprised,

and also suspicious. "When did you meet him?"

"Morning after I escaped from the ranch."

"Just happened to bump into him, eh?" the older Prescott said with sarcasm.

"Yes," Taylor answered quietly. "I said you wouldn't believe me."

"You were right. I don't." Clint laughed harshly. "That's a good one. Clem did it. And I reckon Clem shot Steve too. Might as well go the whole hog with your story."

"He did," the Texan replied evenly. "You won't believe that either."

"Do you take me for a plumb fool?" the ranchman asked. "Where do you get all this stuff about Clem? You claimed you didn't know him."

"I didn't then."

"Your story is not even plausible. Why, Dug Peters saw you come running out of the cabin with your gun smoking. He saw you fire and knock Steve out of the saddle."

"He didn't see me do that last. Walsh threw himself out of the saddle to make a play he was wounded. It was later Oakland shot him."

"Don't believe a word of it," Clint exploded. "I got some sense. Maybe you know Oakland. I'd expect you and him to be friends. But you can't shove this off on him."

"Tell me one thing," Taylor said. "Why did I

211

hunt up Peters and send him to the ranch for help? Why did I stay with Walsh for hours, if I shot him? Why didn't I just light out?"

"You didn't hunt up Dug. Probably you were trying to make a getaway when he got the drop on you. Then you persuaded him to go to the ranch, so you would have a chance to pull your freight. And if you ask me, you didn't stay with Steve one little minute after Dug left."

"Is Walsh badly hurt?" the prisoner made abrupt inquiry.

"Yes, damn you, he is, and if he dies you'll be hanged right here in Montana!" Bob cried angrily.

Taylor lifted his shoulders in weary resignation. Nobody would believe the improbable story he had to tell. Already he was convicted. He had to admit that his own statement would not help him even if it should be believed, up to a certain extent. It would merely serve to explain how he came into possession of a rifle. For that part of his tale about being forced to attack the sheriff to save both their lives would gain no credence at all.

Birds of a feather! Any sane hard-headed jury, if it accepted his story that Oakland had been with him when Walsh was shot, would conclude that two bad men had thrown in together to destroy the man who had become a menace to them both. Taylor could find no out

212

for himself, no matter from what angle he looked at the situation. The admitted facts, fitted one to another, made a perfect case against him, no less damning because it was false. There was something diabolic in the way details could be built up into a structure that was a colossal lie.

The Prescotts took turns guarding the prisoner that night. They camped in the open, with the stars close and the rustle of the pines in their ears.

"I get the best of this," Taylor said ironically. "Sorry to keep one of you awake all the time."

"Don't worry about us, fellow. You've got plenty of grief ahead on your own hook," Bob told him, with youthful ferocity, remembering what he had done to Steve Walsh.

At breakfast they untied the hands of the prisoner, to permit him to eat. One of his captors watched the Texan every moment.

"Know a fellow called Ed Flannigan?" Taylor asked the ranchman as they smoked cigarettes before packing.

"Ought to know him," Prescott answered. "Worked for me. Stole my stock. He went to the pen for holding up a stage."

"He was with Oakland."

"No news. He threw in with Clem soon as he got out."

"They mentioned another fellow named

Dean. I didn't see him. I gather he was up at the Featherhead Dam looking things over."

The hard eyes of the Quarter-Circle X Y man bored into his captive. "So?" he grunted.

"Maybe you're not interested," Taylor said.

"I'm listening."

"You'll believe only what you want to," the Southerner went on. "You're a stubborn fool. But you'd better believe this. Clem wasn't at Seven-Mile on a picnic. He was there for business."

"Meaning what?"

"He didn't say, but he's one of these busy-puss fellows that run off at the mouth. Not happy unless he's bragging. Says he's not going to wait for the law to ruin you. There might be a slip-up."

"What's he aim to do?" Clint demanded brusquely.

"I'm guessing. I'll tell you what he said. Then you can guess, too. He said you'd think the whole Missouri had flooded down on your ranch."

Taylor felt sure he had struck home, that the spirit winced behind the hard leathery face and the grim resolute eyes.

It was the son who put that fear into words.

"God! If he blows up the dam!" He added, swiftly: "Maybe he's done it."

The thought was in the mind of the boy, as it

214

was in that of his father, that anyone who chanced at the time to be in the country just below Box Cañon would be drowned in the flood.

"No," Taylor said.

"No what?" Clint asked, harshly.

"I mean he hasn't done it. He's gone home to take care of his wound."

"What wound? Did Steve wound him?"

"No." Taylor smiled again his bitter smile. "Another fairy tale you won't believe. I shot him."

"You? Why?"

"No need to go into that. I'm a big enough liar already by your way of it. Point is, whatever deviltry he had in mind has been postponed. You can tie to that, unless the man Dean went ahead on his own. And that didn't seem to be the plan."

"It's the most balled-up thing I ever heard of," Bob said, frowning. "Unless it's all tommy-rot what you're spilling. Clem shoots you and Steve, and then you plug Clem, after you and that scalawag have got thicker than thieves and he's talked over his plans with you. It don't make sense, and the reason is it's not so."

"Which disposes of that little matter," Taylor said ironically.

"Why would you stick around looking after Steve, like you claim you did, when he'd come to get you and it was up to you to beat it out of the country fast as you could?"

"Doesn't seem reasonable, does it?" the Texan scoffed. "Though naturally I'd stick around at Seven-Mile from midnight until three or four o'clock next afternoon waiting for a chance to kill Walsh after I had made a getaway. A lawyer ought to get me off for insanity if I did that, don't you reckon?"

"You either stayed there or you came back. Neither one looks sensible."

"Unless I didn't come back of my own choice."

"You were a free man, weren't you?"

"No more than I am now."

Clint Prescott was as puzzled as his son. He knew the Texan was not cutting a lie out of whole cloth. There was a substratum of truth in his story. It was probable that he had met Clem Oakland. That would explain his possession of a rifle. It was more than possible that Clem had designs on the Featherhead Dam, just as it was likely enough that this fellow would betray Oakland to curry favor now that he was in a jam. The account of the shooting given by Taylor could be rejected, of course. The outlaw would naturally try to put the blame on the first man handy, and if Clem was in the vicinity he would be the one to pick. Dozens of men knew he had made threats against the sheriff.

The ranchman found himself milling over again the circumstances of the Texan's tame surrender. Barnett had a reputation as a desperate character. Life and death hung in the balance for him. There was strength in the carriage of the muscular body, virility in the masculine saturnine face. He gave the impression of one who would choose to take his fighting chance and go out if necessary in a blaze of fire rather than be dragged back to the rope. Yet he had not lifted a hand to save himself. Clint was not satisfied he had got to the bottom of the thing.

"What you mean you weren't a free man?" he asked.

"I bumped into Oakland and Flannigan. They asked questions about that C O sorrel I was riding. My explanation did not entirely satisfy, so they collected me and took me along with them back to Seven-Mile."

"Clem giving you his rifle to carry," Clint said incredulously. "You being a prisoner."

"He gave me the rifle later."

"Do you surrender every time some bird yells for you to stop?" the ranchman jeered. "Thought you were supposed to be a fighting man."

"Just a quiet law-abiding citizen maligned by the newspapers," Taylor answered satirically.

"Give a dog a bad name, you know."

"And hang him," Bob added viciously. He could not get Steve Walsh out of his mind. The sheriff had been a hero to him, and this ruffian had perhaps murdered him, had certainly tried to do so.

The Texan looked at the boy and his eyes hardened. The strong jaw of the prisoner clamped tightly. Since that was the way they felt, he would tell no more. Let them think what they pleased.

CHAPTER 20

Molly Has a Change of Heart

To Molly the news brought by Dug Peters about Steve Walsh was a shock. While her father went out to bring in the wounded man, she telephoned for the doctor, prepared her room for the patient, and made ready dressings for use. Beneath her surface activities the girl felt stunned.

She was responsible for what had occurred. Bitterly she blamed herself, for if she had not released the man Barnett, this could not have happened. But she was so willful. She knew so much more than others and always had to have her own way. That the prisoner was a desperate outlaw, wanted for murder, she had understood fully, yet because of a personal reason she had freed him.

Molly hated the fugitive for what he had done to Steve. His crime had been so dreadfully deliberate. There was no way to explain it except that he had waited for hours under cover to assassinate the sheriff. On any other hypothesis he would not have been at Seven-Mile, but a day's journey distant.

Her heart failed when she saw Walsh. There seemed such a tiny flicker of life in him. It might wink out any moment. She wished desperately the doctor would hurry, though she knew he could not arrive for hours. After Steve had been looked after, she prayed wildly.

As she sat by the bedside watching Steve, his eyelids quivered and opened. He lay looking at her, a ghost of a smile in his brown eyes. His lips moved. She leaned forward to catch what he said.

"I didn't get him this time," he murmured faintly. "Walked into a trap like a fool kid."

"Don't talk, Steve," she begged.

"No. Only I'm going to make the grade."

It was a promise, she felt, made because he had read the fear in her face. He was trying to make it easy for her, who had betrayed him to his death. A river of woe flowed in her bosom. All her being was quick with emotion. The words were like a dagger-thrust, and yet they comforted her.

It was not only that he understood and forgave. She clung to his promise as a prophecy. He had said he would get well. Stricken though he was, his supple body lax and weak, his strong will had no intention of giving up the fight. He meant to win.

She was called out of the room by her father.

"We're going after this Barnett, Bob and I," he told her. "Starting tonight, inside of fifteen minutes. Check Charley up on the grub. Your aunt will stay with Steve till you get back."

"Must you go?" she asked unhappily.

He did not discuss that. "See he gets salt and coffee in the sack. I've known him forget both."

From the window she watched her father and brother ride into the night. It was zero hour for her spirits. One or both of them might not come back. She hoped they would not find the man they hunted. At least three other posses were already in the field. Let one of them take him if someone must. She wanted her menfolks to come home safely.

Doctor Wagner arrived late at night. Jim brought his saddle-bags to the door of the room. The physician was a fat cheerful man, and he had fought many a battle with death for those who lived in his territory. At sight of him Molly felt renewed confidence.

He went about his work efficiently and swiftly. Until he had finished doing what must be done, his only words were crisp orders.

Molly followed him from the room when he went to wash his hands.

"What do you think?" she quavered.

"Can't tell yet. Not sure how much damage the bullet has done inside. I'll know better in a day or two. But men like Steve take a heap of killing. Inside of forty-eight hours he may be headed for recovery."

He did not finish in words the thought in his mind. "Or he may be dead."

"Save him, Doctor," she begged.

He was by nature a gossip, interested in the affairs of a hundred people. Now his round eyes twinkled with curiosity. Was she in love with the sheriff? Nothing would be more likely. The eyes of more than one girl followed Steve Walsh as he passed carelessly on his gay way. This vivid slender young thing might be one of these.

"Maybe you can do more than I can," he said slyly. "Make him want to live."

She was looking at him through a film of sudden tears. "It's my fault he was hurt," she explained.

"How was it your fault?"

Molly remembered in time that this was a secret. "It just was," she said vaguely.

"I reckon young folks quarrel," he probed.

"That doesn't matter," she answered, brushing aside his eagerness. "Only if he . . . if he doesn't get well . . . it will be terrible."

Wagner was a man who let attractive young women occupy his thoughts. It was a compensation to him for being fat, fifty, and double-chinned. Molly Prescott had impressed him as being hard as nails; friendly enough, but almost insolent in the confidence of her vital youth. Now anxiety had smudged her eyes with carbon, had distended the pupils with a helpless look of tragedy.

"We'll do our best," he said cheerfully. "I'll stay right here until the crisis is past. There's no sense in you worrying. I'll save him for you if I can."

Molly did not take the trouble to correct any wrong impressions he might have. She was not sure they were wrong. It seemed to her now that nobody mattered but Steve. She would have given up anything in the world for him.

As she stood by the window and looked out at the stars, there came to her a realization of what an insignificant atom she was in the billions of miles of space through which the earth whirls. It frightened her. She had gone her willful way, as though what she wanted mattered, must for that reason come to pass.

Naïvely, like a child, she flung into the night her tortured cry, meant to placate the half-malign, half-beneficent force she conceived as God.

"Please, God, don't let him die! I won't be like I have been. I'll be good . . . if you let Steve live, I'll be humble and . . . different." The word *contrite* came to her mind. She murmured it, so that God might understand how she meant to change herself and that he could depend upon her not to try to run His universe again.

From long experience Doctor Wagner knew there would be no rest for her in bed until she was physically tired. He let her guard the patient until long after midnight. His watch showed two o'clock when he tiptoed into the room to relieve the girl. He was still rubbing sleep from drowsy eyes.

After he had looked at the patient and felt his pulse, Molly beckoned him to the door.

"How is he?" she whispered.

"His heart is strong. That's a good sign . . . I want you to go to sleep and leave him to me, young woman, if you think I'm competent to look after him."

"Yes, Doctor," she said dutifully. "If I can."

"You'll find you can, if you don't start worrying. Listen. If you don't look rested by morning, you can't nurse my patient. I don't want to see any more of you until ten o'clock. Understand?"

She nodded that she did. A penitential pleasure stirred in her. Since she had promised to be humble, it was good to take orders.

CHAPTER 21
Dragged Back

From the Lost Dog Ranch word came to the Quarter-Circle X Y that Clint Prescott and his son were bringing in the escaped outlaw Barnett. They expected to reach home before nightfall.

The punchers at the Quarter-Circle X Y were jubilant.

"I done knew Clint would get the son of a gun!" Buck Timmins cried with a whoop. "The old man is a top hand on a trail. A guy sure has to keep faggin' to make a getaway from him. I recollect once when he was sheriff, back in the old days —"

"I'll bet this Barnett thought hell was coughing when the old man throwed down on him," Peters interrupted. "I'd ought to be sore because Clint took the kid with him instead of me, but I reckon he wanted the kid to taste smoke an' see how he liked it."

"Maybe he figured this Texas bird might talk you into letting him go again after you had him covered," Buck suggested, with wild malice.

"How about that, Dug?"

Peters flushed to his bald dome. "Clint told me I done just right. If you've got any different notions, Buck, I'm the *hombre* that's ready to show you where they're wrong."

"No, Doug, I've got no medicine on that subject," Buck assured the big puncher hastily.

"This bird Barnett is a bad egg," Slim Hodges said wisely. "I knew it soon as I saw him, out at Seven-Mile Camp where he stayed with Miss Molly during the blizzard. Right then I said —"

Dug Peters broke in curtly. "Who the hell cares what you think about anything, Slim?"

"I was only saying, Dug, that where there's smoke most usually you'll find fire. This here outlaw Barnett fooled Miss Molly and Clint and Steve Walsh, but he didn't fool me none. I read his brand *pronto*. When I saw how he had fixed it to be alone with Miss Molly, I was hep to him mighty quick. I says to myself —"

"Funny how a buckaroo will talk himself into a chapping spite of hell and high water," Peters mused aloud. "I'm thinking about one alleged waddy who is going to be a leathers case in about steen seconds if he doesn't shut his trap."

"Why, Dug, I ain't said a thing —"

"You never do, Slim. You just start your fool mouth talking and go off and leave it. If I was you I'd go hook up that team before you take in

226

too much territory in your gab."

Slim did as suggested, though reluctantly. He did not see why someone was always riding him.

Her cousin Jim broke the news to Molly that the outlaw had been captured by her father. She did not share the pleasure of the ranch riders in the triumph of the Quarter-Circle X Y. Her dearest wish, as far as the Texan was concerned, she told herself, was never to see him again. He had been the inspiring motive of the most distressing and humiliating episode of her life. Why did they have to drag him back to the ranch?

During the past forty-eight hours Steve had more than held his own. He was not yet out of danger. Doctor Wagner would not make her any definite promises, but she was convinced he felt far more hopeful than he had at first. Her interest was centered in the wounded man. She told herself so with convincing energy.

Yet she could not keep away from the window of the room as the day began to draw to a close. Her gaze swept the road up which three riders would soon be moving. She discovered that her interest was shared by everyone at the ranch. Some of the punchers rode out to meet the returning trio. Doctor Wagner was as restless as a toad on a hot skillet. Even Jane Macmillan was excited out of her usual calm.

The sun was setting when the group of horsemen reached the ranchhouse. At first Molly could not make out which was the prisoner, but the mass opened and she saw him. He was riding Steve Walsh's buckskin, his hands tied behind him, a rope fastening him to the horn of her father's saddle. When he looked up at the window of her room, as though expecting to see her there, Molly's heart was like a drum answering the call for quicker time.

In the long hours she had told herself many times that he was a villain, and she had half-expected to see evil written on his face, since now she would view him with eyes not blinded by folly. He would be abashed and crestfallen, a ruffian stripped of all pretense of decency. So she had thought.

And he was not like that at all. One lifted look had been enough to tell her his soul was unshaken, that though they had dragged him back at the end of a rope, he carried himself as only the undefeated can. The bitter mocking smile she remembered so well had flashed up at her, and in an instant it had shaken all the well-schooled precepts out of her mind. She felt herself trembling and was unable to control the weakness. Within her a tumult of emotion stirred.

They took him from the horse, roughly. She heard her father's voice.

"Go easy, boys. This is no free-for-all. Let go, Slim. He's been wounded in that arm."

Molly could almost feel the heat of the cowpunchers' hate beating up to her. Steve was popular, and this man had shot him from ambush. If her father had said the word, they would have strung the outlaw to a cottonwood. She saw fists shaken in the saturnine face, heard the sound of low savage curses. The fury appalled her. It was her first experience of the mob psychology which moves without reason to destruction.

"Ought to hang him right here and be done with it," Slim cried.

"Y'betcha!" another voice assented, excited anger vibrating in it.

Prescott turned on them swiftly. "That'll be enough from you buzzard heads," he told them harshly. "When I need any advice from you, I'll ask it. There won't be any hanging unless it's a legal one. This man is Steve's prisoner, and I'm going to see he gets to Tincup safe."

They took the captured man to the bunkhouse. Clint left Peters in charge and came into the house. Molly met him as he entered.

"How's Steve?" he asked.

"He's doing very well, Doctor Wagner says. Better than he expected. I'm almost afraid to say so, but I believe he is going to get well."

"Bully for Steve! We can't afford to lose that

boy. He's one in a thousand."

"Yes, Dad. Are you and Bob worn out?"

"No. I reckon we'll sleep round the clock when we start in. Had to take turns riding night herd on this fellow."

"Did he make any fight before you took him?"

"Not none. Gave up like a lamb."

"You said he was wounded in the arm?"

"That was done in the fight with Steve." Clint blurted out a confession. "I don't understand this fellow Barnett. He quits soon as you throw down on him. Yet I've got a hunch that he's dead game. You saw him when the boys got notions a minute ago. Or did you? Anyhow, he never batted an eye. When they were yelping to hang him, he just turned that impudent grin of his on them. How does he get that way — soft as putty one time, hard as hammered iron another?"

"I don't know. What are you going to do with him?"

" 'Phone in to Tincup to Owen Martin to come and get him. The sooner I'm shet of the fellow, the better pleased I'll be. How long till supper? I want a bath."

"About three quarters of an hour, I think. I'll find out."

Prescott stopped on the landing before he turned into his room. "Better ask Doctor

Wagner to take a look at this fellow's arm," he said.

"Yes," she promised.

Molly was glad her father had suggested this. She had meant to get the doctor to do it, anyhow, but she preferred to be merely a messenger.

"Didn't know he was wounded," Wagner told the girl, his beady eyes twinkling. He was delighted to be brought professionally close to this notorious outlaw. "Certainly I'll look after him. Did your father have to shoot him before he would surrender?"

"No. Dad says he was shot in the fight with Steve. I don't know whether Steve or Dug did it. Maybe you'd better go now, Doctor. Supper will be ready in about forty-five minutes, Charley says. I know you like his hot biscuits."

"Will you stay with Steve?"

"Yes."

The doctor departed with his bag. From the window she watched him waddle across the court to the bunk-house. Molly wished fiercely she was a boy and not a girl. She longed to walk into the bunk-house and to see the prisoner, to hear the drawling mockery of his voice. Perhaps if she could listen again to the sardonic derision with which he flouted honest folks, she could whip her scorn of him to a heat that would destroy the ridiculous feeling in her heart.

She was one of those silly sentimental women who send flowers to brutal murderers condemned to death. The hot blood of shame poured into her cheeks. It seemed that even yet she was not cured of her infatuation for this villain.

CHAPTER 22
"On Shooting Terms Only"

Webb Barnett, or Jeb Taylor if that was his name, sat on a bunk and looked coolly around him, disregarding entirely the fact that he was the focus of eyes curious, angry, or jubilant. His manner was almost *insouciant* in its carelessness. He might have been an honored guest instead of a hunted outlaw at the end of his long crooked trail.

The Quarter-Circle X Y riders discussed him openly, with no regard for his feelings.

"He looks mean," Slim said. "When you see a fellow with that look in his eyes, you can tell he's a killer."

"He's not such a hell-a-miler as a killer," Buck Timmins dissented. "Seems he's one of the kind that's sudden death with a gun when he's got the drop on another fellow, but when it's an even break he's not there."

"That's so," Hank agreed with disgust. "Clint and Bob met him even steven and he folded up like a yellow coyote."

"A bad man had ought to have sand in his

craw, don't you reckon, Dug?" Frank Oyler commented. "This bird is a quitter."

Peters was not so sure of it. The evidence pointed that way, but there was something cool and flinty in this man's gaunt unshaven face that indicated anything but weakness. It was a determined face, marked of bone, with salient jaw, and the gray eyes in it were hard steady, and searching.

"Is he?" the red-faced, bald-headed puncher asked.

"Sure he is. Plays a hand great when he holds four aces, but not there when the other guy holds cards too. He's proved it a-plenty. With a gun in his hand he gave up first to you and afterwards to Clint, didn't he?"

That was true as to the facts, but Peters felt a perplexed uncertainty as to the interpretation. When the outlaw had thrown away his rifle in the bed of the creek, there had been no fear written on the man's face. It had seemed rather a matter of expediency, the easiest way to approach a temporary armistice.

"Would you say he was scared to death now?" Dug asked derisively.

"You bet he's scared," Slim retorted. "And he's got a license to be. That grin of his don't mean a thing but worry."

Doctor Wagner came wheezing into the room. "I've been sent to look after a wounded arm," he announced.

"How's Steve?" asked Peters.

"Steve is a long way from being a well man," the doctor answered. "I don't want it thrown up to me later if I'm wrong, young fellow, but it looks to me like he would fool the undertaker this trip."

"Hurray!"

"Better slip your coat off," Wagner said to his patient.

Taylor laughed grimly. "I'm no Houdini."

"Free his hands," the physician ordered.

"Who says so?" blustered Slim.

The doctor glared at him. "Clint Prescott says so, that's who. Are you scared to leave him untied a little while with only about six of you here?"

Peters stepped forward, grinning, to undo the knots. "You'll have to excuse Slim, Doc. If you knew him better you'd understand that anything he says doesn't count."

The prisoner removed his coat and rolled up the sleeve of his shirt. "If you do anything less than amputate my arm, doctor, you'll be mighty unpopular around here," he said caustically.

As the doctor worked, be asked questions.

"Who shot you?" was the first.

"A man with a gun."

"I reckon I was the man with that gun, Doc.

235

Unless it was Steve." This contribution was volunteered by Peters.

"Where were you standing when you shot at him?"

"First time I was on my horse. Second time I cracked at him was down in the creek."

"Was he running away from you when you fired?"

"No, sir. When I shot from the saddle, he was coming right spang at me. Down in the creek we were facing each other, though I couldn't rightly see him for some brush."

"But he hadn't turned his back to you."

"He had not. Why, Doc?"

"Only that you didn't shoot him. Maybe Steve did, but not you. The bullet that hit him went in at the rear and out at the front of the arm."

Peters frowned. "You sure, Doc? I certainly didn't fire at him from behind, and I don't see how Steve could have."

"I explained all that to Prescott and he wouldn't believe me," Taylor said casually. "I know who shot me."

"Give him a name," Buck Timmins said suspiciously.

"The same man who shot your sheriff."

"You claim you shot yourself?"

The prisoner looked at Timmins hardily.

"Get ready to laugh. Clem Oakland shot us both."

"He done told me that once before," Peters said. "He sure sticks to a crazy story. Like I told you boys, I saw this fellow plug at Steve and knock him from his horse. Any other way he tells it is out."

"How does Clem get in this?" Buck asked. "Are you one of his warriors?"

"We're on shooting terms only."

"Then howcome Clem to be at Seven-Mile — if he was?"

"I'm a little tired of answering questions that get nowhere," Taylor drawled insolently. "Have it your own way. I'm a killer and a quitter and a liar. We'll let it go at that."

After supper Doctor Wagner drew his host aside. "Something I don't understand about this, Clint. Barnett was shot from behind. Peters says he was facing the man all the time."

The Quarter-Circle X Y man led the way to his office. He pushed the cigar-box across the table to his guest, selected one himself, and lit up, then put his boots on the desk and tilted the chair in which he sat.

"Several things I don't understand, Doc. You sure about Barnett being shot from behind?"

"No doubt about it."

"Maybe he's telling the truth when he says Clem Oakland shot him. One thing we can't

237

get around. He left here with Steve's six-shooter. When next seen he had a rifle. Where did he get it? Someone gave it to him. Why not Cem? Let's say they met and threw in together, then went to Seven-Mile and lay in wait for Steve. This Barnett's story is that Clem took him back a prisoner. I don't give that a thing. It doesn't gee with his having a rifle when next seen. But it's possible Clem and the outlaw quarreled after Barnett had shot Steve. By the way, this fellow claims he wounded Clem. I'm taking steps to find out whether that is true."

"How?" asked Wagner.

The eyes of Prescott told nothing. If he had a spy in the enemy's Camp, he did not intend to discuss the fact. "Never mind how," he said curtly. "Barnett's story is that Clem was here to blow up the Featherhead Dam."

"Good God!" the doctor cried. "Would he do that?"

"He'd do any deviltry that would hurt me," the cattle-man answered harshly. "Don't make any mistake about that."

"But innocent people might be caught in the flood below the cañon. Lives might be lost."

"What does Clem care if he can get away with it? But we don't know this Texan is telling the truth. He's in one hell of a hole. Maybe he was trying to win me to his side. I've known prisoners do that before. This fellow is a regular cross-word puzzle I can't solve. He is a mighty peculiar proposition any way you look at him. I don't reckon there's any doubt we've got the right fellow – Barnett, I mean. He hardly takes the trouble to deny it. But, by jacks, he's got me guessing. If he is a bank robber and a killer and a general bad *hombre*, he is certainly a new breed of the varmint. I've seen plenty in my time, the same as you have. But I never met up with one like this bird."

"Nor I. Oh, another thing, Clint. While I was dressing his arm, I found a scar on his shoulder. It looked to me as though he had been shot there, rather recently."

"Barnett was wounded in Texas while he was escaping. I'm reasonably sure this fellow is Barnett."

"If he is Barnett, he is a killer and an outlaw, so there we are, all round the circle and back where we started from."

"Then why in Mexico didn't he blaze away with his Winchester at Bob and me when we ran him down, the same as he did at Steve? Unless he is yellow. Is that the answer? If I hadn't seen him quit, I'd pick him out of a thousand to go through." Clint thumped his fist down on the desk. "Hell, what's the use? We could ask questions till midnight. We'll know all about it some day."

They had to let it go at that.

CHAPTER 23
An Old-Fashioned Girl

Molly was reading a magazine when Peters shuffled into the living-room and stood awkwardly clinging to the broad rim of his Stetson as though it were a life-belt.

"Sit down, Dug," Clint said. "Mr. Martin wants to ask you a few questions."

Dug sat down on the edge of the most uncomfortable chair he could find and began to twirl the hat in his big red freckled hands. He looked expectantly at the deputy sheriff.

Owen Martin was a heavy-set man of middle age. He looked like the small-town professional politician type. Most of his adult life he had held office in one capacity or another. Once he had gone as far as warden of the state penitentiary.

"You were with Steve when he got shot?" Martin asked.

"Yes, sir."

Molly listened intently, but she did not stir. She tried to make even her thoughts inconspicuous, lest her father might remember she was in the room and send her out.

240

"I'd like to know just what happened, Peters."

"Well, sir, as we came up from the creek, Steve was in the lead, the pack-horse was next, an' I was behind kinda proddin' it along. We wasn't looking for any trouble, y'understand. We figured this curly wolf had vamosed hours ago. First I knew there was a shot from the cabin, then this Barnett come a-bustin' out like a crazy man, fogging as he came."

"With a rifle?"

"With a rifle. Steve's buckskin went into the air right off. Fact is, all the horses got scared. The one with the plunder started bucking for fair, and my roan got the bit in his teeth and bolted through the bush along the rock-rim."

"So you didn't get in the shooting at all?"

"Sure I did. Plugged at the fellow quick as I could get my gun out. That was before my horse lit out."

"Did you hit him?"

"Doc Wagner says I didn't, since Barnett was shot from behind."

"But you saw Barnett shoot Steve."

"Yes, sir, I did. His shot lifted Steve clear outa the saddle."

"Was Steve doing any shooting?"

"He hadn't time. The fellow got him right off."

"What happened then?"

"Don't ask me," the big puncher said disgustedly. "My roan got him a man. I was pitched off on my head into the creek an' didn't know any more for quite some time. When I come to, I started up the creek an' met this bird Barnett comin' down. I took another crack at him an' he threw down his gun. We went back up to where Steve was, an' we decided I would have to hustle back to the ranch to get help for Steve."

"Why didn't you take this man with you?"

"Someone had to look after Steve. That was the most important thing. I could see somehow that this guy wouldn't do Steve any more harm an' that he would stick around an' nurse him till we got back. It was neck meat or nothing. I wasn't in no position to be finicky."

"Dug did right, his employer said decisively.

Peters looked at Prescott gratefully. "Maybe I was dumb, but that's how it looked to me. 'Cause I know I lost two-three thousand dollars reward by not taking the fellow in."

"You won't lose all of it, Dug. If there's a reward, you'll get your share," the Quarter-Circle X Y man said.

"Mr. Prescott says this Barnett claims he didn't shoot Steve, that Clem Oakland did it," the deputy said.

"That ain't so. I know what I saw."

"Did you see Clem around there at any time?"

"No, sir."

Molly knew that Dug Peters was honest and open as the day. He had been with the Quarter-

Circle X Y for fifteen years. Since he said he had seen the outlaw shoot Steve, that ended it as far as the girl was concerned. When Taylor told a different story, it was because he was trying to dodge responsibility.

She relieved her aunt in the sick-room just before lunch. Walsh was improving rapidly. He was beginning to eat soups and custards. Doctor Wagner had departed to look after the rest of his patients, with the promise that he would return in two days unless a telephone call brought him back sooner.

"Has my favorite nurse had her lunch yet?" he asked.

"She is eating it now," Molly answered demurely.

"No," he denied, and looked into the laughing eyes that teased him. "Miss Macmillan has been very kind. I'm real grateful. But I can't honestly say I give her first place."

"No?" she asked, politely casual.

"It's no fair for a girl to get a man down, so he can't run away, and then be so sweet and dear and patient, and all the time so doggoned pretty."

She flashed a mocking look at him. "Are you slipping?"

"I've slipped. What can you expect? I've known you steen years, as a hoyden, and a little vixen, and an entertaining young lady who was always shooting off fireworks, and all the time as a friend. Now —

"Could I be all those things and your friend too?"

"Yes, Nurse. You were the little girl with the curl on her forehead. I liked you even when you were very very bad. But I claim you're taking advantage when you let me find out, me having nothing to do but lie here and notice it, that all this rep you've built up on the red side of the ledger is nothing but a fake."

"I suppose you know what you're talking about," she said suspiciously.

"Yes, ma'am. I'm not going to give you away, but your red hair doesn't mean a thing. Nor that hard finish you like to put on. I don't like to knock you, but you're an old-fashioned girl."

"I'll have to go to Denver or Seattle and see what I can do about that," she said, in mock alarm. "If you're sure it is true. I must have been too long in the country."

"Nothing but a bluff," he went on. "Fooling the world into thinking you're hard as nails, and all the time you're soft and gentle. That ain't all. You're sweet as pansies, and you tuck a fellow up with tenderness till he loves the ground you walk on."

She smiled down at him, attempting derision, her face a warm and shining oval. "Do I tuck you up more tenderly than Aunt Jane?"

"Question is, what are you going to do with me

now? I'm sunk." He, too, was smiling, but seriously.

"You're running true to form," she mocked. "It's the proper thing for a patient to feel quite a flurry of interest in his nurse when she's under fifty. I'm awf'ly relieved. It's a sign you're getting better."

"Your hair isn't really red," he said. "Nor golden. Nor copper. Depends on if, as, and when the sun strikes it. I'd call it Tokay, the way it looks when you hold your glass up to the light."

"That sounds very pretty. I believe you're a poet. Unless your mind is still wandering. We weren't talking about my hair, were we?"

"No. I just happened to notice it. I do sometimes. You'd he surprised how much I observe. When you make little movements — bend your head to read, or start quickly across the room — when laughter bubbles up in your face — I think of a verse Masefield wrote, 'The music of her dear delicious ways.' "

Molly flashed a surprised look at him. She felt herself blushing. "Good gracious! Do you read Masefield as well as catch criminals?"

"You mean let them go," he amended ruefully. "But why worry about that? Often we don't know bad luck from good at the time. If I hadn't been your patient, I wouldn't have had a chance to find out what a fraud you are."

She wrinkled her freckled nose at him in a

derisive *moue.* "Don't be silly. The available girl. Propinquity. Add a little repentance on her part that makes her seem gentle, and a little gratitude on his, since he is sick and susceptible. Stir them all up. Season to taste."

"And after you have cooked on a slow fire, you have a pudding called love," he grinned.

"Or enchantment," she amended. "Which is just a glamour that doesn't endure. After you're well and get back to your job, where you can listen to man-talk, you'll be glad the cactus-spiked vixen you were telling me about didn't take you too seriously."

"Those cactus spikes don't fool me any more. I reckon you have temper enough so sometimes there's a breeze in your neighborhood. I wouldn't want a wishy-washy girl."

"I remember Dad once said, after I had put on a hoity-toity act, 'And some day I reckon you'll marry a well-meaning man and ruin his life with your infernal temper.' "

"I'm a well-meaning man," he told her cheerfully. "And I always did believe in taking a chance."

She was not nearly as cool as she pretended. Always she had admired him. During the past days she had been nurse and mother to him as well as friend. His welfare had very deeply engaged her interest, the more because she felt responsible for what had occurred to him. Her

246

heart had yearned over his splendid youth which lay so lax and stricken. If he really wanted her, would it not be a wise answer to all her worries to anchor her life to his? It would snatch her away from the folly which of late had been so disturbing. He was so sweet and lovable, so very much a man.

"Are we talking nonsense, Steve?" she asked.

"I'm not," he assured her.

"Isn't this what they call flirting?" she asked suspiciously, "Weren't you telling me once how quickly the heart recovers?"

"It's what they call proposing."

"Oh! I wasn't sure." Molly felt a warmth beating into her bosom. The brown eyes plunged so disturbingly deep into her blue ones. In self-defense she continued to parrot mockery. "How long ago was it since you had a case on a girl one week and had forgotten her the next?"

"I always did talk too much," he admitted gayly. "I'll say this. Some girls you can forget; some you can't. I like the way joy comes bubbling up from away down deep in you into your eyes."

"Did it bubble up in the other girl too—the one you forgot at the end of a week?"

This he ignored pointedly. "I never saw anyone more alive. It's not only your face that gives you away. Just to see you walk across the room is enough. I lie here and think up things you'd laugh at me if I told you."

"Put them in a poem," she derided.

"Maybe I will. I'll call it 'Youth of the World,' and it will be all about a young singing meadowlark experimenting with its wings and with ecstatic songs about the wonderful world it lives in. When one listens, one can hear life throbbing from its throat. In the last stanza —"

"Let me write the last stanza, Steve," she interrupted. "I know that young lark flapper better than you do."

None the less, in spite of her flippancy, excitement stirred in her. He was laughing a little at his own extravagance. Maybe he did not entirely believe in his fairy tale. But she wanted to believe in it, if he could give her assurance.

"You're not even certain yourself," she reproached.

"If you'll tell me what you mean by certainty," he flung back with *insouciance*. "Only yesterday you read a poem to me about certainties and what a dusty answer the soul that must have them gets."

"I mean — you don't know how long this is going to last. Maybe some day we might not feel the way we do now," she demurred.

"I haven't used the word forever, Molly. I don't ask you to use it. If you care for me now, isn't that enough? We live only one day at a time. Let tomorrow take care of itself. We won't worry about that."

She looked down at him with grave eyes, dubiously, and yet somehow comforted by his philosophy. Lovers' vows, she had supposed, had to be so dreadfully final. But Steve did not seem to think so. He was smiling up, with that touch of devil-may-care charm which endeared him to women. Perhaps love was like that, cheerful and gay and reasonable, rather than a wild and primitive passion tearing at the heart.

Yet even then, on the verge of surrender, a doubt quirked through her mind. Partly, at least, she was coming to him for escape, as women who have sinned go to a convent. But she would find no refuge from love with Steve Walsh. It came to her, like a flash of light, that if she married him, a day would come when love for him would storm through her veins.

His arms went around her warm slender body as she dropped to her knees beside the bed. A tendril of hair, fine as a silk thread, brushed his cheek. Her soft lips turned tremulously to his.

CHAPTER 24
A Self-Invited Guest

After Clem Oakland and his satellite Flannigan had withdrawn into the creased hills back of Seven-Mile, they did not turn south toward the Picket Wire country, but continued to ride deeper into the Black Buttes Range. Clem's rage abated sufficiently to permit him to declare his intention.

"I'll hang out at old Mosby's while you go get a doctor for my leg," he told Flannigan. "From there I'll start something. You're damn whistling. If these knotheads think they can do me a meanness and get away with it, they can guess again."

The lank man turned his chalky eyes on Oakland. "What do you aim to do, Clem?"

"Plenty. I'll show 'em who is the big auger around here."

The broken teeth of Flannigan showed in an evil grin. He was not sorry his boss had got a bullet in the thigh. The old man, as the gaunt man called his chief, was an overbearing bully. Naturally the puncher was pleased, though he was careful to let no evidence of this appear.

"Y'betcha. They'll be climbing trees before you've finished with them. Do you reckon it was Steve Walsh or this scalawag Taylor who plugged you?"

"Taylor. I got Walsh. This county will need a new sheriff right off," the big man boasted.

"And they'll run down Taylor sure. He will be blamed for bumping, off Steve. Looks like things will work out our way after all."

Oakland glared at him. "Seeing it's not you that got wounded. You took mighty good care of that."

"I was lucky," Flannigan said, with mild suavity. He did not care to dwell on the subject of his discretion.

"Ed Flannigan, a cur with a big yellow streak," Clem summed up bitingly.

"That's no way to talk," his companion protested. "I was there right behind you all the time."

"You're lucky I've got this busted leg. Wasn't for that I'd quirt you till you yelped," Oakland told him, with an oath that leaped out furiously.

"You wouldn't treat me thataway, after all I've done for you, Clem? You're sore now. I don't blame you. Anyone would be, with that game leg. But you hadn't ought to act like I'm responsible," the other whined.

The cabin of Mosby was in a hill pocket far from the usual path of travel. It was reached by a cañon cut like a sword-gash in the range. In front of the entrance to the gorge was a rock wall which concealed the approach. Many years since old Jess Mosby, then a young man, had found this retreat and settled there. He was urgently wanted by the law and he had lived furtively until the memory of his crime had worn thin with the passing decades. Now and again he and Oakland had done much nefarious business, though with small profit to the nester.

He stood in the doorway of his cabin and watched the approach of the horsemen. Mosby was a little man with a small pointed face that looked sly and sullen. His welcome to the travelers, when he learned they wanted to stay with him, was far from cordial.

This did not trouble Oakland. His sensibilities were obtuse. It gave him pleasure to override the feelings of others.

"We're welcome as a pair of skunks, looks like, Ed," he said, with jeering sarcasm. "But here we are and here we'll stay."

With difficulty he eyed himself from the saddle so as to favor his game leg.

Mosby watched him limp toward the house. "Howcome?" he asked.

"A wolf bit me."

"A wolf?"

"Didn't you hear me?" the wounded man growled. "If you want to know, I'm going to hang his hide on my barn one of these days. Look after my horse, Jess."

Flannigan walked with their host to the little mountain corral. On the way he told briefly what had occurred.

"Clem acts like he's sore as a toad in a frypan," Mosby mentioned.

The lank man chuckled. "You'd ought to have heard him an hour ago when the lid came off'n his private can of cuss words. He sure was thorough. Between you an' me an' the gatepost, Jess, I can bear a wound in Clem's leg a heap more patiently than I could one in my own."

Mosby laughed slyly. "Me, too. I'd make out to be cheerful over any trouble he bumped into."

"I never saw his beat for meanness," Flannigan contributed. "Runs over his best friends, or those that would be if he'd let 'em. He'll get his one of these days, sure as hell's hot."

The nester slid a curious look at the C O rider. The tone of the man had been venomous, his face a map of active hate. What he had said sounded less like an impersonal prophecy than a threat.

Jess Mosby understood the emotion that inspired such resentment. He knew nobody with anything but dislike of Oakland. The man was a bully, wholly selfish, entirely ruthless. He trampled down the pride and the rights of his own associates. Only because he was powerful, strong, and fearless could he impose his will on others. Personally Mosby was not hunting for trouble, but if someone else should dry-gulch Clem, he would not go looking for evidence against the man.

They found the C O boss lying on Mosby's bed, a bottle of gin on the floor beside it.

"Fix me up some dinner, Jess," he ordered. "Ed, you hit the trail for town and get me a doctor. Don't tell him who has been hurt. I'm not aiming to put it in the *Tincup Courier* that Clem Oakland was shot by a scalawag who doublecrossed him."

"Soon as I've had a bite," Flannigan assented.

Oakland's gross face took on an ugly look. "So you figure on sitting here to guzzle food while my busted leg waits. That the idea, Ed?"

The lank rider withdrew his suggestion instantly. "Maybe I had better start right off. I was figuring on giving the bronc a rest, but we can make it all right."

"You'd better," the big man said harshly. "I want Doc Hart. He's one fellow can keep his mouth padlocked. Both you fellows get this: I'm here on business strictly private. Nobody is to know I'm in this part of the country."

"Suits me," Mosby said sulkily. "But if you're

thinking of staying long, Ed had better buy supplies in town. I'm about out of everything."

"Give him a list of what you need for two or three days," the wounded man said. "We'll play freeze-out to see who pays for it after Ed gets back."

"Not me," Mosby retorted flatly. "You're here on your own invite. I won't pay a thin dime for the grub."

"That's right," Clem jeered. "I'd forgot you're tighter than the bark on a blue spruce. All right. The grub's on me, but I'll okay the list."

"If Doc Hart's out of town?" Flannigan asked sullenly.

"Get him. On your way to town, stop off at Brad Dean's and tell him I want to see him tonight. Tell him not to start till after dark and for him to bring the stuff along."

"What stuff?" Mosby inquired.

"Are you in this Jess?" his big guest asked with cold insolence.

"In what?"

"My business. I'll let you know when you're to sit in the game. That will be soon enough."

"I don't expect to sit in, Clem," his host flung back. "I've been in quite a few propositions with you. They finally work out with me holding the sack. I'm through."

Oakland looked at him murderously. "We'll talk about that, Jess, after Ed has got started.

Maybe you can see your way to change your mind."

They talked of it, at length. Mosby fought like a large trout that has been hooked, but in the end he was landed high and dry. The C O man knew too much about his past. If he gave the word, the nester would be hailed into court, tried, and convicted on the evidence furnished by Clem. Murder is a crime that time does not outlaw.

A man on horseback arrived at the Mosby cabin late that night. He hailed the house.

"Brad Dean," Oakland said. "Let him in, Jess."

Dean was a heavy-set bowlegged man. He had gambler's eyes, pale, shallow, expressionless. With him he carried a sack. This he put down carefully in a far corner of the room.

"That the stuff?" the wounded man asked.

"Yes." He looked at Oakland. "Ed says you been shot up."

"Did he tell you he quit on me when the scrap began?"

"Didn't mention that. He met me as I was coming back from Featherhead. I stopped off at Mumper's and bought some cigs. Looks to me from what I heard there like you overlooked a bet, Clem."

"What you mean?" the big man growled.

"This bird you jumped riding your stolen

horse. Why not collect him when you had him so handy? Or doesn't three thousand dollars interest you?"

Oakland sat up in bed abruptly. "What in Mexico you talking about?"

"Seems to me it would have been good business to turn this Webb Barnett over to Steve and claim the reward. But I reckon you had other views."

"Barnett! Who's he?"

"The fellow that robbed a bank in Texas. Down there they want him three thousand dollars' worth. Didn't you know your friend the horsethief was Barnett?"

The blank eyes of Dean told no stories. Oakland guessed angrily that the man was jeering at him, but he could not prove it.

"I don't know it yet," he blurted. "Claimed his name was Taylor. Said he came from Wyoming."

"If he told you so himself, that settles it," Dean replied, lighting a cigarette. "He ought to know."

"Don't get funny with me, Brad." advised the man on the bed. "It's not considered safe."

"Wouldn't think of it, Clem." The bowlegged nester did not raise his voice. There was no challenge in his even gaze, nor was there fear in it. He was a tough customer, one of the few associated with the owner of the C O outfit who would not give ground before him.

"How do you know he is Barnett?"

"Steve Walsh ran him down. That's the story his deputy, Owen Martin, is sending out from Tincup. He managed to slip away, but several posses are after him."

Oakland cursed, fluently and with feeling. He had let the man talk him out of three thousand dollars. Later he had been outmaneuvered and outfought. One of the posses would probably pick the fellow up and collect the reward, the three thousand dollars which Clem had had in his pocket for several hours if he had only known it.

CHAPTER 25
Two Men

While at the ranch Taylor ate with the Quarter-Circle X Y riders. Usually they were not all present. The ranch covered a lot of territory, and the land leased from the Indians added a pasturage of a good many miles. The punchers traveled far afield, and often several of them were absent from headquarters for days at a time.

During the day and a half Owen Martin was at the ranch, he and his special deputy, Spike Malloy, put their legs under the table with Dug Peters, Buck Timmins, and the prisoner.

"Heading for Tincup soon as I've had lunch," Martin told Peters. "It's fine out here, boys. I like your grub, your scenery, and your company. But we've got to beat it back to town now. Mr. Barnett is getting anxious to see what kind of a hotel I keep."

"Wish I was going to town with you," Timmins grumbled. "I haven't been to Tincup for a blue moon. Seems like I don't ever have any luck."

"Expect Barnett would let you have his place in the car, Buck," the officer said with heavy jocosity. "How about that, Webb?"

The captured man lifted his eyebrows in mild surprise. "Meaning me?" he asked.

"Is there any other Barnett present?" Malloy asked with a grin.

"The name is Taylor," said the prisoner. "Thought I mentioned that before. If you're feeling so friendly you have to call me by my first name, try Jeb, not Webb. Not that it matters to me what you call me."

"Just so we call you in time for the hanging," Timmins said cruelly.

"I've a notion you'll answer to the name of Webb Barnett when you get back to Texas," Dug Peters suggested.

"If, or when?" the prisoner asked casually.

Peters scratched his bald head in search of light. "Far as I'm concerned, young fellow, you're a mystery man, as the newspapers say. Down in Texas, when you were making your getaway, looked like hell and high water wouldn't stop you. A regular Billy the Kid brought down to date, they said. Now every time a fellow points a finger at you and yells, 'throw 'em up,' you reach for the sky quicker than scat." He grinned, amiably enough. "I don't get you, none a-tall."

"Clint got him," Buck jeered. "That's good

enough for me. Only regrets I've got is that Texas is so darned far I can't go to the necktie party."

"Too bad Sheriff Walsh didn't die," Taylor said mordantly. "Then Montana would have had first claim."

Timmins looked as though he were going to swarm across the table at him. "Fellow, if Steve had died, you would never have left this ranch alive!" the cowboy shouted excitedly. "We would have finished the job right here. As it was, hadn't been for Clint, that's the way it might have been, anyhow. Don't you go to making your brags you wished you'd been more thorough with Steve. I'm his friend. Understand?"

"Go jump in a lake and cool off, Buck," Peters advised good-naturedly. "He didn't mean he wished Steve had kicked in. Don't you know sarcasm when you meet up with it? And say, while we're talking about lakes, didn't the old man say you were to go up to Featherhead and take turns watching with Frank?"

"I'm on my way, soon as I'm through dinner," Buck replied. "Don't push on the reins, Dug. I'm taking the night shift at the dam."

The deputy Malloy harked back to the previous question. His mind worked slowly, and he had just thought out this one. It was too good not to give his companions.

"Barnett is his Texas name and Taylor his Montana one. He's got an Arizona one too, don't you reckon? And maybe another in New Mexico."

Peters slapped his woolen chaps in enthusiastic endorsement. "Sure! I've got him pegged now. Can't fool me any longer. This bird is Jesse James when he is in Missouri. He's Bob Dalton in Oklahoma. In New Mexico He's Billy the Kid, and when he roosts in Arizona he's Curly Bill. The same guy traveling under different names."

Slim Hodges had drifted in and was busy stowing away food. He stopped to correct the big bald-headed man.

"Couldn't be, Dug. Every one of these fellows got killed by someone or another. Man named Pat Garrett bumped off Billy the Kid. Bob Ford shot Jesse James. There's a song about it. Don't you remember? About how they laid Jesse in the grave."

The face of Peters registered disappointment. "So there is, Slim. Maybe I'm wrong about him being Jesse James. Your mind sure works thorough."

"Besides, this Barnett is too young to be any one of 'em," Slim added, reaching for the potatoes and scooping what was left in the dish into his plate.

"That's right," Peters admitted sadly. "I got to

give up the whole idea, looks like. And it was such a darned good one too."

"We'll be leaving," Martin announced, rising front the table.

A puncture in one of the rear tires of the car delayed them. It was a slow leak, and the air had gone out of the tire since reaching the ranch. The deputies changed the tire and repaired the leak while Peters kept an eye on the prisoner.

The door of the ranch-house opened. Someone came out, descended the steps, and moved toward the little group around the car.

"Miss Molly going for a ride," Slim announced.

This was self-evident. The girl was in riding-boots, trousers, and coat. She wore a beret set jauntily on her red wavy hair.

Taylor had been aware of her from the moment the door had opened. He knew no other woman under heaven who walked with the resilient step of untamed joyous freedom. There were probably others, he would have admitted if pressed, but he had never seen them. And no other would have brought the mystery of enchantment as this one did.

Was it some trick of old Nature designed to serve her purpose of perpetuating the race? Out of a thousand women one filled the world for a bewitched man with her delicate and penetrating fragrance of personality. Her movements charmed him. The lift of her head was unique and beautiful. The lights in her hair held all the garnered warmth of the sun. To catch sight of her was to be stirred with a strange excitement. Absurd, of course, this irradiation of love, but none the less a reality vital as breathing. So Taylor felt, in a flash, exultantly, as Molly approached.

Until she was close, Molly did not know the prisoner was among the group. This was clear, for she pulled up in her stride, startled eyes fastened on Taylor. Through the tan of her cheeks a rose glow beat to the surface.

He was staring at her, hungrily, as though he must fill himself full of her for a storehouse of memories to carry him through the drear future. His feet touched earth again. He remembered they were not alone, that curious eyes might guess too much.

"How is Sheriff Walsh getting along?" he asked, in a husky voice he scarcely recognized.

"He is better."

"Don't you talk to Miss Molly, fellow," Slim ordered.

Molly did not look at the cowboy. "Please," she said in a low voice, clear as a silver bell.

"I didn't shoot him," the prisoner said. "I've been wanting to tell you. I tried to save his life."

Slim laughed, skeptically. "Too bad Dug saw

you do it. Can't get away with that."

The girl's eyes never left the handcuffed man. She ignored what the Quarter-Circle X Y rider had said.

"What do you mean?" she asked.

"Oakland had me covered. I had to pretend to shoot at him—at the sheriff, I mean. I didn't hit him. He was shot by Oakland later."

Her mind had refused to accept this story when reported to her second-hand, but she believed it now. Not for a moment did she doubt it. Looking into the steel-gray eyes, so shadowed by the disasters that had swept over him, she gathered reassurance that blew a trumpet of joy in her. She knew he was Webb Barnett, an outlaw, wanted in Texas for two cowardly murders. The chain of evidence, as she had read it in the newspapers, ran strongly against him from the moment of the bank robbery to that hour when they had met in the blizzard. He had fled, wounded, from the scene of his crime. Here and there he had been seen during the course of his flight northward. It was impossible not to be sure he was the man pointed at by the reward. Why, then, was she certain he had not shot down Steve, closing in on him, to drag him hack to justice?

She did not know. All she knew was that she rejected all evidence against him, as far as this last crime was concerned, when she looked into that steadfast gaze. He must have shot Steve, since his unsupported word stood alone, all the evidence against it. So her reason told her. But something more sure than reason told her the evidence was not true. He had said so. That was enough. He might be a killer, but he would not lie to her.

"You hadn't ought to talk to this fellow, Miss Molly," Slim said virtuously. "He's a bad *hombre*. You don't need to be scared of him none though. We're here to see he don't do you any meanness."

A tremor passed through her. She would never see him again. They would drag him away to his death. Bad *hombre* he might be, but he was the man who had stormed the inner fastnesses of her soul.

"I believe you!" she cried to the bound man. "If you say so, I believe it."

"Much obliged, Miss," he said gruffly, and turned away.

But his eyes had told another story. Out of them gratitude had poured across to her. And not gratitude alone. He had turned his back on her brusquely for the sake of her reputation. In her life he could be nothing but a liability. He would give no ground for gossips to connect their names. She understood that.

Molly walked straight back to the house and upstairs to the room where lay the man to whom she was engaged. Her heart was beating as though she had been running far. She had engaged herself to fight a hopeless cause.

"You haven't gone yet," Steve said when she opened the door.

"Not yet. Steve, I haven't wanted to trouble you, not while you were so sick. But I have to know something. Who shot you?"

He saw that her small face was charged with emotion. Five minutes before she had left him with laughter. What had taken place?

"Sit down, Molly," he said gravely. "I've been wanting to talk with you about that. I'm not quite clear myself."

"Did this man, this Taylor, shoot you from your horse?"

"No, he didn't. He missed me, either two or three times. I flung myself out of the saddle to fool him, then I scuttled through the brush down the bank of the creek."

Three words burst out of her. "I'm so glad."

He could not understand why, but he did not ask her. Presently he would find out.

"He came tearing down into the creek and I covered him."

"Taylor?" she asked.

"Yes. Then someone yelled to me. I thought it was Dug and climbed the bank, still keeping him covered. It all happened in a split second. Someone shot at me, and that's all I knew till I

267

opened my eyes and looked at Taylor. We were down in the creek-bed, or on the edge of it."

"Then you don't know he shot you."

"That puzzles me, Molly. I don't see how he could have done it. I had collected his rifle, and I thought I had an eye on him all the time. But if he didn't do it, who did?"

"Clem Oakland."

"Clem. Was *he* there?"

"So Taylor says. And Dad thinks it may be true. There were tracks of horses near the house. Besides, there is the rifle to explain. Where did this Texas man get it? He didn't just reach up and pick it out of the air. Someone gave it to him."

"He and Clem stuck around to ambush me. That it?"

"No. Oakland made him shoot at you, but he didn't try to hit you. He tried to save you."

Walsh shook his head doubtfully. "Maybe so. It doesn't sound reasonable, though, does it?"

"But it's true. He told me so."

"Why would he shoot at me because Clem said so?"

"Clem and one of his men had him covered."

Steve smiled incredulously. "And Mr. Webb Barnett with a rifle in his hands?"

"Oh, well!" She pushed that aside impatiently. Her mind was closed to details which did not support her view. "He could have killed you any time he wanted to while Dug was bringing help. Why didn't he, if he was so anxious to get you out of his way?"

"I don't know. He certainly did the best he could for me then. I'm not saying he shot me, Molly. Don't see how he could have. Only I don't swallow that story about Clem making him shoot at me."

"I do," the young woman replied loyally. "He told me so, not ten minutes ago. I believe it."

"You've talked with him," Walsh said, his brown eyes resting on her.

"Only for a minute. Mr. Martin is taking him to Tincup. They're going to start as soon as a tire is fixed. Steve, I feel sorry for him."

He let his gaze continue to rest on her with a dry sardonic humor. The mockery was not for her but for himself. In her exciting personality he saw a promise that one day she would be the crown of some man's life. She was so swift and eager. The freshness of her was internal, born of the spirit. This flamy young creature was engaged to him. Her scarlet lips had turned quivering to his. For a moment, at least, she had clung to him, as a drowning man does to a life raft. But he had no confidence that he had entirely won her heart.

"I've felt that way myself sometimes," he confessed. "But he's a man. Don't worry. He's tough and hard. He'll carry through."

"I know. That's just it, Steve. When I saw him there, handcuffed, wounded, with it those men almost spitting on him, I knew they couldn't break him. There's a look in his eyes. He isn't afraid. They'll never get a whimper out of him. How can a man like that be bad? Why did he rob that bank in Texas and kill those men? Tell me that."

She flung out her question almost fiercely, her slender bosom panting. It was like her, he thought, that she did not at all consider what he would conceive to be the source of her interest in the outlaw, that she did not attempt to conceal the emotion moving her.

"I can't explain it," he confessed. "But we know there are men like that, with a lot of good qualities in them, destroyed by some devil inside driving them to ruin."

"Is he like that? When he is so quiet and strong and, — oh, you know — master of himself?" She seemed to be pleading with him to refute his own hypothesis.

"I don't say he is, Molly. I'm trying to find an explanation of him. It doesn't satisfy me any more than it does you. But I've noticed one thing. There's a weak link in the chain of the character of every man who goes wrong."

"I suppose so. There must be." She threw up her hands in a little gesture of despairing surrender. "Well, I must go for my ride, Steve.

I had to come up and ask you though I knew when he told me so that he had not shot you. I'll be seeing you when I get back."

"Don't worry about it too much, Molly," he advised. "You can't make it any better by doing that."

"No," she assented, frowning at him absently.

"I'll stay here and wait for you," he said, with the winning smile so gaily boyish and yet a little wistful too.

"That will be good for you," she nodded. "Mostly girls wait for you, don't they, Steve?"

"None of them have yet," he denied. "While you're milling this over, dear, give my case some attention, too, please. Just a poor sheriff trying to get along, but if it will help me any with you I'll go out and rob a couple of banks."

"Don't, Steve," she begged.

He understood what that "Don't" meant. She did not want him to make fun of what was so important to her.

"All right I won't," he promised "If you'll kiss me before you go."

The kiss she gave him was hardly lover-like. Her mind was not on it. Steve rather wished he had not suggested it.

Yet, as Molly rode into the hills, her thoughts were not entirely occupied with his rival. Steve was in the foreground of her broodings, too. He was so satisfactory. That was a poor word to express all she meant. How good a friend he was! How full of understanding! He had listened patiently to the evidences of her infatuation for this outlaw. He had not even hinted that she was a romantic fool. Some day she would make up to him a thousand fold for his kindness.

Molly would have called herself a modern. She had been two years at a good school in the East. One summer she had gone abroad with the family of her roommate. Naturally she read a good many books of the young cynics who are the intellectual vogue. But she was essentially simple, as far as a woman may be. Now, as she stood outside of herself and looked at this strange Molly Prescott whom she had recently discovered, the vagaries of the human heart disturbed her.

If she understood herself at all, she was in love with two men. None of the books she had read had prepared the mind for this. For experience cannot he assimilated vicariously. The fact was astounding. A coquette played with one man and another. But she was not a flirt. The trouble was that both Steve and the Texan dragged at her emotions, though in distinctly different ways.

Steve was so human, so far from a plaster saint, and yet contact with him gave her an odd sense of mobility. Life, the mere living, was a fine thing. It sang a song in the veins if one went out eagerly to meet beauty. She knew that Steve would have smiled whimsically if she had told him this. Such a reaction was inconsistent, since he lived by experience and not in maxims. But there it was.

Her feeling for the outlaw was so much more violent, so much more variable. She pitied him from the bottom of her heart. She hated him passionately. When she looked at him, strange flashes in his somber eyes burned her. Because of him she had known the tightening of the throat that fear brings. As she had gone to his arms, on the night she freed him, it seemed to her that the fluttering soul within had poured from her body into his. If this was not love, what was it?

CHAPTER 26

"I See You're Walking Lame, Mr. Oakland"

Owen Martin had telephoned into Tincup the hour when he might be expected with his prisoner. The two deputies discussed together the reception they would be likely to receive.

"I'll bet the whole town is lined up to meet us," Malloy predicted. "You don't reckon they'll make us any trouble, do you?"

"No trouble," Martin assured him. "I've kept Tincup posted on how well Steve is doing. But the boys will be some curious to see this fellow after all the talk there has been. If I could exhibit him and sell tickets of admission at twenty-five cents per, I'd have money to throw at the birds."

To Taylor it was apparent that Martin intended to make for himself a Roman triumph of their arrival. The deputy was a grandstander. Publicity was meat and drink to him. Moreover, he understood mob psychology. After a time the crowd would forget that Clint Prescott had captured the bandit. What voters would remember was that they had seen Owen Martin bring the man into town handcuffed to Malloy. Politically the capture of the Texas bank robber would be valuable capital for the chief deputy. Walsh himself had failed; Martin had succeeded. That was the slant to be put out as propaganda among the citizens.

Martin intended to stress this angle by apparently making light of it. Steve Walsh was a young fellow without much experience. He ought not to be blamed because he had carelessly walked into a trap set for him. It took an older head to figure out the tricks of a wolf like this Barnett. Steve was all right. Maybe he needed to ripen awhile yet. But he would make a first-class deputy under the guidance of someone who *savvied* the ways of criminals.

From remarks made by the chief deputy to Malloy, the prisoner guessed the line of his campaign. That Martin meant to be a candidate for sheriff at the coming election was quite evident. No question of loyalty to his chief disturbed him. In politics it was every man for himself.

Since the prisoner was handcuffed to Malloy, the chief deputy descended from the car to open the poor man's gate★ between two pastures.

★"A poor man's gate," in parts of the West, means one constructed of three strands of barbed wire and three more or less crooked sticks. – W.M.R.

"Better leave the gate open." Malloy said. "I see Miss Molly is heading this way. She'll close it."

Taylor did not look back, though he wanted to do so. He knew he must register no interest in her that might set tongues wagging.

The road wound across the pasture and up into a hill crease, following the line of least resistance.

"Going by Elk Creek Pass, I see," Malloy commented.

"It's shorter," answered Martin from the front seat. "Like to get in before dark if I can."

He went into second to take the grade up the long steep hill. The summit was a rocky hogback. In the course of millions of years erosion had eaten a gap in it through which Elk Creek tumbled.

The car drew near the top. Great boulders flanked both sides of the cut into which the road vanished.

"Kinda like to get in early myself," Malloy assented, referring to the remark made by his superior ten minutes before. "Expect the boys will want to hear all about how we got this fellow."

From the rockrim above a boulder had crashed down and blocked the road.

Martin looked at it with annoyance. "Ain't that a heck of a note? You'll have to help me,

Spike. I can't roll it away alone."

He unlocked the cuff around the wrist of Malloy and fastened it instead to one of the spokes of the spare. "That'll hold him till we're through," he said.

The officers put their shoulders to the rock. Front the blue sky of sunshine above a harsh voice fell on them in menacing mockery.

"Don't work yourselves into a sweat, boys. Take it easy and . . . stick 'em up."

The fat hands of Martin wavered into the air. He was alarmed, but not convinced yet that his alarm was justified.

"Quit your fooling!" he said, with a sickly grin. "That's no way to act. We're officers of the law."

"Put your right hand in your trouser pocket, get the key of the cuffs, and drop it on the ground," the grim voice ordered.

The deputy sheriff saw the barrel of a rifle directed at him through a cleft in the rocks. Back of the weapon he glimpsed a pair of glittering eyes. The rest of the face was hidden by a blank bandanna.

"Now, looky here, fellows," Martin protested. "No fooling. A joke's a joke, but this has gone far enough. I could make you trouble if I'd a mind to, but I won't."

"Do as I say . . . or I'll drill a hole in you."

The cold chill of fear shivered through Martin. The threat in that voice was deadly. It came to the deputy that only the crook of a finger stood between him and death. If he hesitated, he was doomed.

His trembling hand slid into the pocket of his trousers. It seemed to him that his lax nerveless fingers would never find and grip the key.

"Sure . . . sure," he quavered. "Anything you say, Mister."

The key dropped to the ground.

"Skedaddle!"

"You mean—go?"

A bullet plowed into the ground at Martin's feet. He did not wait for further confirmation of the order, but went down the pass with all the speed a middle-aged fat man in fear of his life could contrive. He had traveled a hundred yards before Malloy caught up with him.

Two men emerged from the rocks. One of them was big, rangy, and swaggering, the other lank as a shad. Both were masked. As they came toward him. Taylor recognized them instantly.

"I'll bet you're plumb tickled to meet up with us again," the thin man jeered, showing his black rotten teeth in a grin.

The shackled man did not answer. He was looking steadily into the opaque eyes glittering through the mask of the big man.

"Know who I am?" the larger one asked, a

threat riding heavily in his voice.

"Yes," answered Taylor evenly. "You're Oakland."

"Thought you'd remember me." The swaggerer ripped the mask from his face and laughed cruelly. "This time I aim to give you something to remember me for, a foretaste of hell before I push you in. Fellow, you're bucked out."

The Texan did not bat an eye. With hardy effrontery he drawled a statement that was a challenge. "I see you're walking lame, Mr. Oakland."

Fury purpled the face of the man from the Picket Wire. He lashed out with his left, almost blindly, at the dark sneering countenance of the outlaw.

Taylor ducked. The big brown fist drove past his temple and crashed against the metal body of the car. So great was the force of the blow that the steel was dented.

Oakland gave a roar of pain and rage. With the fingers of his other hand he caught the throat of the prisoner to press the life out of him. Flannigan leaped forward and seized the hairy wrist of his companion, flinging his weight on it to break the grip.

"Hell's bells, Clem, go easy" he shouted. "We need this guy in our business. Don't kill him now."

The big ruffian brushed Flannigan aside, with a sweep of the arm that seemed effortless. It flung him against the rock face of the wall hemming in the road. For a moment he hung there limp, then dropped to the ground

But the diversion had served to check for an instant the lust to kill. Oakland locked his upper and lower teeth together in a violent struggle to subdue his passion. What Flannigan had said was true. He needed this man alive . . . for the present.

Thickly he spoke, his voice rough with the storm that boiled in him. "Fellow . . . I'll tear you to pieces . . . if you devil me."

"That ought to be easy and safe, since I'm handcuffed," the Texan said contemptuously.

"Thought you could make a fool of me and get away with it," Oakland roared. "Thought you could play in with Walsh and Prescott by shooting me. I'll show you, fellow, whether you can double-cross Clem Oakland."

The cold narrowed eyes of Taylor did not attempt to conceal scorn. "One couldn't make a fool of a man who thinks as crooked as you do. He is one already. How did I double-cross you? Didn't you keep me covered while I was to do murder for you under threat of death? Didn't you intend to shoot me down like a dog whether I did or didn't kill Walsh? You're rotten, to the core. There isn't a streak of decency in you."

The big ruffian glared at him, for the moment too astounded by this attack to find words. It was Flannigan who answered, on his lips the evil grin that did not warm the chalky eyes.

"You're a fine bird to talk like a Sunday-School teacher, Barnett," he sneered. "We know all about you; how you robbed that Somerton bank and killed two men doing it. You lied to Clem and me from the start. Said your name was Taylor. Said you didn't steal his horse. Claimed you were from Wyoming. Then, when Clem gave you a chance for your white alley by letting you plug Walsh, you threw him down."

"Figuring that was the last you'd hear of trying to kill me," Oakland broke in. "Hell of a chance! Me, I sleep on a trail till I've made my kill, whether it's a hot or a cold one. Get that key, Ed, and unlock this cuff. We'll be on our way."

The boss of the C O had for the moment leashed his rage, though on small provocation it might break out again instantly. He had never disciplined his passions, but had let them ride him unchecked.

The two men put their prisoner on a horse and tied his handcuffed hands to the horn. They mounted their own horses. Oakland led the way. Flannigan brought up the rear, to make sure the bound man would make no attempt to escape.

They followed the ridge, dipped down from it into a draw, and wound up into the hills.

Taylor's mind was busy trying to digest the situation. They needed him in their business. So Flannigan had said. What for? If Oakland had been merely satisfying a grudge, he would have shot down the prisoner and made an end of it. The Texan knew that. His captor was a villain with no regard for human life. Since he has not killed, there must be a sufficient reason for it.

There was a reward of three thousand dollars. No doubt Oakland would like to collect it. But it would not be possible for him to get it by taking Taylor from the officers and later returning him to them. No, there was something more devilish than that in the mind of Clem Oakland.

CHAPTER 27
Molly Guesses

It was a day of wintry sunshine, with a touch of warmth in the air that made riding pleasant. To Molly's mind there flashed a memory of that contrasting day when Webb Barnett had first come into her life. The storm had flung them together. Was there something symbolic in the blizzard? She had lived in tumult ever since, the sane standards of her life disturbed by violent tempest.

Well, all that folly was at an end. In the distance she could see the car of the deputy sheriff climbing up the draw to the rockrim. In a few moments it would vanish into the pass. She would never see again this outlaw who had so jeopardized her peace. They would take him away to the punishment he deserved, a thought so satisfying that it stabbed her like a knife-thrust.

The hours of the days and nights that had been so full of him would be empty now. She could think of Steve, who was so admirable, so worthy of love. His smile was gay and his laughter not bitter. He was such an indulgent friend. It occurred to her, with self-contempt, that perhaps she would have loved him more if he had been less kind, since she was the victim of an infatuation for a man who had flogged her with a quirt.

A shot sounded, from somewhere up in the pass. This held her interest for a moment without alarming her. Probably one of the deputies had shot at a rabbit. The men she knew were always shooting at something.

One could not, she perceived, measure life by time. She had spent so many years that now seemed unimportant. They had flowed along like a sluggish river, with scarcely a ripple to disturb them. She had been happy because she had not known emotion. Then the stream had plunged into rapids turbid, unsafe, and fascinating.

The heart of the girl gave a jump. Two men were running down from the pass. Something in their haste suggested fear. She recognized the fat figure of Owen Martin scuttling along ludicrously.

What had taken place? Had Webb Barnett somehow escaped from them? Were they flying from him?

She put Gypsy to a canter and swung into the road leading to Elk Creek Pass. As soon as she reached the men, she dragged the pony to a halt.

"What's the matter?" she cried.

Martin gasped for breath, not yet able to speak.

"Held up," Malloy told the girl.

"Held up! By your prisoner?"

"No. By a fellow with a rifle. He shot at Owen."

"Who was he?"

"Don't know. He was hidden in the rocks by the roadside. Ordered us to light out."

"Didn't rob you?"

"No, Miss. Took only the key to the handcuffs."

"Who could he be? Barnett hasn't any friends in this part of the country—if so, I haven't heard of it. Who would want to free him?"

"Search me! I'm telling you how it was."

The chief deputy managed to make his voice heard. "We'd better — get back — to the ranch."

"Yes," Molly agreed. Then, as a horrible thought jumped to her mind: "Perhaps it was someone who meant to . . . kill him."

"Whyfor would anyone do that — now they know Steve will make the grade?" Malloy asked. "Folks ain't so crazy for lynching as all that."

Molly thought of Timmins and Hodges . . . and discarded them. They were not thorough enough for that. Who then, supposing these were enemies and not friends? For of course there were more than one. That she took for granted.

Clem Oakland and his gang! The idea sent a sickness shivering through her. Not for a moment did she doubt that her guess was correct. The Texan had wounded Clem. She knew how vindictive the man was. He had poured bitterness into his fight against her father. Because Steve Walsh had refused to be intimidated, he had tried to murder him. What more likely than that now he was getting revenge upon this outlaw? His vengeance would be ruthless. She reeled under the shock of what her imagination pictured vaguely.

"Clem Oakland!" she cried, sharp pain in her voice.

"What you mean, Clem Oakland?" Martin asked.

"He held you up. Get back to the ranch, Mr. Martin, and tell my father. Hurry, please."

"Why would Clem hold me up?" Martin wanted to know irritably. "He's got nothing against me – not a thing. I didn't ever do him any harm."

"It wasn't you he wanted, but your prisoner. We've got no time to talk. Please be sure to tell my father I said it was Oakland."

Martin gave no weight to her positive conviction. Just like a woman to jump to the first notion that came into her head.

"Have to borrow your horse, Miss Prescott," he said, "You're right, I'd better get back to the ranch soon as I can."

"Sorry. Can't let you have Gypsy. I'm riding up to the pass." She spoke quietly enough, but fear flooded her. Already that villain Oakland might have satisfied his lust for revenge.

"Not now," Martin said, startled. "You're not aiming to go up there now, with those fellows up there."

"Yes. And I've got to hurry." Molly swung the pony's head toward the rockrim.

"Hold on, girl!" Martin called. "You can't do that! I want your horse, in the name of the law." He followed her a step or two, protesting. "Listen. Don't act crazy. You can't go up there now."

Her answer was to touch Gypsy with the spur and set the pony to a canter. Above there, in the pass, the Texan might already be lying lifeless in the road. An urgency, tumultuous and chaotic, filled her bosom.

She pressed up the slope to the cut and rode into it. At sight of the car she stopped. Her eyes swept the pass fearfully.

Nobody was in sight. There was no evidence that a crime had been committed. So she thought at first, with a deep breath of relief. Then she caught sight of a black handkerchief with eyeholes cut in it. The muscles of her stomach collapsed. For on the mask was a moist red stain.

Molly set her teeth to steady herself. She must not get panicky. All her energy must be directed to help the prisoner — if help was not too late. She would have to think coldly and clearly, unshaken by emotion.

What would her father do now? He would pick up their trail, of course. She slid from the saddle and dropped the bridle-rein to the ground. Carefully she moved forward to the car. In the cut, shaded from the sun most of the day, the ground was still moist and soft from the recent snows. There were scores of footprints, many of them cut up by others pressed upon them. Some of these must have been made by the deputy sheriffs. She could see where two sets pointed down the road toward the Quarter-Circle X Y. The toes of the boots cut more sharply than the heels into the mud. Martin and Malloy, running for dear life, had made these.

Others led to the rocks beside the road. She followed these, being careful not to get too close. Her father would be here soon, questing over the ground to cut sign. She did not want to make the pursuit more difficult.

Once among the rocks, she was helpless. The marks of the boots were too slight for her to see. In a small pocket she found evidence that horses had been left there, but how many she could not tell.

Then, on a sudden inspiration, she climbed swiftly a small hill in the rimrock and stepped from one bolder to another to the summit. Her gaze swept the panorama of huddled hills at her feet. They rolled away, a sea of great land waves, to the white mountain range on the far horizon. Except for small draws they were bare of timber.

Her keen eyes picked up a bunch of cattle grazing in a valley. No other sign of life was visible. As she was about to turn away, a little glad cry leaped from her throat. Three horsemen moved out of a crease in the hills, crossed a draw, and vanished into a gulch beyond. Two of the men were armed. Molly could see glints of sunlight reflected from the barrels of their rifles. The third one rode between these two. He carried no rifle, and he leaned forward in the saddle, as one might whose hands were bound to the horn.

Swiftly she ran back to the road and swung into the saddle. She guided Gypsy up the rimrock and along the edge of it, gradually working down into a draw as opportunity offered. A little bank of snow, in the shade of a huge outcropping of boulders, had been trampled by the hoofs of horses.

Molly felt a lift of the heart. They had come

this way. She was on a hot trail. She would follow it to a finish.

Her mind was working clearly, all the panic pushed down into its subconscious depth. She tore her handkerchief into small fragments and at intervals dropped pieces to show her father which way she had come.

The girl rode across the draw where she had seen the horsemen and into the gulch beyond.

CHAPTER 28
No Chips in the Game

There were three men at the campfire. One of them was a prisoner. He observed the others sedulously, but with studied indifference. It was important to him to know exactly what kind of men they were. That his life was at stake he knew. To make a correct diagnosis of character might be of vital moment.

His interest in the big man standing with straddled legs in front of the fire was not psychological. Roughly speaking, Taylor had Clem Oakland catalogued. He was the most ruthless human being he had ever met. His cruelty went back to the basic fact that he was unmoral. In the mind of the Montana ranchman the Texan was already dead, except for the slight detail of blotting him out. What the prisoner wanted to know was how and when. For the ruffian had not yet shown his hand. He had not explained why he had taken the trouble to drag a condemned man so far.

The name of the twisted little man with the sly pointed face and the pig eyes seemed to be

Jess Mosby. Plainly enough, he hated Oakland even though he joined in his evil projects. How far would that hatred carry him? No distance at all in open opposition, the Southerner decided. The old man was afraid of the domineering bully.

"We're now going to talk turkey, Texas Man," Oakland began, a jubilant note in his heavy voice. "You're scared to death. You're 'most ready to break down and beg. Go ahead and see what good it will do you."

The steely eyes of the handcuffed man looked steadily at him. "Thought you said you were going to talk turkey. You sound to me like a four-flushing fool."

The streaked red of Oakland's beefy cheeks deepened to the purple of anger. He glared at the man who dared to lie there on an elbow and jeer at his threats. Barnett, if that was the fellow's name, set boiling in him a fury he could not suppress. Already he had cut open one of the Texan's cheeks with a slash of the quirt. But his exhibitions of rage left him with a strange sense of defeat. The outlaw was unconquerable. No shadow of fear rested in the bitter sardonic eyes. The man would go through with head up.

Flannigan rode into camp, snaking a log for the fire. One end of his rope was attached to the log and the other to the horn of the saddle.

"This will be all we need," he shouted.

The big man turned his ire on the rider. "Better go up to the hilltop and holler that we're here. Invite the whole county. Put it in the papers, you lunkhead."

"There's nobody anywhere near, Clem," protested Flannigan in an injured voice. "What's the use of getting scared?"

"Scared!" the opaque eyes blazed at the lank man. "Did you say scared?"

"I didn't mean scared, Clem," apologized the other. "I meant het up. Seems to me you're riding me all the time."

Oakland strode toward him. "Claim I'm scared, do you? Climb down from that horse and I'll wear you to a frazzle."

The shallow eyes of Flannigan reflected panic. He could not turn his pony and bolt, since the log at the end of the rope anchored him. Swiftly he swung from the saddle and backed away.

"Don't you, Clem! Don't you!" His whimpering protest lifted to a shriek of pain. The quirt was winding around his legs with savage cruelty.

He tried to break away. He screamed for mercy. At last Oakland flung him away. Drunkenly, he swayed to his horse.

"You're staying right here, fellow," the big bully told him harshly.

293

"A pleasant time was had by all," an ironical voice jeered.

Oakland swung around heavily. "So you've come," he snarled.

Brad Dean lounged forward, his pale cold eyes on the big ruffian. "Thought you were expecting me. Dropped in a moment ago while you and Ed were doing your act."

"Time you got here," the other growled.

The bowlegged man laughed, without the least expression in his eyes. "Or you'd have got busy with your quirt again when I arrived," he suggested.

"You trying to ride me, Brad?" Oakland demanded.

"No, Clem. But when I go into a deal, I want to know where I'm at. Is it your idea you can go around whaling us all with a quirt?"

Mosby picked courage from Dean's challenge. "Y'betcha! Clem has got no license to go off the handle thataway."

The C O man knew he had gone too far. He stood frowning at the ground, then blurted out a gruff explanation that might be considered an apology if one wanted to take it so. "He said I was scared. Can't any man alive tell me that."

"I told him I didn't mean it," Flannigan groaned. "I'm through."

Oakland strode across to him. "I'll show you if you're through. Unsaddle that horse."

Flannigan looked at him, venomously. If eyes could have killed, the bully would have been exterminated. But the lank man had not the sheer nerve to face the issue. He began, slowly, to strip the saddle from the horse.

To the prisoner Dean spoke derisively. "Just a little difference of opinion, Mr. Barnett. The boys are real fond of each other, but once in a while they liven things up with a little argument."

"You're one of this ruffian's gang, I suppose," Taylor said quietly. "Have you come here to help him murder me?"

Dean sat down on his heels, cowboy fashion, with the manner of one ready to discuss an interesting problem.

"Has Clem declared intentions?" he asked.

"He doesn't need to declare them. What else did he bring me here for except to kill me?"

"I wonder," Dean mused, with callous indifference. "He must have some notion in his nut. Have you asked him?"

"I'm serving notice on you and these other men here that you'll be held by the law guilty of murder just as much as Oakland himself," the prisoner went on, still in a low even voice untouched by excitement.

"You're quite a stickler for the law, aren't you, Mr. Barnett? When it's on your side, of course. I've been hearing some lately about two bankers you left dead in Texas when you went in to cash a check or something. Weren't you stretching the law a little bit then?"

"I didn't kill those men."

"Meaning you didn't fire the shots yourself," Dean said. "But the law holds you just as guilty as if you had, like you've just been telling us. Sauce for the goose, Mr. Barnett."

The steady eyes of the handcuffed man did not falter. "You're back of him, then, in this business?"

"If you mean the business of Mr. Webb Barnett, I haven't a thing to do with it. I've got nothing against you. Far as I'm concerned you could live to be a Methuselah. I'm not sitting in. No chips in the game. Unfortunate for you that Clem holds all the aces, but strictly none of my affair. If you get me."

"I get you," Taylor said. "No nerve. Afraid to stand out against him."

Oakland stood on the other side of the fire, looking down at both of them sulkily. He listened, without interrupting.

"Is that quite a fair way to put it, Mr. Barnett?" asked Dean. "I'm not one of these altruists who go around butting in. That doesn't get a fellow anywhere, and he's apt to die of lead poisoning suddenly. So I paddle my own canoe."

"You can't beg out of this, Texas Man,"

Oakland said brutally. "It's going to be my say-so."

Taylor did not even look at him. He spoke to Dean, coolly, as though it were a business deal, though he knew that his suggestion might bring a bullet crashing through his brain.

"There's one point, that three thousand reward for my arrest. It would split nicely three ways."

"Three ways?" Dean asked.

"I'm not counting Oakland. He's out, since he took me from the officers. But the rest of you. Why don't you take me to Tincup and collect? I'll back your play to a fare-you-well. It's a lead-pipe cinch."

"And how would we arrange this with Clem?" Dean wanted to know, blowing out a fat smoke wreath.

Oakland glared angrily at both of them, uncertain as to what effect this proposal would have on his confederates.

"Pay no attention to him," Taylor advised. "If he objects, bump him off. Unless Flannigan is so fond of him that he can't bear to have his pal hurt."

"That'll be enough from you, fellow," the big man roared in fury. "Say any more and I'll gun you now. Listen. Your're the one that's in a jam, not me. The boys aren't taking any orders from you. When I get good and ready, I'll rub you out. Don't make any mistake about that. But first you've got a job to do. Soon as it's dark enough."

"Which is?" Taylor asked.

"You're going to blow up the Featherhead Dam."

So that was what the villain was saving him for.

"Never in a thousand years," the prisoner said.

"We'll settle that right damn now!" Oakland shouted, and he dragged out a forty-five Colt's revolver.

Dean moved a little farther out of the line of fire. "Just a moment, Clem," he suggested. "Not butting in or anything, you understand. But no harm in making your proposition clear. If Barnett blows up the dam, you send him to kingdom come. If he doesn't, you do the same. Just what does it buy him if he does as you say?"

"It buys him about five more hours of life."

"Five hours," Dean repeated, with a lift of the shoulders. "Not so much. You're bargaining like a tight-wad."

"I'm not bargaining. I'm telling him. Which is it to be, fellow? Will you take orders from me? Or shall we finish this right here? Take your choice."

The bowlegged man watched the Texan, his

impassive poker face veiling the interest he felt. He had never seen this outlaw before, but the man's self-containment amazed him. The prisoner's cool gaze did not waver, though he looked straight into the barrel of the revolver. Though his heart must be hammering fast, no hint of fear lay in the steel-gray eyes. Much more than his swaggering enemy, he had the assured poise of victory.

Mosby interrupted shrilly. "Hold your horses, Clem! No hurry about this. Let *me* talk to him."

For purposes of avoiding possible legal complications later, Dean filed a formal protest against the murder. "I wouldn't do that, Clem. We'll talk this over reasonably."

"He's making his choice now," Oakland said obstinately. "Which is it, fellow? Will you blow up the dam or won't you?"

Taylor leaned forward a little, to make his refusal more emphatic. "I'll see you in hell first, you scoundrel."

"Look!" Flannigan warned.

Somebody was riding down the slope toward the camp. It was Molly Prescott.

CHAPTER 29
Clem Changes His Plans

Molly flung herself from the horse and ran forward. The man in handcuffs had his back to her and did not know what the interruption was that had saved his life. He saw Oakland lower the point of his revolver with an imprecation. He observed the amazement in the sly fox face of Mosby. Then a never-to-be-forgotten voice, with the sweet pure timbre of a silver bell, sent life pouring once more through his tensed veins.

"Thank God, I'm in time!" it cried.

"Who is this woman?" Oakland asked hoarsely.

He felt the shock of the interruption, too, though not as much as his intended victim. A moment ago he had been keyed to do murder. The slim figure of the flying girl had flung him out of his mental stride. From where had she come? Was she alone? What did she want? Questions trooped into his mind.

Mosby answered him. "It's the Prescott girl."

"Clint Prescott's brat?"

"Yes."

"What in Mexico you doing here?" Oakland demanded roughly of her.

She did not answer. She did not look at him. Her eyes were fixed on the prisoner. A strange weakness swept through her.

"I didn't know!" she cried. "I was afraid! I thought at first—"

She broke down in a sob.

"You came to save me," the Texan said in a low shaken voice.

"I lost my way. I wandered in the hills. It was terrible," she wailed. "Then I saw a man on horseback and followed him. He came this way. I lost him, too. At last I saw the smoke."

"I said it was a fool idea to light a fire," Mosby complained. His words were a slap at Oakland. With his usual recklessness the C O man had ordered it built.

Molly choked back a sob. The anxiety of the long hours, culminating in the joy of finding Taylor alive, had left her unnerved. She cried again. "Thank God . . . . Thank God!"

"For what?" scoffed Oakland.

The question was a threat, sinister and savage. Molly looked for the first time at the man with the forty-five.

"Because he is still alive. Because . . ."
The girl interrupted herself to throw an accusa-

301

tion at the ruffian. "You are Clem Oakland!"

"Right you are," he admitted. "Do you know who this fellow is? His name is Barnett. He's a killer from Texas, wanted for murder and bank robbery. He tried to kill Steve Walsh. He 'most finished me when I wouldn't stand for it and interfered."

"That isn't true!" she cried.

"No use to argue with him, Miss Prescott," the prisoner said quietly. "The truth isn't in him. He was just ready to kill me when you came, because I refused to blow up the Featherhead Dam."

The girl turned, with quick animal grace, in eager appeal to Dean. A note of panic was vibrant in her voice. "You wouldn't let him do such a terrible thing, would you?" she begged.

A second time Dean took occasion to register a perfunctory protest. It might some day be advisable to have unimpeachable testimony in his favor.

"I told Clem he had better not kill this fellow," he said.

"Told him he'd better not!" Molly flamed. "Would you stand by and see murder done?"

Taylor explained to her, sardonically. "Mr. Dean paddles his own canoe. He doesn't butt in on his friend's little murders. That wouldn't be good form. Oakland is cock of the walk here. What he says goes. You can ask Flannigan if that isn't true. He has had experience."

The unsolicited answer of Flannigan was a curse.

"I've had enough of this," Oakland broke in roughly. "Like this Texas killer says, I'm boss. You weren't invited here, young woman. Since you came, sit down over there and keep your mouth shut. You've got nothing to say. I've heard all about what a hellion you are, living in a cabin alone with this fellow and all. Maybe you can run your father. Well, you can't run me."

The hot blood stained the face of the girl from throat to forehead. Without another word she sat down beside the fire.

"When you're standing there with a forty-five in your hand, it's safe to insult a good girl," Taylor said, his steel-barred eyes challenging the bully. "Especially when the only man who might resent your lie is handcuffed."

"I've known Clint Prescott twenty years and more. That's about what I'd expect of his daughter. Like father, like child, I say."

"Hold on, Clem," Dean objected. "The young lady isn't in this. Leave her out."

"Put herself in it by coming here, didn't she?" Oakland retorted.

"Not that way. Barnett is right. You don't have to insult her. I reckon it's well known I've got no use for Clint Prescott. Been against him ever since he posted my name as a cowthief. But I'm not fighting women, let alone girls. Clem doesn't mean anything, Miss Prescott. He's hot under the collar, that's all. No reflections on your character anyway."

"Have I lost my tongue, Brad, that you have to speak for me?" the big cattleman jeered.

"I'm speaking for myself first of all, Clem. Apologizing for being with you when you make such a break as you did," Dean told him hardily.

"What break did I make?" Oakland bullied, the dark blood flushing his beefy face. "All I know is what you told me. You said—"

"I said Miss Prescott got lost in the storm and this man found her. I said they put up at Seven-Mile Camp till the blizzard gave them a chance to get to the Quarter-Circle X Y. You don't have to put any meaning in my words that wasn't there, Clem."

The big man glared at him in savage fury, half-minded to let himself go and have it out with Dean. But he had enough discretion left to know that if he did so, all his plans would be wrecked. He put a curb on his passion.

"All right. All right, Brad, if you're such a child of the forest. Me, I'm not. I've noticed that when a person gets a rep for being so and so, they most usually deserve it. Take this Texas man here. He's one bad *hombre.* You can tell it

304

to look at him. If this young woman wants to pass for a nice goody-goody girl, she'd better change her ways. That's all I got to say."

Oakland, after this long speech, relapsed into sulky silence. Things were not going to suit him. He had made a mistake in flogging Flannigan. The man never would forgive him. He would have to get rid of him at the first opportunity. The arrival of this girl was another piece of bad luck. Either he would have to give up blowing a hole in the dam, or else he must fix it so that she could never tell what she knew. Old Jess Mosby hated him. Brad Dean was about ready to break into open defiance. What in time had suddenly gone wrong with his world?

Though Dean's impassive face gave no indication of it, the drama of the situation appealed to him. He was a hard man. For years he had followed crooked trails. Often he had gambled with his life as the stake. The two things he respected were courage in men and virtue in women. Barnett was game. The cowthief had never seen an exhibition of cooler nerve than that with which the Texan had faced almost certain death. As for Molly Prescott, he gave her the benefit of the doubt. She had the look of a thoroughbred. No doubt she loved this outlaw. A woman's heart was like that; it was as likely to go out to a bad man as a good one. But he had noticed how her eyes had winced at Clem's coarse innuendo, almost as though he had struck her a blow in the face.

He wondered what Clem would do now. He could not blow up the dam, with Molly Prescott as a witness against him. Dean was not sorry, though it would have been a profitable stroke of business for him to ruin the owner of the Quarter-Circle X Y. He never had liked the proposition.

While Dean made talk with the others, Oakland mulled the thing over in his mind. He listened to what was said, even though his brain was full of impressions and fugitive flashes of thought out of which a new scheme of action was beginning to evolve. Greedily his eyes took in the vivid beauty of the girl. Was it, after all, such bad luck that she had followed them to the camp? Perhaps . . .

He was a man whose gross mind dwelt much on women. Furtively he watched this girl now, and as he did so he felt stirring within himself a dull excitement that would quicken with time, his experience told him. The quivering life in her reminded him of that in a wild young colt. There was the same look of dainty untamed fierceness. It would be great sport to give her the whip and hold her with a tight rein when she tried to bolt. He liked the rhythmic way her long slender legs moved. He liked her small flamy head, the soft peachy glow that had crept out under the brown bloom of her cheeks when he had sneered at her virtue. To break her would be triumph enough to thrill his jaded nerves.

He prided himself that he knew women. It was plain that she was in love with this outlaw. On that fact he would trade. In a moment, without the least regret, he swept from his mind all the plans he had made for the destruction of Featherhead Dam. He knew a revenge on Clint Prescott a hundred times more crushing than that. But he must move carefully. He must make sure there was no flaw in his scheme to bring the trap down upon himself.

For he was dealing with very brittle stuff when he took into his plans the wooing of a woman in love with another man, the daughter of one enemy and the sweetheart of another, with the deliberate intent of bending her strong young will to his until her splendid pride was crushed.

His sulky, half-shut eyes gloated on the figure of slender fullness. She was aware his look was insulting and moved restlessly beneath it.

He grinned in anticipatory triumph.

CHAPTER 30
Horse Neighs

Given the glow of high adventure, a man may face death with racing pulses. Excitement quickens all his nerves. The heart is lifted. A thousand humdrum hours are less full of zest than this one shot through with the stir of conflict.

But to sit, hands bound, and look into the cold eyes of death without collapse is another matter. The iron will of Taylor had beaten down the paralyzing fear rising like a flood within him. Yet it had been there, ready to sweep away his courage if given a chance.

Then a girl had flashed into the picture and brought him life. This in itself was miracle enough, but because the girl was Molly Prescott drums of joy beat in his breast.

She had come to save him. He would never forget the look in her eyes in that moment when the cry of thanks had been wrung from her white lips. Its meaning was beyond mistake. In spite of everything—the rough impact of their first meeting, the clash of temperaments, his reputation as a murderous outlaw—she amazingly offered him the glamorous gift of her love. No wonder the drums sounded tumultuous music within him.

Presently, back to earth, he took stock of the practical effect of Molly's arrival. Dean was making cheerful, casual talk. At something he said Mosby's splenetic laughter crackled ironic mirth. The black opaque eyes of Oakland watched the girl. From across the campfire Flannigan poured furtive hate at the ruffian who had beaten him.

Taylor knew that the confederates of Oakland would not have turned a hand to save him. What the fellow did to a hunted outlaw, with no unfriendly witness present, was something they would not make their business. But with Clint Prescott's daughter on the scene, the equation was wholly changed. They would not let her come to harm, scoundrels though they were. He could depend on two of them for that, Dean and Mosby. Since his own safety was involved in hers, Flannigan, too, would protest against injury to her, though his support might be ineffective. Yet they dared not release her to be a witness against them. The plan of blowing up Featherhead would have to be dropped.

The Texan did not deceive himself as to his own danger. Oakland had no intention of giving up his revenge, though he might be forced to postpone it. The man was still a menace, even if his hatred was just now leashed.

In spite of his reliance upon Dean, the prisoner was anxious about Molly. What disturbed him was Oakland's preoccupation with her. He had seen men look at women like that before, insultingly, as though they saw them stripped of clothes. Evil ideas were taking form in the man's mind.

Presently Dean broached the problem before them. "Where do we go from here, boys?" he asked.

"I been thinking," Oakland replied. "We'll kinda let things go up above, if you know what I mean. I reckon I'll turn this fellow in to the sheriff's office at Tincup. You fellows can drift on home."

Dean looked at him a moment before he answered mildly. "Not so good, Clem. It would be better for us to take him to Tincup, on account of the reward. Split it four ways, you understand."

"Good of you, Brad," Oakland jeered. "But I'm the fellow who picked up this guy roaming around the hills. I reckon I'll deliver him, seeing I collected him."

"I'll go with you, then," Molly said quickly.

"That'll be all right with me," Clem agreed. He had expected her to insist upon going, too. Otherwise he would not have suggested the plan.

"Not quite all right with us, though," Dean demurred. "Best thing is for all of us to go. Eh, boys?"

"Y'betcha," Mosby assented. Flannigan nodded his head sulkily.

"What's the idea?" demanded Oakland harshly. "I got this bird. He's my prisoner. Where do you fellows come in?"

"Ed was with you, wasn't he?" Dean mentioned. "But that's not the point. We started out to do a job today, all four of us. If we change our minds and do something else, we're still partners, Clem."

"I didn't say I wouldn't divvy the reward if I get it," Oakland responded sullenly. "But what's the sense in four of us wasting our time taking this fellow to town?"

"I've got time to burn, and I'd kinda like to go to town, anyhow," Dean said.

"Me, too," Mosby chirped up.

"You're not going!" Oakland exploded angrily. "You fellows can't ride herd on me. I've told you I'll go share and share on the reward. That's all there is to it."

"What's your objection to our company, Clem?" Dean asked.

Taylor spoke crisply. "His objection is that you would probably interfere with his deviltry. For one thing he means to murder me."

"I don't reckon so," Dean said, with a glance at Molly. "We're all law-abiding citizens except you, Mr. Texas Man. You've got Clem wrong. His bark is a lot worse than his bite. Tender-hearted as a child, Clem is . . . Now here's my idea. We'll cut across and drop Miss Prescott just above the Quarter-Circle X Y and the rest of us will drift along together to Tincup."

"No," snarled Oakland.

"Doesn't suit you, Clem?" Dean murmured. "Want to play a lone hand, eh? I expect the boys think that's not quite reasonable."

"It's the way that it will be," Oakland said doggedly.

The cold eyes of Dean were entirely without expression. "I wonder," he said, in a low even voice.

The two men looked at each other, steadily, unwinkingly.

Then one of the horses nickered, and from a distance came an answering whinny.

CHAPTER 31
A Free Prisoner

The explosion of a bomb could not have banished more effectually the difference of opinion between Dean and Oakland. The two men had been one moment moving vigilantly toward the ultimate appeal of roaring guns; the next the quarrel was dead, forgotten, as though it had never been.

The five men and the one woman in camp listened attentively. Once more Gypsy lifted his head and whinnied, and a second time there came an answer.

Dean spoke. "Quarter-Circle X Y horses likely," he said quietly.

"That's what we've got to find out," Oakland replied. "Jess, you go up the gulch with Barnett and the girl. Wait for us near the top, and see they don't either one of 'em get away. Ed, you saddle up and hold the broncs at the head of the draw back of the plum trees. Brad and I will take a look-see and learn who has jumped us if we can."

All accepted his orders without protest. As

Mosby herded his prisoners into the gulch, Molly raised a low-voiced question.

"Had we better shout so Dad will know we're here?"

"I'll plug this bird Barnett if you do," Mosby said flatly. "You can't run any shenanigan on me."

"You weren't meant to hear that," Taylor said to the guard, with a disarming smile. "But since you did I'll mention that the idea was in the discard even before you disapproved. When a man has the drop on me, I do as I'm told."

They moved in single file up the little cañon. Molly led, the handcuffed man followed, and Mosby brought up the rear. It was a steep trail, rock and bramble-strewn. At times Molly had to fight her way through a tangle of bushes.

"Keep moving," the little man ordered.

"When I can," the girl protested. "It's rough going. If you can do better, maybe you'd like to lead."

"No, Miss. I'm not complaining. You're doing fine."

The sound of a shot came to them. Two or three more, at intervals, followed the first. To Taylor it seemed that the sound of the later ones was less clean. He was sure of this when a far faint pop drifted to them after several minutes. Someone was on the run.

Molly turned and looked at the prisoner for reassurance.

"They're fighting," she said. "Dad and Bob are probably there."

"Don't worry," the Texan said. "They're on horseback and could spill a quart of lead without anyone getting hurt."

"I reckon Clem and Brad are leading them away from here. After a while the boys will come back and pick us up," Mosby explained.

"Unless you decide to keep going with us to Tincup and get that reward for yourself," Taylor suggested.

The little man glared at him. "What you take me for? I never did throw down on a partner yet, and I don't aim to start now."

The Southerner laughed ironically. "Clem Oakland wouldn't throw you down, of course."

"I'm not thinking of Clem," Mosby said shortly.

That he was toying with the temptation suggested, Taylor knew, though it was almost certain that he would reject it. To double-cross Clem would be too dangerous.

The gulch grew steeper toward the top. It was difficult for the shackled man to clamber up without the use of his hands. More than once he stumbled and almost fell. Once he staggered back against Mosby.

"Tough going," he said. "I never knew before

315

how much use a fellow's arms are to steady him."

"You'll make it," the nester encouraged.

"Sure I'll make it. If I don't fall and break an arm or a leg first."

They came to a rock slide, at a place where a smaller gorge ran into the first. Great boulders had crashed down from the summit a million years before the earliest inhabitant had opened his eyes to blink into the blue sky.

Molly turned. "Maybe I can help you. Without using your hands you can't get up, can you?"

Their eyes met. She read a message in his.

"If I don't slip," he said. "Much obliged, but I reckon you can't help any."

"Not far now," the little man said.

Moving up carefully, Taylor put his weight on a round boulder half the size of his head. The stone shifted a little and the Texan's foot slid from the rock. He gave a little cry of alarm as he staggered back and clutched at his guard.

With both hands Mosby tried to hold him up, but the prisoner could not seem to find secure footing. His bound arms encircled the neck of the old man and dropped down past the shoulders to the waist.

"Here. Get away, fellow!" Mosby protested, struggling to keep his feet.

Together the two went to the ground and

crashed down the slope, rolling over each other as they went. A clump of bushes stopped them.

Mosby, underneath, found breath to gasp an order. "Get off me, Texas Man!"

"Pretty soon," Taylor agreed with a grin, then called to the girl.

"Are you hurt?" Molly cried, as she descended.

"No casualties," the handcuffed man answered cheerfully. "Can you reach underneath and get his gun? It might go off and hurt him."

The nester struggled desperately to draw the weapon. His fingers could just touch the butt, but were unable to close on a grip. For the elbows of the Southerner pressed against his side so tightly he found it impossible to move his arms. He heaved and tossed wildly. If he could slide his right arm down two or three inches and get it free for an instant, he would stop this fellow's clock. Taylor shifted his weight to the left, so that it rested on the forearm trying to work down.

"Don't get too near," Taylor shouted to Molly. "Wait."

He braced a foot against a rock to give him purchase and crowded down upon the straining muscles of the arm.

Mosby collapsed. "I give up. You're breaking my arm," he groaned.

The man on top did not relax. "Now," he told the girl.

Molly's hand slipped across the body of the Texan to the butt of the revolver. "If you could lift him just a little," she suggested.

Taylor lifted, and the weapon came clear of its holster. After making sure the nester had no other gun, the handcuffed man freed him.

Painfully Mosby rose and felt his bruised and abraded anatomy.

"You might of killed us both." he reproached. "If we'd gone over the bluff."

"We would certainly have got bumped," Taylor agreed gayly. "The good life you've been leading probably saved us."

"You did it on purpose," Mosby accused.

"Now would that be reasonable — after all your kindness to me?" the Southerner mocked.

"Clem will be sore as the devil when he comes back. You better gimme back my gun, Barnett."

"It will be too bad if Clem is annoyed. That will worry me a lot. Good old Clem, as tender-hearted as a child. Testimonial of Mr. Dean. I don't reckon friend Flannigan will go quite that far, but he may be prejudiced."

"When he finds you —"

"If he finds us," corrected the Texan.

"He'll take it out of you and the girl sure. My advice —"

"Can't use it. Give it to Clem."

"Now, looky here, fellow. I can't go back and tell him you got away. He'd skin me alive. You know how he is." Mosby spoke in a persuasive whine, as though trying to argue the other out of an unreasonable position. "And of course you can't get away when you're handcuffed. You know that your own self. Might as well give up right now."

"No use. I've given up four times in the last few days, once to the sheriff, once to Mr. Prescott, and twice to Clem. Everybody turns me loose. Nobody wants me. Now we won't detain you, Mr. Mosby. You know the way down to the camp."

The nester looked poisonously at him. "If I had that gun —"

"Condition contrary to fact," Taylor interrupted. "I learned all about that in Latin Prose Comp. It never got me a thing. Jog along, Mr. Mosby. Pleased to have met you and all that, but we understand you are in a hurry."

Mosby said no more. He turned and went limping down the gulch.

The Texan looked at Molly with a smile, then at his handcuffs. "I'm what you might call a free prisoner," he said.

Her eyes sparkled with animation. "I never saw anything like it before — the way you planned your fall and took him by surprise. If you hadn't done it just right, he would have killed you."

"I had luck," he said. "We'd better be getting out of here before Oakland gets back – if he does. We've only got Dean's word for it that his bark is worse than his bite."

"His bite is pretty bad," she said. "Let's hurry. Which way shall we go?"

He had already decided that. "We'll follow the little gulch. If we have any luck, we'll be lost in the hills before Mr. Oakland arrives."

"I hope so. If he finds us –"

"He might be the one out of luck," Taylor finished cheerfully. "It was about fifty-fifty on the luck last time we swapped shots. By the way, you'd better drop that gun in my coat pocket."

Molly had never seen him light-hearted before. The sardonic bitterness she had been accustomed to associate with him had gone. There was something almost boyishly happy in his manner. She could think of only one reason why he had changed. He was still a fugitive. Since he was handcuffed, he must inevitably be caught. Justice still awaited him in Texas. Only one factor in the situation was different. Her eyes had told him that she loved him. Was that so important to him? Did it mean enough to make him forget the evil fate toward which he was marching just now so gayly?

He was hampered by the handcuffs, and now and then she stopped to wait for him. A new shyness suffused her. Southern women were dependent. Their men liked them to be clinging vines. Very likely he thought her bold for following them alone in to the camp. No doubt he despised her, in spite of himself, for having shown her love so openly. Nice girls waited to be pursued — fled from their lovers — denied them — yielded to persuasion. That was silly, she felt, but it was what men liked. They wanted to be conquering aggressors.

"There isn't any way to get those things off your wrists, is there?" she asked.

"Clem has the key," he answered. "Even if he were here, I doubt if he would take them off."

"I don't see what we can do, then," she frowned. "Whoever sees you first will know who you are."

He lifted his shoulders in a shrug. "What must be must. Why worry now? Half an hour ago I shaved death by a finger crook. Now I'm free, in a way of speaking, and alone with you in the hills. I'm satisfied."

A faint crimson streamed through her cheeks. "It doesn't take much to satisfy you, then."

She did not wait for his answer, but turned again to the climb.

It was delightful to watch the rhythmic reach

of her long slender legs, the easy movements of the supple body. She was as lithe and light-footed as an Arizona antelope. When she reached above her for a hold, chin lifted, poised for a fleeting instant from finger-tip to toe, the unbroken line seemed to him the ultimate of grace.

Her young loveliness stabbed him. She was so soft and fragrant, yet so strong. Why be a fool and yield to impossible dreams? Her dear delicious beauty, her sweet reluctant love, were not for him. His race was run. The cuffs on his wrists were symbolic of his future. He was a hostage of misfortune. As far as she was concerned, he had no rights. What in Heaven's name had he been thinking about to let her care for him? He had taken advantage of her years, of her interest in his desperate fate, to let her weave some pattern of love about him. Yet he had not intended, Heaven knew, such a result. His own passionate longing for her had leaped out at him, surprisingly, like a sword snatched from its scabbard.

The spell of her had been over him glamorously since the touch of their lips in the first kiss. Because he was what he was, a lost soul, it had filled him with burning misery as well as joy. On the dodge, sleepless under the stars, she had been always near. Her voice had come to him, low and far, like distant church bells in the early misty morning.

They reached the tableland above. To the north there was a roll of wide hills; to the south and west a more rough and broken country.

"This way," he said, and lifted a hand toward the sunset. "Better chance to find cover if Oakland comes looking for us."

At the edge of the mesa they dropped down into a gorge that led from one hill pocket to another.

CHAPTER 32
Under a Crescent Moon

"Tired?" the Texan asked.

Molly scoffed at the question. "Not a bit. I could go on forever." She modified her answer. "If it weren't for these riding-boots."

The poise of her slender body, still elastic as a rapier, backed the words. Taylor looked down at her feet.

"The boots are hurting?"

"Well – a little," she admitted.

"We'll stop in this draw," he decided. "No use trying to find our way in the darkness, anyhow."

"No."

"It's getting cold already. We'll build a fire."

"Will that be safe?"

"Probably there is nobody within miles of us."

They found dead wood in the timber just above. Together they dragged it to the place they had chosen for a camp. Soon fire was blazing merrily.

The stars came out, myriads of them, clear and cold and infinitely far.

She asked him if he had a pipe and would like to smoke.

"Haven't even a cigarette," he told her.

"I have," she told him.

With the same match she lit first his and then her own, cupping her hand in front of his mouth that the flame might not be blown out by the wind.

He settled down on an elbow contentedly. "Not the first time I've had only a cigarette for supper. You're hungry?"

She grinned, showing two rows of even teeth between the red lips. "I'll say I am – hungry as a wolf. Will you take me to dinner, sir?"

Their cigarettes glowed companionably. "You should be content with the goods the gods provide. We're at a smoker, with all the universe as fellow guests – if every star is a cigarette tip."

"You make us sound awf'ly unimportant," she said. "I suppose we are, and yet –"

"– each one of us is the center of our own world," he concluded for her.

"We matter to ourselves immensely," she frowned. "Is that just our little egos, vanity clamoring in us?"

"Rather a mystery, our personalities, aren't they? We're here, out of all the millions of years of the past and the future, for such a little time. It's something more than vanity that makes us want to find individual expression."

"We're getting into theology, aren't we?" she asked, and her radiant smile flashed at him. "You're the strangest bank robber I ever met."

"How many have you met?" he asked cheerfully.

"I met today four men, any one of whom may be, for all I know. If Clem Oakland and that shadow of his, Flannigan, never robbed a bank, it's because they've been afraid they couldn't get away with it."

"They're a sweet pair to draw to," he admitted. "But why play favorites? Why not include the others, too?"

"There's a difference in villains. I rather liked the one they called Brad Dean. He wasn't afraid of that big ruffian Oakland, anyhow."

"I'm glad you think there is a difference in villains," he said, grinning at her.

His grin was of the surface only. She was sure of that. Taking her courage in her teeth, she asked a question.

"You *are* Webb Barnett, aren't you?"

"Yes," he said simply.

"I felt sure of it," she sighed.

"Yet helped me just the same," he murmured gratefully.

She lifted her hands in a little gesture of despair. "I don't understand. I don't see how a man like you could — could . . ."

"I didn't."

"Didn't rob the bank?" she breathed, starry-eyed.

"No."

A tide of joyous excitement raced in her blood. Not for a moment did she doubt that he was telling the truth. How could she have ever have believed it of him? The thing was incredible on the face of it, since he was the kind of man he was.

"It was all a mistake!" she cried. "Someone thought it was you, and it was another man!"

He shook his head. "No. It's not as simple as that. I was there and was wounded during the fracas."

"But — why didn't you tell the officers you weren't one of the robbers? Why did you try to escape? If you had stayed and explained —"

"That's just what I couldn't do. I helped one of the bandits to escape. A dozen men saw me do it."

"Helped one of them escape," she repeated. "Why?"

"That's the one thing I can't go into. I knew him. He was a friend of mine. I can't tell even you more than that."

"How did you help him?"

"Got him out of a side door of the bank and into my car. Instead of going with him, I stopped to give myself up and explained I wasn't one of the robbers. But half dozen men were firing at me. I was hit, and saw I would be killed if I stayed. So I ran across the road and jumped on a horse hitched there. I galloped out of town. It was too late to correct my mistake then."

"How terrible! You just happened to be in town and got tangled up in the dreadful business. Was that it?"

"No," he answered, choosing his words carefully. "Some information reached me. I was worried about my friend, and I hurried to Somerton to stop him from going into the crazy business. I was too late."

"You must go back and tell everything," she urged. "Your friends will believe you. The truth will come out. It's bound to."

"How?" he asked bluntly. "Two of the bandits have been killed. The third is in hiding. My story would be laughed at."

"That's what you thought when you said you didn't shoot Steve. You didn't expect to be believed, but we put this and that together. Now we feel sure Clem Oakland shot him. Even Steve thinks so."

"Miracles don't happen twice," he said skeptically. "I've been over this a hundred times in my mind. There's no way out for me."

"Not even if you told who the robber is that escaped?"

"I can't tell that."

"But you must. Of course you must. If he's that kind of a man, you oughtn't to sacrifice yourself for him. It's absurd."

"If I told who he was, it would not help me. I would be held in contempt the more for trying to get out at his expense."

She argued and pleaded, eagerly and vehemently, but she saw that she did not move him from his decision. Womanlike, she apparently abandoned the attack. She asked him questions about himself, and he answered them.

Presently, by that campfire in the hills, with the wind soughing through the pines and a crescent moon riding the heavens, he told guardedly the story of his life to the woman he loved. She listened like a charmed thing, her eyes lost in his, her heart in a wild alarm of passionate sympathy for this man who had been so greatly wronged. A hundred unseen wires, tentacles of emotion, vibrated between them. Solitude and darkness engulfed them. They were as much alone, one man and one woman, as were Adam and Eve in the primeval days of the Garden.

The facts he actually told were very few. His father had been a Texas cattleman, an old-timer who had driven the Chisholm Trail with a herd more than once. Webb was an only son, and after the death of his mother an aunt had come to take charge of the household at the ranch. She was a widow and she had a baby son several years younger than Webb. This aunt had been a mother to the little orphan boy as he grew up. She had given him love and care, just as she had to her own child. A few years before this time she had died, about three years after Webb's father had passed away.

"And her son — what became of him?" asked Molly.

"Alan. Oh, he — drifted away."

"He didn't live at your ranch?"

"Off and on. Young fellows are restless, you know." He said it very casually.

She would not let it go at that. "And wild?" she added.

His grave smile was enigmatic. "I reckon you know boys as well as I do."

"Not this particular boy, and yet I could guess a good deal," she flashed.

"If we were interested enough to bother with him just now," he fenced.

"He fell into bad company and came under the influence of some older man who had no moral scruples against crime," she said. "I think the older man's name was Lewis."

Barnett was surprised out of his impassivity. "What do you know about Lewis?" he asked.

"His name was Buck Lewis, and he was about forty years old. He had been a cowboy and was in the World War. Officers killed him near Good Cheer the day after the bank robbery at Somerton."

"I see you read the papers," he said, with a touch of amiable sarcasm.

"We keep a lot of old papers in a closet. I dug them out and read the story of the Somerton robbery."

"And then did a lot of guessing," he smiled.

"I did some of it in the last five minutes. You can't deny I'm right. The man you helped into your car at Somerton was your cousin Alan."

He looked at this straight slim girl, so very much alive, so possessed by a determination to fight his battles for him, and a wild primitive rapture poured through his arteries.

"It's been worth all I've gone through!" he cried. "Worth it a hundred times, to have met and known you!"

Along the unseen wires between them emotions flashed. The girl's bosom began to rise and fall fast. In the fire-glow her red hair was aflame, her eyes pools of light.

The barriers he had built between them because of his plight began to tumble. Her courage was contagious. He had lived so long the victim of a combination of damning circumstances that he had lost hope of proving the

331

truth. But perhaps her fresh view of the case was more just than his. He would go back and try to clear his name, hopeless though it seemed. If he succeeded, if he escaped the net entangling his feet, he would come back and offer to her the life she had given value.

"I never believed you were bad," she told him, her rapt young face shining valiantly out of the shadows. "I knew there was some explanation, though I didn't act that way when I flew at you."

"I've never known anyone like you," he said, and somehow the remark sounded like a superlative. "Never. It's you or nobody for me."

He heard a little rustling movement in the shadows where she was, but no words came to him.

"I'm mad," he went on. "It's you — or the night — or something. I've always known it was no use. I'm smirched, always will be, even if I persuade them not to shut me up for life. Just now I thought for a moment — but that's sheer folly. I've nothing to offer you — nothing that would not drag you down."

"You mean — because you've been unfortunate?" she said, in her low melodious voice.

"Yes. I should be a coward to ask a woman — and you of all women — to share my disgrace."

"Don't you think she might be proud to do it?"

"All her life she would be pointed at as the wife of a man who ought to have gone to the gallows."

"O, my dear," she murmured, "as though that would matter."

"Your daughters, if you had any —"

"— would be proud of their father," she interrupted, a flag of color in her cheeks.

"A murderer and a thief who had got off by the skin of his teeth."

She put her warm fingers over his mouth to stop the hateful words. They trembled against his lips.

The tide of feeling in them rose to flood.

She heard him whisper, as to himself, "My love! My love!" Her strong arms went about his head and snatched it to her warm, tender bosom. He was her man, in desperate need of love and comfort. She would fight for him against the world.

CHAPTER 33

Molly Remembers a Prior Engagement

They had talked long, in the fashion of lovers, less with words than with smiles, kisses, silences, and the contact of warm flesh. Her eyelashes swept his cheek and sent a strange delicious tingle through his blood. His fingertips touched her temple and set music pulsing in her.

"We're all alike, we women," she laughed tremulously. "We think we want to be free, but what we really want is a mate and a home."

"The tragic thing is that you're all so sure you're going to be happy when you've found him," he answered, smiling at her.

"That's not the important thing," she denied. "Maybe we'll be happy with him. Maybe we won't. But we have to walk with him, anyhow. We can't help it." She added, after a moment: "And wouldn't if we could."

Her lips turned to his in the semi-darkness.

Presently she began to laugh. "Good gracious! I had forgotten. I'm engaged to Steve

Walsh." She said it as though it were a matter of not the least moment.

"You'll have to get excused on account of a subsequent engagement," he told her cheerfully.

She smiled at her Texan with sweet derision, to test him. "Or from the subsequent engagement," she said.

"Already!" he cried in mock alarm. "You're worse than our Southern girls."

"It was after I thought you had shot him," she explained. "I was trying to hate you, and he was so sweet while he was sick. So I thought I would stop all that foolishness of my heart going pitty-pat when outlaws were around."

"And, glory be, it didn't work."

"It sort of half-worked — until I saw you again, with all our boys screaming at you." A rueful little laugh rose from her soft round throat. "That scared me, the way I got silly about you again. So when Steve said his little piece I told him 'Yes, sir, thank you, sir.'"

"An anchor to windward," he suggested.

"Yes, but that wasn't all," she went on, determined to make full confession. "I've always been awf'ly fond of him. Sometimes I've thought maybe, if he wanted to —"

"And of course he wanted to," her Texan interrupted.

"There was no 'of course' about it. All the

girls want him. He's a dear. With him so near, how could I let my thoughts stray to anyone else, especially to —"

She stopped, looking at him with a smile radiant and derisive.

"Perversity of the human heart," he guessed. "Why any woman, not bewitched, would look at me with young Walsh around is more than I can see."

It did not matter much what they said. All roads of speech led to love. They talked of many things, laughter on their lips, the wonder of this experience always near the surface. They caught each other's meaning in swift plunging glances, in fragmentary phrases not necessary to complete.

Molly was surprised at the tenderness that warmed and irradiated her. Always she had been more than a little sharp. She would have defined herself as hard and cool, encased in the shellacked finish of the modern young woman. Men drawn to her by her good looks and by the spirit with which she attacked life impinged upon a mocking insolence of untenderness discouraging to them. She would have nothing to do with sentiment and had promptly turned her back on those who sighed. Now she was a well of emotion. Probably the next time she read a mushy novel, she would weep over it, Molly decided with a fugitive smile at her surrender.

The night was cold, though mild for Montana at this time of year. They dragged in more wood to keep the fire going, laughing at the awkwardness with which he helped. Before the fire one side of them toasted while the other side grew chill.

"We'll have to turn round and round like chickens on a spit at a *rotisserie*," Molly said happily.

She had never before plucked such a thrill out of life. They had escaped from Oakland. Together they shared the adventure of being alone in the shadows of the great hills. Molly looked up at the stars. They were so far away, but no farther than that world they had left with its censure and its violence. She and Webb so deeply belonged to each other. In spirit their marriage was irrevocable, she felt, even though a fastidious instinct held her from yielding too impulsively to the impassioned tenderness with which she longed to surround him on this last night before they took him away to pay the penalty of another's crime.

For they had decided that he must give himself up. They would return to the Quarter-Circle X Y in the morning, as soon as they could find the way. He would surrender and face the charge against him. This was the only chance their love would have for any future, though they recognized it as a bleak one.

Behind the hills the moon disappeared. Into the sky sifted the faint gray light of coming dawn. Sitting before the hot live coals, her head against his shoulder, they slept a little at last. Their slumber was light, broken by starts as their bodies slumped and recovered.

Out of their sleep a raucous voice snatched them stridently.

"So here my lovey-doveys are!" it jeered. "I'm glad to death to meet up with you."

Neither of those in front of the fire needed to look around to see who was speaking.

CHAPTER 34
His Pound of Flesh

Under the shock of that voice Molly's heart went down like a plummet into icy water. He had found them. In all the vast welter of hills and hollows he had stumbled on the one pocket where they had hidden. It was a thunderclap of disaster.

Oakland straddled forward, spurs jingling. "Well, well, well! Here we are again, our little family happily reunited. I reckon you'd say Providence sent me here to look after you, Missie. As a chaperon I'm a little late, I expect. But as the old saying goes, better late than never."

Molly shuddered. Her shoulders sagged. She did not look around. All the plans they had made were gone agley.

Webb Barnett turned his head. The man was eight or ten feet from them, a revolver in his hand. The Texan realized that there was not a chance in the world for him to reach the weapon in his pocket.

"Just waiting here for me, like babes in the

wood," Oakland went on. "Fine! Couldn't get along without good old Clem, could you? Speak up and tell me how pleased you are I dropped in on your honeymoon."

"I'll make you a proposition," the Texan said quietly. "Take these cuffs from my wrists and we'll settle this. One of us will stay here. The other will go."

The big ruffian laughed triumphantly. "Do I look like that kind of a fool? Me, I know already which one of us will stay and which one will go — with the lady."

"Keep her out of it, unless you want to be shot down like a wolf," Barnett advised.

"Who by?" the other sneered.

"Every honest man in this country would rise against you. Don't forget that. You'd never get away — not even for a day."

"You're worrying about me, for fear I get in bad. That the idea, fellow?" Oakland flung at him with a cruel grin.

"I'm telling you what will happen if you make a mistake."

"Yeah! Well, I won't make a mistake. What's eating you, Texas Man, is that you're scared stiff. I'm sitting pretty, and you know it. First, I do my little business with you. After that — the lady. Turn about is fair play. You've had your chance. Now I have mine. I'd call that reasonable." He jingled forward till he stood in front of Molly, tilted up her chin, looked down into her fear-filled eyes, and laughed.

Barnett's shackled hands moved slowly toward the lower right-hand pocket of his coat. The muscles of Oakland tensed.

"Hold on, fellow. Hands still, or I'll pump lead into you," the man with the revolver ordered harshly.

The moving hands stopped.

"Do you think I picked a gun from a cherry tree?" Barnett asked lightly.

"I don't know." The forty-five in Oakland's hand covered the prisoner. "Where's Jess? What did you do with him?"

The question crackled explosively.

"He went home."

"Home! Did you bump him off, fellow?"

"How could I — without a gun? Use your brains, man."

"Without a gun? We'll see about that. Don't move, or . . ."

From the coat pocket of the prisoner Oakland drew the revolver. He gave a whoop of savage glee.

"You'll tell me now what you did with Jess and how you got his gun," he said.

"I didn't do anything with him. He went down the gulch soon after we started. I took his gun — fell against him and got it. "

"Likely that's another lie."

Molly spoke for the first time, wearily. "No, it's true. I helped him."

"Oh, you helped him!" The ruffian's eyes gloated on her. "I'll bet you're a great little helper."

The girl felt a chill shiver through her. Nothing she could say would matter to this villain. No appeal would reach him. He was feral, entirely outside of her experience.

"It wasn't Mosby's fault," Barnett explained, partly to divert the man's thoughts. "I stumbled on a rock and slipped my arms over his head. He couldn't get at the gun."

Oakland paid no attention to what he had said. His ribald eyes were fastened on Molly. "How would you like to help me awhile? Would that listen good to you, my dear?"

"We were going home," the girl said hurriedly. "As soon as it was light, we meant to start. Back to the ranch."

He shook his head in mockery. "Too far. I wouldn't want you to have to go so far. I'll look after you, little girl. Don't you worry."

"She's not worrying," the Texan answered hardily. "She knows you daren't do her any harm."

The big man turned bleak eyes on him. "You're not in on this, Barnett. It's between me and her, understand. I don't aim to hurt her any — not if she's reasonable. I'll go farther. I

342

wouldn't hurt her, anyhow. If she wants to leave, she's welcome to go down the road any time."

"You mean — both of us?" she asked, white lips trembling.

"Why, no. You wouldn't expect that." His black opaque eyes were full of unholy mirth. "I've got to protect you from this outlaw. You can go. He'll stay."

Her eyes dilated with fear. "You mean — What do you mean?"

"I said he would stay."

"Yes, but —"

The words faltered on her lips. She did not dare to say what she dreaded, lest the mere expression of it might give it reality.

"He's getting ready to bully you, Molly," her lover said quietly. "Remember this. He daren't lift a hand against you. You're quite safe."

"She doesn't have to learn that from a Texas criminal," Oakland blustered. "She knows it. Because I'm telling her so. Me, Clem Oakland."

"Are we . . . both safe?" she asked,

"You and I? Sure we are," their captor said with heavy jocosity.

"I mean — this man."

"Him! Don't worry your pretty head over him. What's it matter whether he gets bumped off now trying to escape or whether the law gets him after a while? He's in the discard, my dear. Take a look at a live one for a change."

"If we took him to the ranch or to Tincup, I'd help you get the reward," she pleaded.

His lecherous grin appalled her. "I've got all the reward I want right here, dearie."

"I don't know what you mean."

"After me rescuing you from this scalawag, you'll be grateful, I reckon."

"You'd better go, Molly," advised Webb in a low voice.

"Sure. Go right along," jeered Oakland. "Then I'll settle my business with this Texas killer."

"Pay no attention to what he says," the shackled man urged.

"When you get through giving orders, maybe you'll let me do the talking, seeing that it's going to be my say-so, fellow," Clem scoffed angrily. "I'm boss of this round-up. What I say goes. She'll do like I say, and so will you."

"Maybe we will; maybe we won't. Depends on what you say," Barnett answered composedly, meeting the black eyes steadily. "You can kill me. That's as far as you can go."

"Isn't that far enough?" Oakland demanded, with that odd sense of defeat this man gave him. "You're dead right about it, too. For a plugged dime I'd bump you off right now."

"No!" Molly cried in terror. "I won't let you! Anything but that."

344

"Now you're talking sense, girlie," the ruffian grinned. "I don't like this bird. He double-crossed me, and I promised to hang his hide up to dry. But I expect you're the one person could persuade me to change my mind."

"Don't listen to him," the Texan insisted. "He's trying to blackmail you through your fear."

Molly needed no warning. She was dreadfully aware of the direction in which this man's mind was moving. He was serving notice on her that she could save her lover's life – at a price.

Clem spoke to the prisoner. "Keep your mouth shut. You've got no chips on the table. This is between her and me."

"I won't have it. You can't drive your rotten bargain with her for my life. What good would it do you anyhow? Her father would kill you like a coyote."

"Would he kill his own son-in-law?" Oakland asked.

"What do you mean?" Molly cried.

"I'm making a *bona fide* proposition to marry you. Being a generous guy, I'm making a complete rescue. I'll save your name and make an honest woman of you."

"You dog!" the Texan cried.

Molly drew back, as though the ruffian had struck her in the face. She was white to the lips. "That's ridiculous!" she said. "Why would I marry you, when I've never even seen you till yesterday?"

"Up to you, Miss," he said, with a derisive wave of his hand. "But remember I'm a go-getter. I do things on the jump. Soon as I saw you I made up my mind."

"But it's absurd! I wouldn't think of it. And you — what in the world would you want to marry me for?"

"I've got my reasons. They're good enough for me." He decided to offer one, ironically, which had no place in his mind. "Now there's this feud between Clint and me. It's unneighborly. We'd ought to be good friends. You and I will tie up and cement the breach, as the old saying goes."

"I can tell him you want to drop the quarrel," she said. "I will, as soon as I get home."

He did not want to drop it at all. One of the reasons that most moved him to his offer was the chance it offered for a sweet revenge on Clint Prescott. For this daughter, so near his heart, to be permanently in the power of the man he hated would be a mortal blow at the owner of the Quarter-Circle X Y, one from which he would never recover. Oakland had other reasons, more or less mixed. He would score heavily on the Texan. All the friends of the girl would be incensed, and the man delighted to flout public opinion. His mounting passion counted, too. He wanted to possess her. He wanted to break her spirit, so that when he snapped his fingers she would come running. Moreover, he knew that what Barnett had said was true. The only safe way to take this girl was to make her his wife.

The man ignored her suggestion. "No pressure, you understand. No threats. You can say 'Yes' or you can say 'No.' You're the one that has to decide."

"I'm not even thinking of it!" she cried. "It's wicked even to talk about it."

"Fine. Suits me if it does you." He looked malevolently at the man in handcuffs. "Better say good-bye to Mr. Barnett. He and I will be on our way. We've got some distance to travel."

"I'm going with you!" the girl cried.

"Oh, no." His evil grin beamed at her. "I'm taking him on my horse. You wouldn't keep up. Maybe you'd better say good-bye to him. *It's not likely you'll see him again.*"

"What do you mean to do with him?" she wailed.

"Why, take him to Tincup," he said, still with the hateful smile that mocked her. "Hope he doesn't make a break to escape. That would be just too bad for him. I'm afraid he will, too. Looks to me like he's figuring on it."

"You've done all you can for me, Molly," said

Webb, in a low steady voice.

Oakland laughed cruelly. "If that's the way you and she feel. Not the way I'd look at it, though." His glittering eyes shifted to the girl. "Just as you please, Missie. I wouldn't press you. Well, Texas Man, we'll be traveling, you and I. Don't make any mistake. You're a bad *hombre*, and my nerves are right jumpy. I'm liable any moment to get scared and plug you, understand. You better be good."

Molly understood the ominous threat behind the words. At the chosen moment he would murder the man from Texas and claim that he had tried to escape. Since Barnett was an outlaw, the excuse would probably be good enough to serve.

She cried out her protest. "No, I won't have it! You can't do this! He didn't rob the bank in Texas. It was another man. He's not a bandit at all."

"Talked you into believing that, did he?" Clem grinned. "Must have a good line of palaver. I'll be saying *Adios!* since you're not interested in my proposition."

"What did you mean when you said I could persuade you to change your mind about Mr. Barnett?" Molly asked wildly.

He shrugged his broad shoulders. "Oh, that. I reckon I was thinking that if I were a happy man, my mind all set on matrimony, with a loving near-bride to look after, I probably wouldn't have time to fool with escaped criminals."

"What would you do with him?"

"I might even take the cuffs off him and turn him loose. The county didn't elect me sheriff, anyhow. I don't know why I should do Steve Walsh's dirty work."

"All lies!" the Southerner broke in hastily. "Don't believe a word he says. He'd never free me in the world. After he had you in his power, he'd kill me just the same. Can't you see that?"

"Would you free him now?" Molly asked.

"Soon as the preacher had spliced us, dearie," he answered craftily.

"I told you so," Barnett flung out.

"I wasn't born yesterday," the big man retorted. "Can't anyone leave me holding the sack. I'll send to town for a preacher and we'll he married this afternoon. Then Mr. Barnett can be on his way. Fair enough, isn't it?"

"Why don't you be human?" Molly cried. "I'll do anything I can. I have eight thousand dollars of my own that my mother left me. I'll give it all to you as soon as I can get it arranged."

"You can give it to me to invest for you after we're married."

"What's the use of saying such things? You know I can't marry you. My father wouldn't let me even if I wanted to ruin my life."

"You're of legal age. All Clint would have to do would be to fix up a wedding-feast for us afterward. We'd have a nice quiet ceremony with Mr. Texas Man here for one of the witnesses."

The malicious smile of the man chilled the girl's blood. He was not human. He would have his pound of flesh no matter how much she pleaded.

"No use," her lover told Molly, with quiet finality. "You can't bargain with him. I wouldn't let you sacrifice yourself, anyhow. But if you did, it wouldn't do any good. He wouldn't keep his word. He's a liar as well as a coward."

"What's that?" roared Oakland.

The cold gray eyes looked into the furious black ones.

"Coward was the word I used. You dare make your infamous proposal to Miss Prescott because my hands are ironed. Yesterday you struck me across the face with a whip when I couldn't defend myself. You weigh thirty pounds more than I do, but you daren't take these cuffs off for ten minutes. Not for your life you daren't. For fear I kill you with my bare hands."

Barnett had struck the man's one vulnerable spot. He was vain of his courage and of his strength. It was his boast that he feared neither God nor Devil. As a rough-and-tumble fighter he was a legend in the county. No man had ever faced him without being beaten.

His first savage impulse was to seize his hardy challenger by the throat and tear the life out of him. But once more the look of ironic scorn in the steely eyes held him. To do so would be to prove the man's taunt true. He could not endure that. It stung his inordinate pride too closely.

Yet his rage had to find satisfaction. He must lay violent hands on the fellow and beat from that strong face the contemptuous expression. He must see the Texan lying before him broken and spent, the fear of death written in his eyes. After he had trampled his enemy down, made of him a wrecked and maimed thing, he would put the cuffs back on his trembling wrists. That there could be any doubt as to the issue of the battle did not once occur to him.

Oakland emptied the cartridges from the two revolvers and dropped them in his hip pocket. The guns he flung aside. From another pocket he drew the key to the handcuffs, jerked Barnett toward him roughly and unlocked the steel cuffs.

"What are you going to do?" Molly cried in alarm.

"I'm calling his bluff," Oakland answered

thickly. "He said I was a coward — said I was scared to fight him. I'm going to beat hell out of him."

The girl started forward, but Barnett flung out a hand and stopped her, his gaze fastened to the other man.

"Keep back, Molly. You're out of this," he called brusquely.

While he was still speaking, Clem charged at him like a battering-ram.

CHAPTER 35
End of the Trail

The physical contrast between the two men was notable. Oakland was built with the thick solidity of a concrete post, his antagonist with the undulant grace of a Greek god. The men had thrown off their coats, so that their torsos stood out against the flannel shirts they wore. The chest of the larger man was very deep, his rounded shoulders were immense. The muscles of his arms and legs bulged in knots. His movements had the lumbering awkwardness one observes in a bear, but they could be swift and accurate.

In front of Webb he loomed so terrible that Molly's heart contracted. His face was a map of fury as he plunged at his foe. The girl expected to see the lithe slender figure smashed down at once and annihilated. She caught her hands together in fear, then gave a sigh of momentary relief. The Texan's head had moved slightly to the right and the hamlike fist had just grazed his shoulder as it drove past. At the same time, so quickly that her eye could hardly follow,

Barnett's left moved upward and landed with a jolt under the ranchman's chin.

The giant gave a grunt of pain, and almost simultaneously the other's right pounded against his ribs just below the heart. With a supple dip of the body, Webb was clear of the ruffian before he had recovered.

The swiftness of Barnett's motions and their ease reminded the girl of a mountain lion. His muscles had the same rhythmic flow. They were not bulky, and they seemed to ripple under the skin as they functioned. She noticed now, as she had done while attending his wound during the blizzard, how smoothly and with what a beautiful line the flesh swept down from throat to shoulder.

Oakland turned, let out a roar of rage, and rushed again. Molly was sure that her lover would be overwhelmed this time. It was not possible for anyone to stand up against the impact of that avalanche of force. She heard a quick smack and saw Webb ducking away under a rigid extended arm. On the big man's cheek was an angry mark through which blood crept.

The big man followed, arms working like windmills. He crowded close, intent on crushing his enemy by the violence of attack. Excited and enraged, he ignored defense, sending in powerful blows from the side with both arms.

This left him wide open. Barnett smashed in rights and lefts, straight as he could drive them, with the weight of the body back of them.

Clem stopped for a moment, breathing heavily. He was not in good condition, and the fury of his assault had winded him. His face, swollen and bleeding, was distorted by its expression of baffled passion.

"Come on and fight!" he cried hoarsely.

Barnett did not answer. He watched the bloodshot eyes to read the man's intent, standing lightly on the toes and balls of his feet in order not to be caught flatfooted. He weaved slightly, and as he did so moved lightly from side to side.

The big man flung himself at him, lashing out blindly with right and left. Webb covered, and caught a brawny arm on his elbow in time to deflect it. He ducked, slipped, and met Oakland's fist flush on the cheek. Off balance at the moment, Barnett was flung from his feet to the ground.

Clem rushed forward to pin him down, but he was gone. He had rolled over, got to his hands and knees, scrambled up, and dodged out of reach. His head was buzzing from the blow.

Molly watched them, almost breathless from anxiety. Her heart had jumped when Webb went down. She gave a little cry of joy when she saw him up again, apparently none the worse for the blow. As she saw him sidestepping, breaking ground, and ducking, she did not realize that he was sparring for time to give his head a chance to clear.

But presently she understood Webb was in distress. He was getting the worst of it now, she was sure. His lip was cut and bleeding. The shirt had been torn from his chest in one of Oakland's attempts to seize him and red angry marks showed on the flesh. The big ranchman was swarming all over him, hammering him savagely, beating down his defense. So it seemed to Molly. There was nothing she could do to help. It was to forestall aid that Clem had emptied the cartridges from the revolvers.

The girl saw only the fury of the attack. She missed the Texan's expert footwork carrying him so lightly out of danger. Nor was she aware that most of Oakland's wild blows were smothered or caught on arms and elbows. Least of all did she guess that the big ruffian was badly winded and that his great arms and legs were very weary.

But Webb knew it. His head was growing clearer every moment. All he had to do was to fight off his enemy's frenzied onslaughts and Oakland would defeat himself. He could not keep going much longer.

One of the man's eyes was shut, the other was swollen. He panted heavily. His feet were dragging. To hit him was no difficulty, since he forced the fighting all the time. Webb played for his wind, struck hard clean blows that made him gasp.

To encourage his foe, Webb feigned exhaustion. Oakland crowded in, almost staggering as he came. One — two. The Texan scored twice on the ribs and ducked away.

Clem followed. He knew he was beaten unless he could close with his agile antagonist and throw him down by sheer strength. His knees buckled under him as he reached for the Texan. A right smashed to the point of the chin. His body plunged to the ground.

Webb stood looking at him, breathing heavily. The prostrate man turned half over, then his huge frame collapsed.

"You've won!" Molly cried, and ran toward her lover.

The smile on Webb's bruised and distorted face looked more like a gargoyle grin. The defeated man had decorated him in plenty.

"He was too anxious."

"You're hurt!" she said, clinging to him. "What can I do for you?"

"I'm all right. When we get to water, I'll wash up." Gently he put her from him.

"Business first," he went on. "We'll look after Oakland."

From the man's hip pocket he removed the cartridges and reloaded the revolvers. Then he snapped the cuffs on the hairy wrists of the ranchman.

"So that he won't run amuck when he comes to," Webb explained.

"You don't think he's – dead, do you?"

"You couldn't kill him with a sledgehammer. He's too tough. His eyelids are flickering now. See?"

Molly's blue eyes blazed. "I never saw anything like the way you fought! It was splendid! I was so frightened! I thought he would smash you. Nobody has ever beaten him before. I don't see how you did it."

"He beat himself – wasted his strength. And he'd let himself get out of condition. He couldn't keep going. His legs wouldn't carry him."

"You're sure that you are not hurt?"

"I'm sure I'll be the sorest stiffest man in the county pretty soon – excepting Mr. Oakland," he said, with a laugh. "Let's be going, Molly girl."

They started the climb back to the mesa from which they had descended the previous evening.

Just before the two vanished in a crease of the

hills, Oakland returned to consciousness of his surroundings. He sat up, sick and ashamed, and looked out of the slit of open eyelid that was not swollen shut.

To him the thing that had occurred was tragic. It had been his pride that nobody had ever beaten him in a rough-and-tumble fight. He had been in a score of them, and he had always won. Now an unknown had disgraced him. He put his battered head down in his shackled hands and groaned.

A sound aroused him. He looked up. A man was standing a few yards away tittering at him. The man was Flannigan.

That nervous giggle ought to have reassured him. But it did not. Flannigan was nobody. He was only someone to be ordered about and to be cuffed. Yet the sight of the gaunt puncher standing there full of unholy glee, gave Clem a shock. Ed had never dared to laugh at him before.

"Well, I saw you take it a-plenty," Flannigan cackled. "You weren't one-two-three with him. I was roosting up there in the timber and I certainly enjoyed myself thorough. Every time he socked you, I said, 'That's one for me.' You look like a grizzly had clawed you up."

"When I get my hands loose, I'll skin you alive!" Oakland threatened.

"You don't get the idea, Clem," the other

man said, showing his ragged teeth in a horrible grin. "You're bucked out. I'm bumping you off right now."

"What?"

"You'll never go around quirting any more fellows for no reason at-all. You're through — here — now — like I said."

Clem clambered to his feet awkwardly and lumbered toward the other man.

"If you think you can bluff me, fellow!" he roared.

The threat died on his lips. Flannigan had a gun out, pressed close to his side. The lank man's lips were drawn back from his gums in a terrible snarl. Oakland knew that he had come to the end of the trail.

Webb and Molly climbed a little spur of a ridge.

A faint sound came to them, like the pop of a distant fire-cracker.

"What was that?" Molly asked.

"Sounded like a revolver," Webb answered. "From down in the hollow where we left Oakland. Queer. He didn't have a gun."

CHAPTER 36
Headed for Home

From the summit of a ridge, Clint Prescott caught sight of two figures on the mesa. They were on foot. He raised his voice in a shout and instantly put his horse to a lope. For one of the two trudging toward him was Molly.

He dragged his cow-pony to a halt and leaped from the saddle. His arm went around the agitated shoulders of his daughter. She clung to him, sobbing.

"It's been terrible, Dad!" she cried.

"What made you do such a crazy thing?" he demanded. "Girl, I nearly lost my mind."

"I know! I know! But I couldn't help it. Don't be angry now, Dad. If you knew what we'd been through."

The harshness died out of his voice. "What have you been through, Molly? Has this scalawag here done you any harm?"

He turned to Barnett and his eyes registered surprise.

"No, no! He isn't a scalawag. It's all a mistake. He didn't rob the bank."

Upon that point Clint reserved an opinion. A caught criminal nearly always claims innocence. What the cattleman was interested in just now was his daughter's story, and part of that story appeared to be the bruised and bleeding face of this Texan. He made the same comment that Flannigan had done to Oakland.

"Did a bear claw you up?" he asked.

"Your friend Clem Oakland did that," Barnett answered lightly, smiling at the owner of the Quarter-Circle X Y.

"Clem did! When?" queried Prescott.

"About an hour ago."

"Mr. Barnett had a fight with Clem. He beat him till he was senseless." Molly flung out her news breathlessly.

"You mean Clem beat this fellow!"

"No. He beat Clem. Webb did. He gave him an awful whipping."

"What with?"

"They fought with their fists."

"And Clem took a licking?" Clint asked incredulously but gleefully.

"Yes. His eyes are all shut up. I never saw a face look so bad as his does."

"Neither did I," her father assented dryly. "If it looks any worse —"

"Clem was going to kill Webb unless I married him."

"What!" the girl's father roared.

"Webb was handcuffed. He couldn't do anything. But he called Clem a coward, and Clem took off the handcuffs so they could fight."

"By jacks, I never heard anything like this!" Clint said, his eyes blazing interest. "Begin at the beginning, girl. Tell me the whole story."

Molly told it, leaving out one important detail. She did not mention that she intended to marry a man accused of bank robbery and murder. But she did not minimize by one tittle the unflawed nerve of the man who had been through the adventure with her.

Clint frowned at the Texan. "You've still got me up in the air," he said resentfully. "Will you explain one thing to me? You've got sand in your craw. I knew it soon as I saw you. Molly's story cinches it. Tell me why you always quit and surrender when a fellow comes at you with a gun."

"He didn't quit when Clem was just ready to kill him because he wouldn't blow up the Featherhead Dam!" Molly cried indignantly.

"Shut up, Molly!" her father ordered. "But she's right, Barnett. I mean when officers come to arrest you. What's the answer?"

"How would this do for an answer?" Webb replied. "Say I'm an honest man and not an outlaw. Say that public opinion has already convicted me and that I have to try to escape. Isn't it possible I might not be willing to kill an innocent man in order to get away?"

The Quarter-Circle X Y man stared at him while this sank into his mind. "By jacks, that would explain it," he said at last.

"There's only my word for it," Barnett said, with a touch of his old cynicism. "All the evidence is against me. I'd advise you not to believe anything I say."

From a distance there came a shout. Two riders on a hilltop showed in silhouette. Clint waved them to join him. The horsemen were Jim Haley and Dug Peters.

Jim stared at the Texan. "Caught him again, did you?" he said to Clint.

"Not exactly. I ran into him and Molly heading for the ranch."

"That's what he claims, is it?"

"That's what he says. Jim, and I believe him," the young man's uncle said severely.

"Miss Molly all right?" Dug asked.

The girl's smile was surprisingly contented for one who had been up all night without dinner or breakfast. "Never better, Dug," she said.

"I've got a job for you two boys," Clint told the riders. You know that draw where Slim found last spring the black calf cached by its mother. Mr. Barnett left Clem Oakland there. He's handcuffed. Maybe he's moved out of the draw, but you ought to be able to find him.

When you do, bring him into the ranch. I've got business with him."

"Did you say Clem Oakland — handcuffed?" Jim asked, not because he had not heard, but because he could not believe the fact.

"That's what I said. boy. He'll probably kick like a bay steer about coming, but bring him, anyhow."

Jim found he could not restrain his curiosity. "How come he to be handcuffed?"

"That's quite a long story," Clint said. "The nub of it is that he insulted Molly and this Texas man here licked the stuffing out of him and put the cuffs on so he would be good. You can look as surprised as you've a mind to, Jim. I had to get used to the idea myself."

"Frank is waiting at the cottonwoods below Paddy's Prong with an extra horse, Clint," said Dug. "Better swing around that way, don't you reckon? Far as Clem goes, if he's anywhere near that draw, we'll bring him in if I have to throw a squaw hitch on him."

Prescott lifted his daughter to the saddle of his horse and the three headed for Paddy's Prong. The subject of food was becoming an insistent one in the minds of two of the travelers.

CHAPTER 37
"Bless You, My Children"

Molly knocked on the door and walked into the room occupied by Steve Walsh. She had something very important to tell him. That it would hurt him she was afraid, but she could not help that. It had to be told as soon as possible.

She stopped in the doorway, surprised. A stranger sat in a chair by the bedside. He was a heavy-set brown man in corduroy clothes.

Steve gave a little exclamation of relief. "You're all right, Molly?" he asked.

"Yes, Steve. I've got a lot to tell you. Please excuse me. I didn't know anyone else was here."

"That's all right. This is Sheriff Pincus from Texas. Sheriff, meet Miss Prescott."

The girl acknowledged the introduction with a sense of drenched emotion. He had come for Webb, of course.

"I've got a good deal to tell you, too." Walsh said. "But my news can wait a little while. Did you get lost?"

"Yes. And after a while I ran into Clem Oakland's camp. He had Mr. Barnett there as a

366

prisoner. It was just the way I thought. He took him from Mr. Martin. When I got there, he was just going to kill him because he refused to blow up the Featherhead Dam."

"Kill Barnett, you mean?" Walsh asked, with quick excitement.

"Yes. We've had an awful time, Steve."

"You and Barnett?"

"Yes. Clem Oakland was crazy to kill him. He almost had a fight with that other man Dean about it."

"Suppose you begin at the first and tell us the whole story, Molly."

She told it, again with one vital suppression. She could not go into her feeling for Webb Barnett with this stranger present. Not by intent, at least. Nor was she aware that Steve Walsh, his brown eyes fixed steadily on her, read the meaning of her excitement as clearly as though she had cried out, "I love him." The color in her eyes deepened as she talked. There were strange flashes in them. The flush in her face came and went delicately as she lived again the danger of the adventure.

When she had finished, the sheriff from the South made comment. "That's Webb Barnett you've been telling about all right, young lady. I could have told Mr. Oakland, if that's his name, to lay off Webb and pick on a panther instead to have a rough-house with. But I reckon a fellow has to buy his own experience once in a while. Well, I'm glad Webb is here. Where can I see him. Miss?"

"You're going to take him with you back to Texas?" she challenged.

"I reckon," he admitted, with a curious smile. "I'll tell him all about that."

Steve was lying dressed on the bed. "Let's have him brought in here," he suggested. "You stay, Molly. I'd like for Clint to be here, too."

Molly felt the beating of the pulses in her temples. She felt that something dramatic was impending. It was as though this hard brown man from Texas held her life in the hollow of his hand and by closing his fingers could squeeze all the warm vitality out of it.

She looked at Webb when he and her father entered. His glance hardly rested on her as it passed to Pincus, but it seemed to cry "Courage!" to her.

"Hello, Tom! Run down at last," he said, quite casually.

"Yes, Webb. You certainly gave us a run for our money," the brown man said quietly.

"I suppose we start back at once."

"Yes. We'll have to do that. From what Sheriff Walsh says, I reckon you haven't heard the latest news. Alan White was killed at San Antonio resisting arrest."

The eyes of Barnett flinched, then grew wary

and vigilant. "Poor Alan," he said. "What were they arresting him for?"

"For robbing the bank at Somerton. He made a mistake and reached for his gun. I don't know that it was such a bad mistake at that. When a man goes bad, he's better dead."

"You think so?"

"I think so, Webb." The impassive gaze of the Texas sheriff rested on his prisoner. "I expect you think so, too. Well, you did your best for this boy. That's probably a satisfaction to you. No regrets."

"No?"

"It was a piece of luck for you. He didn't die till next day and he made a complete confession. Said you weren't in the robbery. Said you'd been trying for a long time to wean him away from Buck Lewis. There were letters from you on him that proved it, too."

A sobbing little cry of joy interrupted him. He looked at Molly for a moment before he continued.

"We found other papers. too. They let you out completely, Webb. Of course we know you didn't have a gun out during the robbery. Several witnesses will swear to that. It was dumb of you to try to get Alan away by giving him your car, but if it ever comes to a jury, I expect the twelve good men and true will forget that. You were a kind of father to the boy, and he never did amount to a hill of potatoes."

Clint strode across the room and wrung the hand of Barnett.

"Proud to meet you, sir," he said. "I like a man who stands by his friends."

"So that's that," Steve said cheerfully, and reached for the walking-stick beside the bed. "Have to show you all out of my room except Molly. She's my nurse. You wait a moment, Mr. Barnett. Got something to say to you."

After Clint and the other sheriff had gone, he rose from the bed, leaning on the walking stick.

"Who said you could do that, Steve?" Molly asked.

"I say so. Permission of my nurse, Miss Macmillan." He looked sternly at Molly. "Young woman, to how many men are you engaged right now?"

Molly blushed. "I want to talk to you about that, Steve. You know you told me that if our feelings weren't permanent, and either of us found it out —"

"So that's it." His face creased to a smile. "Give me back my ring, woman."

"You didn't give me a ring," she demurred. "It wasn't so very much of an engagement, was it, Steve?"

"Didn't I?" He made a pretense of looking puzzled. "Must have been some other woman. Well, let that go. Do you think your feelings are permanent now? How can a fickle young chit like you be sure?"

"I don't know how, Steve, but I am."

Walsh transferred his attention to Barnett. "Do you think you know how to handle this explosive young woman gently but firmly?"

"No," admitted Barnett, with a smile.

"Good. I see you have some sense."

Steve took Molly's hand and put it in that of her lover.

"Bless you, my children," he said unctuously, and then hobbled out of the room.

Webb took Molly in his arms. Her warm young lips kissed his battered mouth.

F.

F.